Janet Planet

a novel by Eleanor Lerman

Mayapple Press 2011

© Copyright 2011 by Eleanor Lerman

Published by   MAYAPPLE PRESS
              362 Chestnut Hill Road
              Woodstock, NY 12498
              www.mayapplepress.com

ISBN 978-1-936419-06-7

This is a work of fiction. Names, characters, places and incidents either are products of the author's imagination and/or are used fictitiously. Any resemblance to actual events, locales, persons or coyotes, living or dead, on this plane or any other, is entirely coincidental.

ACKNOWLEDGMENTS

The author is grateful to the Puffin Foundation for a grant that supported the writing of this book.

Cover designed by Judith Kerman. Book designed and typeset by Amee Schmidt with titles in Batavia and text in Bell MT. Author photo courtesy of Jeff Tiedrich.

"What do I seem to know, Don Juan?"
　　　　　　—Carlos Castaneda

Prologue

In the psychedelic days, and even long after, everybody knew the story about the shy young man who met a Yaqui Indian shaman in a bus station in Mexico and became his student. More, became his greatest student and the shaman's successor, the only one who would know all the secrets and master the ancient practices of the Yaqui sorcerers, who would, in fact, become the last nagual. In the beginning, of course, that was not his intention—or so he thought. A graduate student at the University of California, Los Angeles, he was struggling to write his Ph.D. thesis about the use of medicinal plants among the Indians of the Mexican state of Sonora. His advisor urged him to make a field trip, so he got on a bus in L.A. and traveled to a hot, tiny town hundreds of miles south of the border where he hoped that he could find someone to talk to, someone to guide him through the desert and perhaps share Yaqui lore about how to practice the healing arts of the natural world.

When he told an old Indian sitting on a bench in the bus station what he was interested in (though the young man later wrote that it was the Indian, Yamon, who spoke to him first, who said that he knew who his student was as soon as he stepped off the bus), the shaman laughed. "Plants?" he said. "As if what is in this *world is all that important. But if that is what you want," he said, "then we will start with plants."*

And so they did. Two nights later, the young man, whose name was Jorge Castelan, was crouched on the rocky ground of a high mesa—or at least his body was—because his other self was walking behind a spirit animal, a huge coyote that was going to lead him through the passageway from the reality in which the slightly luminous package that contained his skeleton, his bones and blood, was stuck, to the alternate realities that he would soon learn to travel between. And the coyote spoke to him. Mostly what it said was Breathe, breathe. Stop acting so scared!

At first, these trips from the mesa to the places of altered perception required the ingestion of peyote—a plant, certainly, though a particularly remarkable one—but later, Jorge Castelan said, he could summon the coyote on his own, without the use of drugs. Eventually, he came to believe that he had been born for this: to be the student and then the vessel of his teacher's teachings, to tell the story of what he had learned, what he was learning still.

That story became more than an academic paper: it was published as a book called The Peyote Palace, because, said Jorge Castelan, that's what the desert had seemed to him, that first time—a palace, a wondrous place of inexplicable splendor with many doorways, some that he could open, some that had yet to budge. But he was still trying, and everything he learned from the trials he went through to open these doors, he wrote about, publishing book after book containing what he had learned from his teacher. And then he wrote about what he learned afterwards, on his own, when his teacher finally decamped to go "elsewhere." He described what he knew about ripping through the brainless stupidity of the fat, lumpy, wooden, human level of here to get to there, which was better, which was a deeper consciousness of everything, which could be adjusted, controlled, oriented in your favor, which was pure spirit but nasty sometimes, aggressive and perfect and peaceful, all at once.

And even so, he was honest about his failings and his shortcomings. He seemed to have no problem admitting that the great sorcerer who had passed on these secrets to the bumbling boy that he had been had seen the irony in the choice of his successor, which was not a choice but a dictate of the universe, which apparently had a sense of humor, a message in a peyote button that went spinning through time and space, or at least along the bus route that ran from Mexico to California and back again. *The joke's on me, Yamon had said to Jorge Castelan. You are an idiot, but teachable, I hope. I was expecting someone different.*

And now I am someone different, wrote Jorge Castelan. All of you can be, too.

☽

But as for Janet, how was she to know who he was when she met him? He was famous by then, but had become, also, famously secretive. He never gave interviews. He never allowed photographs to be taken of him and even his book jackets never bore his picture. Instead, he was represented, always, by a drawing of a man wearing a backpack and walking on the clouds, with a burst of energy obscuring the features of his face. But it was hardly that being, hardly the last nagual—or so it seemed—who walked into a certain warehouse at the grim, industrial edge of L.A. in the spring of 1970 and waited patiently for someone to help him. Who waited, perhaps, for Janet, in the way that Yamon had surely waited for him.

That was how it started. Janet was barely eighteen, a runaway from an unhappy family in a New York suburb. It was that time, that place: all the music on the radio said the way to escape from the mess and pain of the straight life in a dead town was to just take off, and so she did. What did it matter anyway? She had been working after school from the time she was fourteen and she had saved some money; enough so that at least she didn't have to worry about how she would buy food or cigarettes. That was her temperament: rebellious by nature but careful by instinct. And so it remains.

She had already been traveling for more than a year, starting out in an East Village crash pad and then drifting north to a commune in Canada, and then south to the Haight. Now, she was in L.A., where she had gotten a job with a small manufacturer that sold harpsichords and clavichords in kit form and shipped them all over the world. Many of the parts used by the company, Guttenberg Harpsichords, were handmade and Janet, who had been hired as a packer, was also gradually being taught to cut and wind fine wire, drill pin blocks, shape plectra. To her surprise, the job, which had been a necessity (the culture still ran on money; you couldn't trade candles or hand-dyed tee shirts, yet, for supermarket groceries), was also turning out to be something she enjoyed.

Occasionally, a customer would actually come to the Guttenberg warehouse to buy some needed replacement part. They would ring the bell, and whoever happened to be closest to the front door of the warehouse would provide service. This particular time, it happened to be Janet.

When she walked to the counter at the front of the warehouse, she saw a short, dark-haired man wearing a polo shirt and brown slacks. When he spoke, it was with a slight Spanish accent.

"I'd like to buy a tuning fork," he said.

Janet asked him to wait, walked to the back of the warehouse and rummaged around in a bin, until she found a box of tuning forks. She brought one to him and he paid her. The price was two dollars.

"Thank you so much," *he said gravely, as if she had just given him a long-sought-for object that he was grateful to have found.*

After that, he would show up every couple of weeks to buy another tuning fork. If someone else appeared at the counter, he would ask for Janet. He would tell her that whatever tuning fork he'd bought last time wasn't "right," *and so he needed another.*

Eventually, he stopped coming, and Janet forgot about him until one chilly April day when she decided to buy lunch from a food cart that was always parked a few blocks away. She ordered a burrito, turned around, and there he was.

He was also buying lunch and invited her to join him; there was a small park nearby—an unexpected half-block of greenery amid the otherwise unrelieved brick and concrete of the surrounding neighborhood—and they sat together on a bench. He finally introduced himself, saying his name was Georgie, and she said that she was Janet Harris. Georgie told her that he was a professor of anthropology and that he rented an office in one of the buildings near the harpsichord warehouse where he did some of his research and writing. It was a good place, he said, because it was inexpensive and "away from everybody." *Later, she found out that some of this was true—he did, for example, once have an office nearby where he had done some of the work on his thesis, and when he had taught, anthropology had been his subject—but all that was already long in the past when she met him. So had he indeed sought her out? Had he been led to her? Later, when she might have asked him questions like that, he would have told her they were ridiculous: they were human questions and applied only to this world, to this plane of existence which, of course, was limited and dull and clouded with confusion. He would have patted her on the head. He would have laughed.*

That day, he seemed different from the quiet, even scholarly person who had been coming into the warehouse—he was suddenly telling her silly jokes, acting almost mischievous. She wondered, fleetingly, if he had some sort of designs on her, but she didn't think so; she couldn't exactly have said why but she just didn't get that vibe from him; he was being friendly, not flirtatious, and she thought she was streetwise enough to know the difference. Besides, she thought he was a lot older than she was, though that turned out not to be completely true either: depending on which information you believed, which "discovered" birth certificate that was later turned up by those interested in debunking his teachings, Georgie was probably somewhere in his mid-thirties when they met. He had been born in Chile or Argentina or maybe Peru.

After they'd eaten their lunch, he walked her back to the warehouse and came in with her to buy yet another tuning fork. "Look hard this time," he said to her. "It's up to you to find what I need."

The next day, he came back and told her that he was pleased: she had finally found him the "right" tuning fork. Since it was almost noon, he suggested that they go back to the food cart, buy lunch, and sit in the park again. Which they did, arranging themselves on the same bench as the day before. This time, however, as they ate, Janet noticed that dozens of huge, black crows were massing in the trees around them, flying in, it seemed, from every corner of the sky.

After a while, Georgie reached into his pocket and took out the tuning fork—the "right one"—and held it in front of him.

"Listen," he said. "And watch." And then he struck the fork on the side of the bench. As it vibrated, it emitted the sound of "A," the international concert pitch that is the standard tuning note of orchestras. Almost immediately, all the crows began to make noise; it was as if they heard the sound and were responding to it.

"Did you know," Georgie said, "that the hearing of most birds is in the same frequency range as humans? So they hear the tuning fork in the same way that we do."

Which may certainly have been true, but Georgie was causing quite a scene with his impromptu bird concert. The crows kept on making noise—to Janet, it sounded like they were barking—and the immigrant workers from the surrounding buildings who had also come out to buy their lunch from the cart were disturbed by the commotion. They were chattering away in Spanish and pointing, first at the birds and then at Georgie.

"Those men," Georgie said about the men at the food cart, "They don't like that I'm doing this." But that didn't seem to bother him in the least, because he struck the fork against the bench again, causing the crows' barking to become even louder. And then they began hopping from branch to branch—all of them, it seemed—jumping over each other, shaking the trees as they flapped their wings and pushed each other around, creating a frenzied tangle of movement and noise that whirled overhead.

Then, as a few of the workers started walking toward them (maybe, Janet thought, with the aim of manhandling Georgie if he didn't stop his game with the tuning fork), the crows suddenly ceased cackling and jumping around. All at once, as if they'd heard some other sound, some secret signal—and as if they were one entity, one single, connected bird mind with one intent—they took wing and, all together, flew away.

That is, almost all of them. One single, large black crow kept to his perch on a high branch, where he sat motionless and apparently unaffected either by the disturbance or the departure of the roiling mob of birds that were now completely gone from sight.

"Do you see that?" Georgie said to Janet, pointing to the remaining crow as the men who had been advancing in their direction now drifted away.

"Yes," Janet said. "So?"

"So this is a lesson. The tuning fork, the sound it made, was a distraction—and it worked, yes? It captured the attention of all the birds and got them worked up. It made them crazy. But one didn't pay attention. One knew enough not to think that what was going on around him mattered in the slightest. And it doesn't. There are other things."

"Like what?" Janet asked.

Georgie's answer was a deep laugh. "Ha!" he said. "You sound like me."

Janet looked up at the bare trees and at the one huge black bird—were crows really that big?—that remained stubbornly perched above them. It seemed, she thought, to be watching them. "I don't understand," she said. "What did you do all this for?"

"For you," Georgie told her. And then he tapped her on the head, a hard tap that she felt for the rest of the day, as if he had made her skull rattle. "Janet Planet," he said. "I did this for you."

1

This is Janet now, waking up in her rented house in the town of Woodstock, in Ulster County, New York. And when she wakes up she is instantly alert, instantly aware of her surroundings and engaging in an inventory of what she needs to know, remember, consider, before she even gets out of bed. This is something she has done for years and years, something she was taught and has never forgotten, because it's useful: you need to always be conscious of the forces that may be at work in the day ahead.

She also takes the time to review her dreams. Once, this would have been a lengthy process—she had been taught that she could travel in her dreams, through realities not limited by the way the world is described during daylight hours—so waking from a dream required the review of another kind of inventory, a sort of trip log of the nighttime world. But she had long ago given that up as unproductive: disciplined by day, she was never able to exert enough control over her dreams to think through and manipulate events or locate pathways that she had been told to look for.

Maybe when you get older, that will change, Georgie would sigh when she told him this. Maybe you're like me: it took me forever.

But it never had changed, and Janet does not see that as a fault. Not anymore. So her dreams are just that—dreams, but still interesting, still offering clues, sometimes, to her own hidden feelings, to unexpected notions. The dreams she remembers now—pieces of them, fragmented scenes—are certainly unexpected, because they have been about Georgie. Though she hasn't seen him in fifteen years, she did live in his house for almost as long, and it is hardly a surprise when she dreams about him. But lately, he has been absent from her dreams altogether, so it seems odd that he has been with her all night—and she's sure of that; he has spoken to her, held her hand, played with the tuning fork again, even summoned the crows—dominating every dream.

Soon, she gets out of bed, pulls a sweatshirt on over her pajamas and heads for the kitchen, where the coffeemaker has obeyed its programming and brewed some mocha java. Outside, the stars fade, light brightens the horizon.

   Janet pours herself some coffee, pulls an energy bar out of a box in the cabinet and goes to sit outside, on her back steps. There's a distinct autumn chill at this early hour, but she can stand it for now; in another month, she imagines that she'll be eating breakfast in the kitchen, wearing wool socks and slippers and with the heat turned on full blast. It gets cold up here quickly, in the Catskills; the rocky streams in the valleys that separate the foothills seem to freeze overnight and to the west, the paths through the deep gorges will soon be slippery with ice. But right now, here in Ulster County, it's turning out to be a morning of mixed sun and clouds. Hawks ride the scraps of wind. Janet finishes her coffee and then goes inside to shower and change.

   Half an hour later, she's out the back door again, this time walking across the weedy backyard to a small artist's studio that sits on the property. From the outside, it looks run-down, but inside, the walls are sound enough and there's a space heater bolted to the rafters, so it will be passably comfortable when the weather turns. The studio is a great bonus for Janet because in the year or so she's lived here, she's been able to turn it into a serviceable space for the work she's decided to do and take a chance on turning into something she can make a living at.

   She opens the studio door and, with great satisfaction, regards what is technically just a thing, an object, a musical instrument, but which she has thought of, from the instant she saw it in its original unassembled and somewhat woeful state, as an old friend. In the center of the studio stands a Guttenberg Flemish double keyboard harpsichord, fully assembled and carefully detailed from the hand-carved rose in the soundboard to the uniform strength and color of the pearwood jacks which, with their plastic tongues and brass pins, hold the plectra that pluck the instrument's strings. And the harpsichord has a beautiful voice; Janet has ensured that voice will be long-lived and tonally accurate by the hours she's spent adjusting the tension of the wire strings and shaping the Delrin plectra with an X-acto knife so the interaction of the jack, tongue, plectrum and wire will produce the optimal notes and shadings that an experienced player can produce.

Until about a year ago, she hadn't seen a Guttenberg harpsichord kit for as long as she hadn't seen Georgie. She had been living in New York then, working as an office temp and rooming with some friends who were renting an apartment on St. Mark's Place. The old hippie neighborhood of railroad flats, bathtub-in-the-kitchen tenements, of the Fillmore East, Ukrainian bakeries and head shops had already all but vanished into loft conversions and art galleries; the bars served Cosmos and girls in retro-chic dresses, who had never seen the outer boroughs, teetered on designer heels down the streets once crowded with potheads who had now decamped for oblivion and where the bikers had cleaned up enough to be getting awards for doing good works for AIDS babies and Vietnam vets. One evening, in the apartment on St. Mark's, when no one felt like showing up for work the next day, someone said, fuck it, let's go to Woodstock, as if that was a place that still existed in the way they wanted it to exist, and so a bunch of people, including Janet, got in a car and drove upstate; the next morning, a cold winter morning, wandering around the mess of a house of a friend of a friend in Bearsville, ten minutes down Route 212 from Woodstock, Janet found a pile of boxes in the basement that looked familiar. The boxes were open and their contents were strewn around, covered with dust and the kind of earthy grime that accumulates in badly ventilated basements of houses in the woods. Janet began picking through the pieces and soon found herself wondering if a lifetime ago, she could have been the person who had carefully wrapped these pieces of wood in egg crate foam, counted out the coils of wire, bags of pins and jacks and damping ribbon and packed them into these boxes. Even the case was here—she found it in an unopened crate hidden behind a discarded collection of warped shutters and window frames.

 She couldn't leave it there—she just couldn't. It would have been like finding a neglected pet wasting away in a cage. Hey, she asked the friend of a friend who seemed to be the main tenant of the house, did you know you have a Guttenberg harpsichord kit downstairs? No shit? he'd said, clearly having no idea of what a Guttenberg harpsichord kit even was—just something that had been in the basement forever, with the rest of the crap. He asked if Janet wanted to buy it and she said yes, she'd give him three hundred dollars, which must have seemed like a lot to the friend, but was a fraction of what the kit would have cost when it was new. And maybe it was a lot, because who knew if the pieces, living season after season in the cold and heat and damp, were even salvageable?

And if they weren't, Janet—who had decided that maybe she was going to try to put the kit together herself (Why not? If anyone still knew how, it should be her)—was going to have to make the parts herself, because Guttenberg was long gone from this and any other plane of reality. It had been a kind of hippie conglomerate, run by two refugee brothers who had been instrument builders in some part of Europe that went dark in World War II. In Los Angeles, where they eventually set up their own business, everybody who worked for them seemed to be on the run from something, and they always doled out everyone's wages in cash. But they were competing with the one other harpsichord kit maker in the United States—the best, the only, Fekkenson, which not only made harpsichord kits but also built concert-quality instruments for the retail market—and when one of the brothers died, the other didn't have the heart to keep trying to make the business anything other than marginally profitable. So he sold off the remaining stock—even gave some of the kits away—and closed up shop. He had given each of his few employees five thousand dollars in farewell envelopes, money that Janet had managed to live on for a long time.

Her other problem was that there was no place for her to build the harpsichord, since all she had on St. Mark's Place was a tiny bedroom and use of the kitchen. So, temporarily, she left the kit in the Bearsville basement until she figured out what to do, and what she came up with was that she should move to Woodstock, where it was much cheaper to live than in Manhattan, rent a house and see if, once again, she could live off some small savings while she reoriented her life. The day she decided to do that was the first time she had felt happy—hopeful—in years.

She actually tried to persuade one or two of her friends to come with her, but Woodstock, it turned out, had been a disappointment to the urbanites she was living with: the peace signs and fortune tellers and the bookstore that sold the I Ching, framed copies of the poster for a music festival (the music festival) that hadn't even really taken place there and thirty different kinds of incense was great background for a road trip, but who actually wanted to live like that anymore? Well, Janet thought she might. Her single reservation was that, for most of her forty-eight years, she had almost never lived alone. In that way, she was like Georgie, too, she supposed, but she had also learned from him that you never knew when you might meet your fate. He had met his in a bus station; wasn't it possible that hers—though perhaps not quite so much of a thunderclap, with so many repercussions—could have been waiting in a basement, in some old boxes? It was not just people who could speak, nor spirit animals; objects could stop you in your tracks now and then. And that harpsichord wanted to be built. It wanted its voice.

So she rented a very small house on a dead-end lane in walking distance of town, asked the friend of a friend to bring the boxes over to the studio behind the house and spent the spring and summer at yard sales buying used tools. It was an odd experience for Janet, acquiring things: she was unused to it, since for many years she had moved from place to place, city to city, job to job, and she had learned to travel light. In some ways, she was still living a runaway's life, still traveling the hippie trail that she had started out on before she met Georgie, even though, of course, the trail had gone cold. By the time she was on her own again, the world had changed; the communes and crash pads and youth hostels she had depended on were in the wind, but there were always remnants to be found, always some house full of friends who had an extra room, some kind of relationship to form with someone. Men, women; it was in her nature, perhaps, to have no boundaries, or living in Georgie's house, in Georgie's world, had torn them down. But nothing lasted, and she knew the potential of bus stations and how cheap and easy it was to just get on a bus and go.

In Woodstock, what she couldn't buy, she made, rediscovering not only her neglected talent for woodworking but finding, as well, that she could call upon a hidden wellspring of mechanical ingenuity when that was what she needed. From memory, she created the jig to guide her in drilling the harpsichord's pin block; she reconstructed the spinning machine made of sewing machine parts that they had used at Guttenberg to wind coils of wire for shipping because she found that storing extra wire strings in coils was convenient and kept them from becoming brittle.

It took her more than seven months to construct the harpsichord and when she was almost finished, she stayed for almost an entire night looking at it, checking it, restringing one section of an octave. I really did this, she kept thinking. I really did.

The next morning, she posted it for sale on Craig's List, along with some digital photos she'd taken and the information that she had built it herself using some custom handmade parts. She asked for seven thousand dollars and, to her astonishment, sold it within two hours. What were even more amazing to her were the e-mails she got asking not only whether she had other Guttenbergs for sale but if she could repair existing kit instruments that needed to be worked on or if she could finish off a half-constructed kit that someone's father or son had started years ago but couldn't complete. Apparently, in the years that Guttenberg had been off the map, the company and its instruments had achieved a kind of cult status. Once thought to be basic, workmanlike instruments, they improved with age; their voices grew finer and their sturdy, simple design allowed for upgrades and renovations that included adding extra choirs and elaborate cabinet decoration, if one so desired. Pianists don't generally build their own pianos and most guitar players don't spend their off-hours trying to create a Fender Stratocaster from scratch, but harpsichord devotees seemed to have something in common with ham radio fanatics—some of them wanted to build the thing they loved, or at least try to. Janet, in that one day, and then in the next and the next, began to hear from the failed lovers who needed help.

Within a week, she had put up a website, answered dozens of queries, and shortly thereafter had taken delivery from UPS of two crated sets of Guttenberg kit parts—one completely in pieces, one framed out but missing all its interior action—from two different owners who had made partial payment in advance for Janet to complete the kits. The more difficult of the two projects was going to require her to actually find the lumber and build the cabinet, which had either never been purchased with the kit or had disappeared somewhere along the way, a challenge that worried her at first, but was beginning to seem exciting. She had even received a query from a Fekkenson owner who felt he didn't have the skill to finish the instrument he had started building and wondered if Janet could do that for him. She had never worked on a Fekkenson, but she was willing to give it a try.

Today, the piano movers are coming to take the harpsichord she's sold to its new home two states away. She snaps some more photos of the instrument, uploads them onto the laptop she keeps in the workshop and prints out the pictures; some go in an album she's kept to document the different stages of the project; some get pinned to a corkboard above her worktable to serve as proof that she's built one harpsichord, so surely she can construct more. The projects she has in the workshop now are going to require some ingenuity, and there may be some stretches when she's going to need a reminder of the obstacles she's already overcome.

Janet spends the morning inventorying the harpsichord kit that has arrived in pieces, without its cabinet. Some of the parts are still in their original packaging but someone had pulled most of them out of their different bags and boxes and then put them back carelessly, so much of what Janet finds is mixed up; jacks, tongues and hitch pins are rattling around together in a Ziploc bag; rails are tied together with twine, while hinges—some of them bent or rusted—are boxed together with wire coils.

She's so intent on what she's doing that when she hears a horn honking, it takes her a moment to realize that it must be the movers parked outside, in her driveway, which is not much more than a dirt lane winding through a stand of trees that march up a low hill to her house.

Three men have come with pads and blankets: a driver and two helpers. They enter her workshop, put the harpsichord on a dolly and wrap it expertly; by the time they wheel it out to the truck, which has padded walls and straps to hold the instrument from moving around as they drive the roads, all Janet can see is a big gray bundle on a platform with wheels. It could be a hundred pounds of laundry. It could be a stack of paintings, a pile of kitchen chairs.

It's almost noon by the time the movers are gone and Janet decides that maybe what she'll do is walk into town for lunch. That's one of the benefits of this particular house; besides the fact that the rent is low, it's a reasonable hike—maybe fifteen minutes—to get to the Village Green, the center of Woodstock. Janet has a very used car, bought at a lot in nearby Saugerties, but she does not like driving and as long as it's not raining or snowing, she'd rather walk to town. And lunch in a local restaurant seems like a good idea; just having the affable moving men around for half an hour has made her crave some more human company. Woodstock is a small enough, us-against-the-world-enough kind of place that everyone knows when a new resident has moved into the vicinity, and Janet has become a familiar enough face around town for the Woodstock locals—a mixture of old hippies, artists, craftspeople and an assortment of people who just like their beautiful upstate scenery and relatively low property tax rates to be accompanied by a stubborn left-leaning ambiance—to say hello to her, to stop and talk for a few minutes. She wants that now, she wants to make small talk, eat in a café where people will chat across the tables. And maybe after lunch she'll walk over to the nearby lumber yard and talk to the someone about what it will cost to buy the mahogany for the cabinet she's going to build.

The harpsichord, which is now probably traveling along Route 212, toward the highway, had taken up a lot of room in the small workshop, so when Janet walks back in to get her jacket before locking up, she's struck by how empty the space feels. But she is untroubled by the absence, untroubled by the fact that the one thing that led her here, to this place, this house, this work, is now gone forever. Anyone else would probably already miss the harpsichord, regret having lost it no matter what the financial gain. But that is not something Janet is inclined to do. She feels some sense of loss, but it is a small feeling, something to be acknowledged, certainly, but then dismissed. And so as she turns the key in the lock on the door to the workshop and starts down the driveway, heading for the road into town, she leaves behind her feelings about giving up the harpsichord. It's easy for her; in fact, it's nothing. In fact, there is no comparison to what, to whom, she's walked away from before. In the long ago, the far away.

☽

When Janet went back to the warehouse after her lunch with Georgie—after the scene with the tuning fork and the crows—she told a few of her friends at work about it, but they were all heads and stoners, people who went home at night, ate hash brownies with their beans and rice and then consulted tarot cards before deciding what to do for the evening, so it didn't strike anyone as particularly weird. She did think it was weird, but in a kind of interesting way, so when Georgie turned up again a few days later to take her to lunch again, she joked with him, saying sure, as long as you don't invite any more birds. No, he told her, no more birds. Not today.

They bought lunch at the food cart and sat on a bench in the park. Where do you live? Georgie asked her as he munched his taco and Janet explained that she rented a room in a tract house in Anaheim, on the flatland of suburbs and strip malls near Disneyland. It was a long trip to and from work each day; two buses to L.A., two buses home, usually with a long wait in between. Well, Georgie said, I live in Westwood, with some friends, and we have an apartment above our garage. We could rent that to you, and your trip to work each day would be much shorter. More time to sleep at night, he told her. More time to dream. Janet didn't think she could afford it—he hadn't mentioned the rent but Westwood was fancy enough for her to know it was impossible, beyond her budget, but Georgie said he wasn't planning on asking for rent. What he wanted was help.

"There are four of us," he said, "and we have someone who comes in to clean, but with everything else, except the gardening, we're all impossible. Things break; things need to be fixed, and no one ever seems to know what to do. We're all so busy..." his voice trailed off and he never quite explained what they were busy with, but Janet imagined that he, at least, was studying, writing, teaching. What was it? Oh yes, anthropology. "I bet you could take care of these things for us," he said. "You could call repairmen. Make sure the bills get paid." He sighed, sounding like a man overcome with petty problems that were keeping him from more important concerns. "They forget to do things like that," he said. "My friends. My feeling about you is that you're very organized, very precise, so I think you could manage the household for us, and get everything done without having to take time away from your regular work. We're very quiet," he added as if, suddenly, the tables had turned and instead of offering her what sounded like a heaven-sent opportunity, Georgie was the one being interviewed for a job.

Janet agreed to come look at the place on Saturday. She couldn't think of anything wrong with what Georgie suggested—in fact, it sounded great; a free place to stay, the ability to save a little money in return for what sounded like not much work—but there was still something that made Janet feel uneasy. Just something that seemed a little strange. What if he and his friends were cooking up LSD in their basement or pimping college girls? That was about as far as Janet's imagination stretched in terms of the kinds of things he might—might—be doing that she'd want to stay away from (not that she was against sex or drugs, but she definitely didn't want to get arrested for writing out checks to pay the household bills of an illegal operation; you never knew who the narcs might target these days, even a professor of anthropology).

Janet had expected Georgie to be living in a substantial house—she didn't think there were any other kinds of houses in affluent Westwood—but was unprepared for what she found when, that Saturday, she arrived in the late morning. The address she had been given led not simply to a house but a sort of mini-mansion, a vast, multileveled Spanish-style house with stucco walls and a red tile roof, a structure surrounded by gardens and fruit trees, all nearly hidden from view by high walls and an electronic gate. When Janet buzzed to be let in, she was met, not by Georgie, but by an elfin, red-haired woman in a prim skirt and blouse, wearing a beautiful double strand of pearls. Janet's first confused thought was that she was some sort of secretary—but then, almost immediately, another woman appeared at the door; this one taller, dark-haired, but dressed in an equally conservative style, at least by Janet's standards. Did Georgie have two secretaries? Or was one a wife?

The answer to those questions was not immediately forthcoming. The elf introduced herself only as Lily, and the taller woman as Namuria. They apparently knew who Janet was, and why she was there, so invited her in and took her on a tour of the house. It was a strange place, Janet thought, because the common areas they showed her first—the living room, a dining room, hallway after hallway—were decorated as impersonally as rooms in a hotel. The furniture was very high quality, but there was also very little of it; there were no pictures on the walls, no keepsakes or knick knacks anywhere in sight, though there was a television, a cabinet model with doors that closed across its screen. Then the two women showed her the bedrooms, explaining that there were four of them in the house. These rooms, at least, looked a bit more like people actually used them (there were books on shelves, a framed photo or two on bedside tables), though Janet was still finding it difficult to intuit the living arrangements. Three of the bedrooms had a distinctly feminine feel (so where was the third woman?) and the fourth bedroom, which they told her was Georgie's, seemed to belong only to him, and it was the only one that looked slightly messy. The bed had been made but the main piece of furniture in the room, a massive and clearly very expensive desk topped with a leather writing surface, was covered with piles of papers. On a separate table, next to the desk, was an electric typewriter. But where, at the moment, was Georgie himself? Neither woman even mentioned him, other than to point out which room was his.

Then they took her out to the garage and up the stairs to the apartment that might become hers, which was perfectly nice. It was small, but there was a tiny kitchenette with a stove and a small refrigerator, and the bed was a low wooden platform with a foam mattress on it, covered with an Indian-print blanket, the kind of light cotton throw that was sold in every hippie head shop from the East Coast to the West.

They still weren't finished with the tour, though. Next came the garden, which somebody—maybe everybody in the house?—clearly loved, because it was unmistakably well tended. There were flowers and fruit trees and even a rock garden with flowing water. Greenery protected the entrance to the house and a paved path wound through the plantings that were cultivated in the back.

This odyssey ended back in the living room, where Georgie finally appeared, walking through the front door followed by a woman who looked older than the other two but also leaner, stronger, like someone who worked out a lot.

Georgie smiled when he saw Janet. "Ah," he said. "It's good you're here."

"The directions were easy enough to follow," Janet replied, making small talk.

"What do you think of the house?" Georgie asked. Before she could answer, he pointed to the television set. "That," he said, "has to go. We need a new one, but we're fighting over what to get. They're finally laying cable in the neighborhood and Zella thinks we should wait until they get to us to decide what kind of TV to buy."

Zella was the lean woman with graying blonde hair who had now seated herself on the couch. It was hearing her name that finally—finally!—made something click in Janet's mind. Like just about everyone else she knew, everyone her age, she had read Jorge Castelan's books; in the fifth volume, when he announced that his encounters with Yamon were in the past, he introduced three women who he said had also been Yamon's students at one time or another and had been given sorceric names by the old Indian. Two of them, Lily and Namuria (a name that the woman who possessed it seemed to pronounce differently than Janet had read it in print, which maybe helped to account for how slow on the uptake she had been that morning), liked to be called the witches and the third, Zella-Zed, was known as the Fearless Guide.

Janet tried not to react to the dawning realization of who these four people were, whose house she was in, but she knew that the expression on her face could clearly be read as surprise.

"I know what you're thinking," Jorge Castelan said to her, "but you can handle this. You can."

Maybe he simply meant that she could become part of them, join them, the last nagual and his women. Live a life like the lives they led, which turned out to be nothing like Janet had ever known before. Whatever he was saying, he was right, of course. And being who he was, he must have known that he would be right—why else would he have invited her into their world? A world in which few others were ever so intimately welcomed. But if, at that moment, Janet had known enough about the philosophy of Jorge Castelan, about his teachings, to understand his belief that there were many potential realities, and it was up to each individual to choose the one that he or she would experience most deeply, the one that sealed your fate—then she would also have known that there would come a time when even all Jorge Castelan's magic and mystery could not change the fact that, from the first moment that she walked into his house, he was also very wrong.

)

Janet pulls on her jacket, locks up the studio and begins her walk into town. She's on the side of a local road, passing by stretches of woods and the occasional house set back in the pines, most with weathered decks and porches still displaying the rickety Adirondack chairs and slightly rusty barbeque grills that were in daily use over the summer. In one yard, fallen leaves float in a baby's wading pool; in another, someone has finally taken down their summery garden flag and hung a banner featuring a smiling pumpkin and a peace sign. In the distance, the mountains seem, to Janet, to be leaning down toward the town, closing in just a little as a brisk wind begins to blow. The gray sky of the morning is turning bluer but the sun is still a weak ball of pale light, obscured by scudding clouds.

She passes the old tannery brook at the edge of town that had almost dried up during the summer but is beginning to run again, fed by autumn rains, and then turns onto Tinker Street, the main Woodstock thoroughfare. At a corner near the Village Green, across from the bus stop where the Adirondack Trailways line takes people back and forth to the Port Authority bus terminal in Manhattan, two-and-a-half hours away, Janet decides to stop in at the bakery where she can also buy the local paper and catch up on what the latest outrage is this week. The *Woodstock Times* is always taking a stand for or against something, and arguments rage in the letters to the editor section. Try to move a sewer pipe in town and someone is likely to write to the paper alleging a government conspiracy to poison the water.

In the bakery, she chats for a few minutes with the owner, Meggie Duncan, who's working behind the counter today. Janet and Meggie have determined that both of them had once spent some months at a commune in rural Ontario, though at different times. The commune, which lasted well past the decade when most of the residents' contemporaries had moved back to the cities, found jobs and blended back into the mainstream of American life, is gone now, though neither Janet nor Meggie mourns it. It was hardly an idyllic place, they both agree, due in large part to the fact that though it was a farm-based collective, nobody involved really knew all that much about farming, so they had little income, an unrelieved diet of brown rice and mangy vegetables, and an endless amount of work. The dream of living off the land paled a little when you actually had to do it day in and day out.

As they're talking, the door opens and a small man wearing sandals and a wool sweater over saffron-colored robes walks in and asks for half a dozen cupcakes. Meggie knows him—he's a monk from Thailand, visiting the nearby Karma Triyana Dharmachakra monastery on Overlook Mountain. When Meggie tells him that Janet is a harpsichord maker, the monk—whose name Janet hears as Tenzig, though she can't be sure—engages her in a surprisingly informed conversation about the development of the clavichord, an instrument that must be played with skill and is almost silent; savoring its whispered music is itself an art form. Afterwards, as she's leaving the bakery, Janet wonders about the fact that a monk from the edge of Asia would know so much about the historical antecedents of a 14th century European keyboard instrument. But then who can predict, Janet thinks, what people will take an interest in?

With the newspaper under her arm, Janet continues up Tinker Street, heading for Joshua's, a restaurant not many steps away. The north wind has cleared away the clouds and the surrounding hills, with their paint-box colored trees, are lit by the sharpening sunlight of early afternoon. The air is clear and cool. All lines of sight are open, the town is as mildly busy as can be expected on a weekday, the afternoon is unfolding pleasantly, and Janet is hungry now, thinking about what she'd like to have for lunch.

And then, suddenly, she stops dead. There is a place near the Village Green—the center of town—where the street rises and then falls away again as it continues on to the end of the commercial district and winds back out into the countryside. Just at the top of the rise, Janet sees a man standing in the sunlight—backlit so that his dark hair and stocky frame are dramatically lined by sun and shadow. For Janet, he is an unmistakable figure, a man out of the past who cannot be the man she sees standing just a few yards away from her. He is with a beautiful woman who is probably in her thirties, tall, trim, with spiky hair—not anyone that Janet recognizes. Who is this woman? She is not one of the witches. She is not the Fearless Guide. How can he be here without them? How can he be here at all, in Woodstock? In this tiny town in upstate New York?

But he is. For a moment, as she stands frozen in place, a series of panicky thoughts tumble through Janet's mind: she can run home, throw the few things she really needs into her car and start driving. Or, if she had a weapon—she thinks of a stone from the tannery brook, a knife from the nearest restaurant—she could attack him. But in the end, what she does, when she finds that she can move her feet again, is walk toward him, walk up to him, look into his eyes, and let herself be enfolded into his arms.

"Janet Planet," he whispers as he strokes her hair. "It's good you're here."

II

She was eighteen years old. She belonged to nobody. She was wary, but she was also free, living in a time when everyone—everyone she knew—was sure there was a revolution coming, because they would make one, and their revolution would change the world. Not only the world they lived in but the way that people perceived it, what they valued, what they believed. So why shouldn't she think that anything was possible? That a spirit coyote might have led a young man down the glowing path to infinity? That, older now, and even more advanced in what he had learned, he could teach you to adjust the attention of the universe so that it finally revealed what it had been thinking all along? Why not accept that what you saw and what you experienced were more a product of what you had been told to expect—what had been described to you—than what was really possible?

*In one of Jorge Castelan's books—*A Journey Through Dreams*—he gave an example of how things could be understood in a sorcerer's world that seemed ridiculous in the everyday realm. He wrote this on the typewriter in his bedroom, but Janet did not read it until he gave her a copy of the book, on the day it was published. You would not think, he wrote, that three women and one man can give birth to a daughter, but we did. She had been born into this world long ago, but not really, not until she became our Janet Planet. A spirit that will assemble itself over time. Our time. Our girl.*

Georgie, which was what he liked to be called, wrote in the morning, locked up in the bedroom, sitting at the massive desk. Janet eventually figured out that he rarely spent his nights alone, but there didn't seem to be any pattern to which of the women were with him at any given time. Janet actually asked Lily once—who she had become closest to at first—and Lily seemed to think the question was funny. They were in the garden at the time, so Lily led Janet back into the house and repeated what she'd asked to Zella and Namuria, who also laughed. Look, Zella said, he's powerful and brilliant and a great teacher, but he's also a man. And they all think with their peyote buttons, she said, apparently an old joke between the three of them.

When Jorge Castelan was writing, Lily and Namuria sometimes used the time to go shopping; they were both fond of clothes, though their taste was what Janet thought of as decidedly bourgeois compared to the bell bottoms and tee shirts that were the staples of Janet's wardrobe. (But then Georgie was hardly a fashion plate, either; he rarely wore anything but slacks and buttoned-down shirts.) Zella, on the other hand, often went off on her own. Apparently, she was Georgie's most serious companion and, Janet was told, she had her own spirit guides that led her up into the hills where she hiked and meditated.

They were also holding classes in those days, though Janet understood that Jorge Castelan was becoming less interested than he had once been in trying to share his ideas in any way other than through his books. When classes were scheduled, they always took place in a different venue and were announced only by word of mouth. They were rigorous affairs that could go on for hours, with Jorge Castelan speaking, telling stories and answering questions, but not in the naïve-boy persona that his readers would have come to expect. In person, he could be quite stern, even angry, and if he thought someone was being dense—tonto, he would call them, fool—he was likely to get angry and kick them out. He could also be confusing: he seemed, sometimes, to be talking in circles or making things up on the spot. Lily said it was a way of testing people, because only those who were really ready to adopt the sorcerer's life—a life of heightened attention, of maintaining awareness and being alert to the potential of adjusting experiences and "re-describing" reality, a term used to explain what individuals needed to do in order to reevaluate their visual and emotional perceptions—would be able to interpret Jorge Castelan's philosophy in a way that was useful.

For all of this, the surprising truth about the four of them—at least, Janet assumed it would be surprising to the millions of readers of Jorge Castelan's books; she could only imagine what they thought his private life was like—was that they could be a rather sedate group. When he wasn't writing, Georgie didn't seem to quite know what to do with himself. The women tried to keep him entertained, and together, they could spend hours watching videos—Lily liked musicals; Georgie liked anything with Clint Eastwood or Charles Bronson—or playing card games. When cable television became available, they all became enamored of MTV.

And yet, and yet. Slowly, slowly, she fell in love with them. With all of them, though perhaps to a different degree with each. The women were kind to her, they were sweet and caring. They made her lunch, they bought her clothes (the wrong kind, the wrong size, but they kept trying), they made her go to their doctor when she was sick. They were loving and maternal, and Janet, who didn't know she was missing that, found that she was. In a place that she hadn't realized she was hurt, she felt soothed.

And Georgie was the same. Paternal, loving, funny, and when he was in the mood to talk, endlessly fascinating—very different than the Jorge Castelan who presided over the bizarre teaching sessions. And he seemed to like to talk to her, drawing her into a world in which she was supposed to understand that experience was malleable; that she should live her daily life with the knowledge that there were steps she could take—that he would show her when she was ready—to divest herself of the everyday and become aware of the universal forces that were waiting for her to struggle with them, to flow with them, ride them to the infinite elsewhere that Yamon had revealed to Jorge Castelan.

The problem, however, with enfolding these possibilities into her life was that in the morning, she got on a bus and went back into the day-to-day world that she was supposed to be learning to leave behind her—and went happily enough, because she liked her work. The Guttenberg brothers were teachers as well, and as time went on, they taught her almost every aspect of making harpsichords. It was like belonging to a medieval guild, albeit a quirky one.

There were times when Georgie hinted that she didn't have to work if she didn't want to—money abounded in the household; the books had made Jorge Castelan a millionaire many times over—but Janet kept getting on her bus every morning, traveling from the quiet, expensive suburb of Westwood to gritty southeast L.A.

Sometimes Georgie would sigh and say to her, "It's possible that you are unteachable. I was for a long time, because I was stupid. You aren't stupid, though." He'd squint his eyes, tap her on the head as he had in the park. "You're smart. And you have a strong spirit. Maybe too strong for your own good."

☾

Janet is in her workshop, trying hard to concentrate on what she's doing. She's tired though, and doesn't feel as sharp as she'd like to because she's had a bad night's sleep. At one point, she woke up in the dark and found herself thinking that she'd heard the mountains grumbling. She had been having a dream in which Georgie suggested that inanimate objects such as mountains might have thoughts that can exert influence on us. He is on her mind, of course, because of her encounter with him yesterday, and she was not able to get back to sleep.

The woman he was with had whisked him away before Janet got to talk to him for more than a few minutes, urging him down the street to where her car was parked and then driving him away. Janet was surprised that Georgie had let himself be hustled off like that—she had never known him to allow the witches or the Fearless Guide to make him do *anything*, unless he was indulging them for his own amusement. Perhaps this is a different kind of relationship he's involved in with this woman, though that's hard for Janet to imagine. What she *can* imagine, though, is that he would claim to have not been as surprised by his encounter with Janet as she was; in fact, she can almost hear what he would say: *I knew you were around me, nena. I felt your spirit. My spirit had already greeted you; we had already embraced.*

With these thoughts in mind, Janet sits down at her computer, which is on a table in the workshop, and checks her e-mail. She reads a few messages but they don't hold her attention—instead, she clicks over to a website she has visited from time to time, *www.PeyotePalace.com*, which has been online for years and rarely seems to change or be updated. It remains as spare as the desert landscape that Jorge Castelan first wandered through with his teacher. The only imagery it offers is a squat cactus with a crow flying above it; the crow is a flat, black graphic, a distant V-shape hovering at the edges of the screen. The few pages that comprise the site simply offer links to the publishers that sell Jorge Castelan's many books and contain information about the nagual's teachings. It also includes a very restrained biography of Jorge Castelan, listing his academic degrees, for instance, but omitting both his age and place of birth (somewhere in South America, but which country even Janet has never been able to pin down). The site provides no contact information, no addresses or phone numbers, and gives no hint of who is maintaining it. But someone must be paying attention to it, because a few years ago, below the graphic, finally some new text appeared in a severe, slanted font. It was a notice of sorts, and it said, All requests for information about, or interviews with, Jorge Castelan, Lily Arg, Namuria Beek or Zella-Zed Delacourt will have to wait, because they are traveling.

As she views the website now, Janet sees that nothing has been altered since she viewed it last. The crow is still hovering in the distance, the notice is still there. Well, if they are traveling, wouldn't they be together? If so, where are the women? The new one Georgie was with—new to Janet, anyway—seems an odd type for him, but then all Janet is used to are the witches and the Fearless Guide in their Junior League skirts and dresses. Only Zella ever wore anything else, and that was only when she went hiking; on those occasions she generally put on some of Georgie's old clothes: chinos, usually, and shirts with rolled up sleeves. The spiky haired beauty, who had to be half Georgie's age, if that, was wearing tight jeans and a bomber jacket; it was a sexy outfit, meant to be noticed. When Janet had lived in Georgie's house, on those occasions when he did go out, even to dinner at a restaurant (a treat they all enjoyed, including Janet, though they never all went out together), he prided himself at being able to remain unrecognized. Drawing attention to himself, even by being in the company of someone who, for whatever reason, would stand out in a crowd, had never been on Jorge Castelan's agenda for as long as Janet had known him.

But she can't spend the entire day puzzling about this. She has those two kits to get to work on, and she has to try to keep herself on a schedule. So, though she's still feeling out of sorts, she turns off the computer and sets about the task she began yesterday: inventorying the components of both kits so she can check the condition of every part to see what she may have to replace or repair before she actually begins to put the instruments together.

At mid-morning, she goes back to the house for another cup of coffee, but before she pours it, she decides to get the mail. She opens her front door and almost cries out in surprise to find a woman standing on her porch.

"I've been ringing your bell," her visitor says impatiently. "Didn't you hear it?"

"No," Janet replies. Is she supposed to apologize? "I was out back, in the workshop."

"Well, you should fix up something so you can hear your doorbell," the woman says. "Otherwise, how will you know when someone comes to see you?" Then she hands Janet a dented white box holding what turns out to be an Entenmann's coffee ring that looks like it's been sitting on a shelf for a while. "House warming gift," the woman says. "Can I come in?"

Janet steps back from the door and the woman, whose long, tangled blonde hair hangs down the back of a black velvet dress that ends mid-calf, over a pair of boots with silver-colored heels, sweeps down the hall. Janet follows her; apparently, she's honed in on the kitchen, and that's where she's headed.

Arriving there, she stops and looks around at the rather grungy appliances, the mismatched dishes drying on the drain board, the worn bamboo mat that somebody some long time ago plopped down by the back door.

"So?" she says, pointing at the cake in its lopsided box. "Do you have anything to go with that?"

"Coffee?" Janet suggests.

"Don't you have any grass?" the woman inquires as she seats herself at Janet's kitchen table, a yellow formica relic that had come with the house. When Janet tells her no, she sighs and says, "Alright. Coffee, then. Black."

While Janet pours coffee into two mugs, she is also trying to figure out why this particular woman has suddenly stopped by to see her. Janet certainly knows who she is: Renna Childs, ex-girlfriend of just about every half-famous musician from the way back when, and a few very famous ones, too. Several members of the Band are on the list, which is probably why she's here, in Woodstock, their old stomping grounds. She owns a gallery in town, which is always on the tourist's route along Tinker Street, since the gallery's main stock in trade are prints of photos that Renna, a talented photographer, took during her heyday: backstage revelries, stoned nights under the stars on islands, yachts, beaches or up on Mountain House Road in a rambling house with a recording studio and a heated pool for nude winter swims; Renna in bed with beautiful, long-haired boys that everybody who was over twelve the Summer of '69 can name. There are also drawings of Renna, paintings of Renna, collages inspired by Renna created by former lovers and admirers. Her one mistake, everyone says, is that she never married any of the wealthier rock and rollers whose houses and limos and drugs she used to share; even divorced, she would have ended up with a big pile of money instead of having to run the gallery. It does well, apparently, but she could have done better—though the woman sitting in Janet's kitchen, now, still strikingly attractive, still lively and exuding charm, seems unconcerned about any of that. But what is she doing here?

"Did you know we're neighbors?" Renna says, though Janet doesn't think this is an explanation for her sudden visit. She waves her hand airily. "I live down the road."

"Which house?" Janet asks.

"The one with the gables," Renna replies, identifying, for Janet, a large, rambling Victorian that is "down the road," sort of, but much too far for Renna to have walked here in those boots. Which means she must have a car parked outside. Which is more indication that this is hardly a spur-of-the-moment drop in by a neighbor. Which all becomes clear with the next thing Renna says.

"So how do you know Jorge Castelan?" she asks.

"How do you know I know him?" Janet asks, presenting Renna with her coffee and then sitting down opposite her, at the table. She has brought the coffee cake with her, on a plate; it sits between them, looking like a large brown Lifesaver studded with nuts.

"Are you kidding?" Renna says. "First, he hugs you at high noon on Tinker Street—don't think *everybody* doesn't know that by now. Second, in order to get near him you had to breach the defenses of that hideous Carolee Carter who usually won't let anyone near him. Actually, we almost never see them in town—they just moved into a house she's renting, near Phoenicia."

Phoenicia is a town about ten minutes away. The hills around the town are a haven for wealthy weekenders who have built ski chalets and winter retreats that are guarded by private security patrols when the owners are not at home. The news that this is the kind of place where Jorge Castelan is staying doesn't surprise Janet—a hidden house, a woman protector—that pattern, at least, seems to have remained in place. "Who is she?" Janet asks.

"You don't know her? I guess that's not so surprising," Renna sniffs. "She *was* a kind of flash in the pan. I guess you'd say she's sort of a new-age exercise guru. You know, burn candles, stretch your body, stretch your mind, that kind of thing. She even had a television show for the tiniest little while. And she wrote a book, put out some DVDs, but they flopped and then she sort of disappeared. So lucky us, she's decided to grace us with her presence here." There is what sounds like genuine rancor in Renna's voice, but if she has something else to say about Carolee, she keeps it to herself for now. Lighting a cigarette, she looks around, pointedly, for an ash tray. Janet gets up and brings her a saucer, which Renna accepts with a nod of her head. Then, after a few meditative puffs, she says, "But the real question here is, who are you?"

"Janet Harris," Janet says.

"Bullshit, darling," Renna says. "That's not what he called you."

Challenging her, Janet asks, "Were you standing right there?"

"Carolee must have told someone, and then it gets around. You know how things are here; everybody talks." Then she leans toward Janet. She raises an eyebrow and smiles, as if she's going to reveal a delicious secret. "It must have killed her, you know, to share him with someone else."

"We just said hello," Janet offers.

"Not from what I hear," Renna tells her. "As I said, a big embrace was reported by the local grapevine. And you say Harris, but I hear he called you Janet Planet. That's a bit odd. But nice, in a way. Very retro. Very sixties. Loved them, by the way—the sixties. How about you?"

"That was a long time ago," Janet offers.

"But what a time, right? Very Jorge Castelan, those years: all anyone seemed to be talking about was him and that damn Indian. What was his name?"

"Yamon," Janet says.

"Yamon, right. Yamon and all that fascinating stuff: Alternative realities, tearing away the veil of earthly illusion, past lives and all that." Again, the raised eyebrow, the ironic smile. "Not that I really am the right age to remember all that."

"Of course not," Janet says.

"Good for you," says Renna. "It may just turn out that I like you. Now don't be offended," she continues, "but when I say 'the right age,' I get the feeling that you're teetering on that same edge. Not that you don't look wonderful, darling—I love your hair, for example; long hair, bangs, black eyeliner; very dark, very mods and rockers, true retro, so congrats, congrats, you've got great style—but not exactly like you're young enough to have been Jorge Castelan's baby girl."

You would not think that three women and one man can give birth to a daughter. "I see," Janet says. "So you did read that."

"Well, I Googled you," Renna says. "I was actually very proud of myself. A computer whiz, I'm not. But there wasn't a photo to be found, so I wasn't sure."

"You wouldn't recognize me anyway. At least, I don't think so. I was actually about twenty, when he wrote that," Janet says. Then, tucking the ends of her hair behind her ears, she says "And I'm not exactly trying for a style."

"Then it comes to you naturally," Renna says.

Janet is getting a little confused about this conversation; they seem to be bouncing back and forth between hairdos and mysticism. But one thing Renna said stood out for Janet, and—perhaps from habit—she decides to correct a misperception. "Did you say something about past lives?" she asks. "Georgie thought the idea of reincarnation was ridiculous."

"See? I told you I didn't understand anything he said. Well, not most of it anyway. You'll have to enlighten me."

"I don't think I'd be very good at that," Janet tells her.

"Why not? You already cleared up the whole reincarnation thing."

That makes Janet laugh. "If I could clear up anything about reincarnation, I'd be the one writing books."

"Georgie, hmm?" Renna says.

"What?" Janet thinks she's lost the thread of the conversation again.

"You called him Georgie."

"Oh, well," says Janet, a little flustered. "He liked that. He was taught that people should have sorceric names—something about naming yourself when you began to have more control over your life and your abilities. I think it amused him to be called something so…silly," Janet concludes. "Sweet. I guess it would be like calling the Dalai Lama 'Pops' or something like that."

"Really?" says Renna. "The Dalai Lama? My, my my."

"I'm not explaining this very well."

"Oh, I don't know. I think you're doing fine. So tell me—did you make up Janet Planet for yourself?"

"No. He did." Janet stands up, empties the saucer of its ashes, and brings it back to Renna, who lights another cigarette. "Look," Janet says, "I haven't seen him in a long time, so I'm probably not the best person to explain Jorge Castelan."

"Ran away from home, did you?"

"Something like that." *Something like that. Once from her own home, once from his.*

Sounding breezy, Renna says, "Well, then we're sisters under the skin, because actually, I did the same thing myself. I was fourteen. Left Birmingham, went to London and look where I've ended up. It *was* a long, strange trip—with apologies to the Dead, of course."

Janet suddenly feels an almost palpable wave of panic; she simply doesn't discuss Georgie with anyone, hasn't in recent memory, and is amazed to find herself sitting at her own table, in her own house, talking to a stranger about a subject that between herself and anybody else—friends, lovers, anybody—has always been taboo. But there's something about Renna; something gossipy and maliciously theatrical that seems to be drawing out some side of Janet she's managed to keep hidden all these years. Maybe she is just lonelier than she wants to admit. Maybe she wants to answer some of these questions. Maybe it's time she asked some herself.

"Lovely ring, by the way," Renna says, pointing to a large moonstone that Janet wears on the middle finger of her right hand. "And darling, not to be intrusive, but do you realize that you're crying?"

"No I'm not," Janet insists, even though she can feel the tears welling up in her eyes.

☽

They gave her the ring the night of the adoption ceremony. It was Georgie's idea; this was how three women and one man would give birth to a daughter, bind her to them, and them to her. She had lived with them for several years by then; a period in which the last nagual, the two witches and the Fearless Guide withdrew more and more into their own world, circumscribed by their Spanish-style house with its pink stucco walls and empty rooms, by their gardens, their books and movies, and each other's company. Not that they didn't go out—there were still shopping trips, still dinners at restaurants, days spent at the beach or weekends when all of them, Janet included, would decamp to some luxury hotel in San Francisco or a resort in Malibu to "relax," because the women were always concerned about the toll that Georgie's work might take on him. They traveled under false names and enjoyed the task of rehearsing what they would call themselves for a weekend away. "Now, Florence," or Verna or Annabel, one of the women would say, addressing another, and everyone would burst into laughter. But wherever they went, much of what they talked about was when they would go home, and Georgie, wherever he was, still locked himself in some room, somewhere, and wrote.

This was also the time when Georgie finally gave up on holding classes. Never comfortable in public, he decided that there was no reason to push himself to teach groups of students what Yamon had taught him, out in the desert, over the course of years. It was enough that he was pouring everything he knew, everything he continued to learn through his own struggles along the path to the infinite, into his books, so that was that. Time after time he said that he didn't want to build a cult around himself so it was better that he remain a private person. Of course, the further he withdrew from the devoted legions of people who read his books, who wrote to him, who traveled from all over the world to try to meet him (which was why cameras were installed all around the outside of the house, and a high concrete wall surrounded the perimeter) the more he attracted followers who waited for the next book, the next revelations. But he said he wasn't responsible for that. He said that the choices other people made were up to them.

But his choice was to make Janet part of what he called his family. She was not a witch—she was years away from understanding enough about adjusting the attention of the universe and re-describing reality to be one of them—and certainly, there was only one Fearless Guide. So they decided to make her what she had already become: Janet Planet, the sorcerer's child.

They drove north, into the canyons, in Lily's blue Volvo. They rented rooms in a motel on the highway—a very un-Georgie like place—and as the afternoon turned to evening, Zella, the hiker in the group, led them on a trek into the hills. They walked for about an hour—not much by Jorge Castelan standards; in his books, Yamon often had him traipsing through the desert for days—and finally, after struggling up a steep incline, arrived at the summit of a flat-topped hill. It was dark by now; the stars were appearing in scattered patterns and the moon, a sharp crescent on the wane, hung somewhere in the distance, looking small and unfriendly.

Jorge Castelan led Janet to the edge of the hill, while the witches and the Fearless Guide looked on. "Alright," he said now. "What you have to do is make an energetic leap. We will make it with you, and meet you on the other side."

"The other side of what?" Janet asked.

Jorge Castelan pointed to another hilltop across the canyon, an impossible distance away. "I can't do that," Janet said. She was suddenly terrified. She thought, for a moment, that maybe they were all crazy—really crazy, and actually expected her—in body or spirit or both?—to jump across the canyon. Did they think a great eagle, or maybe one of her old friends, the crows, would swoop down out of the night sky and carry her across? In his book, The Other Side of Reality, she had read about the time that Yamon had made Jorge Castelan take an energetic leap into the infinite, which was his induction into the world of the naguals; he had stood at the top of a hill and jumped off into the darkness below, waking up two days later in Yamon's hut, with not a scratch on him but a remembered experience of walking on black clouds and glowing pathways of energy. But that was Jorge Castelan; even as Janet Planet, she certainly didn't believe there was any possibility that she could accomplish this sorcerer's task.

"You know I can't," she repeated.

"Of course not," Jorge Castelan said. "Not yet. But I want you to have a picture in your mind of this distance when you do jump. This is how far you will really go, from where you are now to where you will be soon."

Zella came up to her then and led her down the hill a few hundred yards to where there was a ridge above a narrow crevasse; on the other side of the crevasse was a high plain with a desert-like landscape of scrub brush and sandy soil. As Janet was looking into the crevasse—and thought she could see the bottom; it wasn't very far—Namuria came up behind her and tied a blindfold over her eyes. Then Georgie took her hand and led her on another walk that lasted for about ten minutes, during which he said nothing but "Listen, listen." For what? Janet asked and he said, "Listen to me breathe. I am breathing the wind for you. I am breathing the wind of a hundred worlds to carry you from here to there. I am breathing the wind that Yamon breathed into me. He made me his pupil and then his successor in an ancient tradition. Now, in that same tradition, I am making you our child."

Finally, he led her back to the ridge and said, "Now. Jump." She knew that she could jump across the small crevasse—and even if she failed, she wouldn't fall far enough to get hurt—but of course, it was possible that he had actually led her back to the top of the high, flat hill, and what she was facing was an uncrossable chasm.

So what did she believe? Was this a test about sorcery or love? If it was sorcery, then Jorge Castelan might lie to her—Yamon had often lied to him to get him to do something he was afraid to do in order to teach him one lesson or another. But if it was about love, Georgie wouldn't do that to her. She believed that deeply; he would not hurt her or put her in jeopardy. He would not ask her to do anything she wasn't ready to.

"Go," he said, pushing gently at her back. "Run ten steps and then jump."

And so she did. She ran fast and jumped without thinking—jumped blindly, jumped as if she was jumping a barrier between life and death, between death and freedom. Jumped, and felt like she was flying. Jumped—and landed on sandy soil, splayed out on the ground, tasting blood. She was afraid to move. For a moment, she thought she might be clinging to a ledge or teetering on the edge of a ravine, in great peril. But very quickly, Georgie and the witches and the Fearless Guide were beside her, helping her up, wiping the blood that was trickling from her lip. They started to lead her down the hill and then, finally, someone remembered to remove her blindfold.

"Now you really are Janet Planet," Georgie said to her. And over and over again he murmured one of his Spanish endearments: he called her nena. Baby. My baby. Our baby.

They decided to drive all the way home that night instead of staying at the motel. At one point, when Lily was at the wheel of her blue Volvo, with Janet sitting beside her and Georgie, Zella and Namuria asleep in the back, Lily whispered to her that actually, the place where Georgie had made her jump was not even at the edge of the shallow crevasse he'd shown her, but an even smaller one—so small that if she had tripped and fallen into it, she wouldn't have done any more damage to herself than stubbing her toe. Zella and the witches had seen to that: they weren't going to allow the slightest possibility that Janet would be hurt.

And then she took the moonstone ring off her own finger and gave it to Janet Planet. "Today is your birthday with us," she said. "And here is your gift. It came from Mexico, a long time ago."

"Did Yamon give it to you?" Janet asked.

"I never met Yamon," Lily said. And then, realizing what she had admitted, she smiled. "Our Georgie," she said. "Sometimes he exaggerates a little bit, but only to prove a point. You understand that, don't you?" Lily asked.

And to celebrate her birthday, Janet said yes.

☾

"Do you have anything to drink around here besides coffee?" Renna asks as Janet wipes her eyes on her sleeve. She cannot remember the last time she cried in front of anyone. And more, she is surprised at herself, at how quickly the feelings that engendered the tears came on. She had been so angry at him—at all of them—for so long. Maybe she didn't notice when the anger began to slip away. But left what in its place? Loneliness? Regret?

"It's eleven o'clock in the morning," Janet tells Renna.

"Oh, excuse me," Renna says as she stands up and stalks around Janet's kitchen, rummaging through drawers and cabinets. "I didn't figure you for the kind of person who has rules about things like that." Finally, giving up, she leaves the kitchen, and Janet hears her front door slam closed and then open again: Renna must have gone out to her car because she comes back into the kitchen triumphantly holding aloft a bottle of white wine. She pours the dregs of their coffee into the sink, gives the mugs a cursory rinse and then fills them with chardonnay. "Go on," she says to Janet, putting one of the mugs down in front of her. "Live dangerously. It always helps."

Janet looks at Renna but says nothing. Renna meets her gaze. "Yes, well," Renna says after a moment. "I guess you know that." She takes a sip of wine and then, restlessly, stands up again, and again begins marching around the kitchen. "What about food? I don't really think we can eat this," she says, poking at the deadly looking coffee ring. "And I'm hungry. Aren't you?"

Before Janet can answer, Renna has the refrigerator door open and is pulling out what few items it contains. She turns on one of the gas burners and says, "The life I've lived, you learn to make a feast out of nothing at any hour of the day or night. When some guy who's been in a recording studio for twelve hours straight says he's hungry, you learn to cook or else some other babe with bigger tits than you is going to fry his bacon for him, if you know what I mean."

Janet can guess. She drinks her wine while she watches Renna crack eggs into a pan, add a bunch of other ingredients Janet didn't even know she had, and then bring an omelet to the table that looks—and turns out to taste—delicious.

"So," Renna says. "Feel better?"

"I do," Janet says. "Thank you."

Renna attacks the food on her plate, quickly finishing half her portion of the omelet, and then says, "So. Were you in love with him?"

Janet puts down her fork. "You just come right out and ask whatever question you want, don't you?"

Renna goes all wide-eyed and fluttery. "Am I out of line? You can tell me that I am and then I'll have to admit that you're not the first person who's ever suggested to me that I can be the teensiest bit aggressive. And nosy. I will admit to nosy without any argument whatsoever. On the other hand, give me a break, won't you darling? I mean, he's Jorge fucking Castelan. You can imagine that I'm curious. I've met just about everybody, but I've never met anyone before who actually lived with him."

"Well, now you have," Janet says. "And it probably isn't exactly the mind-blowing experience you expected."

"Oh, I don't know if I'd exactly say that," Renna tells Janet. "You do seem kind of interesting. Kind of."

Again, they regard each other wordlessly across the table, still sizing each other up. Finally, Janet says, "No, I was not in love with him. Not like you mean. But I was very young and it was... complicated."

"So you're not going to tell me any secrets?"

"My secrets aren't all that interesting."

"Now you are lying," Renna says. "But that's alright. I do it myself all the time. Let me ask you, though—is it a secret what you're doing up here in the hinterlands? Usually, everybody around here knows everything about everybody else, but you're a bit of a puzzle. Meggie—you know Meggie, at the bakery—said you're working on something with pianos?"

"Harpsichords," Janet tells her. "I seem to be resurrecting harpsichords." Resurrecting harpsichords. What a wonderful phrase—now where did that come from? Janet asks herself. She has no answer, but just as she did the day she decided to move to Woodstock and salvage the kit she found in the Bearsville basement, Janet feels a stirring of joy. Real joy. More than that—it's like life coming back to her, she thinks. The life she didn't realize had leeched away over the years is coming back. She turns away from Renna, just in case her face shows what she's feeling, because she doesn't want to explain it right now—but it has occurred to Janet that what she's done, in a roundabout kind of way, is what Georgie was always telling her to do: she's adjusted the attention of the universe. Her universe, at least. She's re-described her reality, changed it so that it suits her better. Is that sorcery? Well, she decides, maybe a little.

They've both finished their food, so Renna takes their plates to the sink, along with the mugs, which they've both emptied. She washes the dishes and sets them to dry on the drain board. "There," she says. "A full service lunch, or brunch, or whatever it was." She remains standing at the sink, looking thoughtful. "You really said harpsichords, right? I didn't quite get the resurrection thing."

"All I meant was that I just put one together from an old kit, and now I'm going to try to repair some other kit instruments that never quite got finished. Why?"

Renna answers Janet's question with one of her own. "Just kits? I didn't know they even made harpsichords that way. But what about one that wasn't made from a kit, but that's broken. Do you think you could fix it?"

"That depends on what's wrong with it. Do you actually have a harpsichord? Is that why you're asking?"

"You sound shocked. I have lots of interesting things," Renna says to Janet, who replies that she doesn't doubt it for a minute. "But in a wonderful confluence of circumstances—which one might say is very Jorge Castelan-like, don't you think?—it happens that I do have a harpsichord and it's broken and if you can fix it, that would be great. I don't know what's wrong with it, but some of the keys don't work."

"Do you play?" Janet asks her.

"No. But it belonged to Robert Plant. He used to play it."

"Robert Plant gave you a harpsichord? Why don't you sell it? Whether it plays or not, it must be valuable."

"I can't sell it because I can't prove it's his," Renna says. "But he did give it to me...only he doesn't seem to remember. They don't remember half their lives, those guys. He seems to think it was stolen from him somewhere along the line."

"Ah," Janet says.

"Never mind," Renna says. "Just see if you can fix it, will you? I'll certainly pay you."

"Well, let's see how big a job it is," Janet tells her. "Wine and omelets may cover the cost."

Janet tells Renna that she can stop by her house later in the afternoon. Renna will be in the gallery then, so she tells Janet to just let herself in; there's a key under a rock next to a gargoyle statue in the garden.

After Renna leaves, Janet goes out to her workshop where she spends the next few hours feeling as out of sorts as she had in the morning, before Renna's visit. She's trying to work but she isn't getting much done: her thoughts are drifting, and she's being clumsy with her tools, which is unusual. Late in the afternoon, she decides she's done, so she cleans herself up and decides to make good on her promise to look at Renna's harpsichord. Correction, she tells herself. Robert Plant's harpsichord. Maybe.

It's a long way to Renna's house, but Janet still prefers to go on foot rather than drive the narrow road with its many sharp turns and blind curves. Fifteen minutes after she's set out on her walk, Janet arrives at Renna's place, a chocolate-colored wedding cake of a house, with stained glass windows and a wrap-around porch painted purple. Hello again bygone days of psychedelic glory. Janet has seen the house before, and liked it from the outside; she's curious about what it will look like inside.

Janet finds the key and lets herself in. She is not all that surprised by what she finds. The interior of the house is a lace-and-velvet fantasy, a rock star girlfriend's brocaded palace circa sometime when Jim Morrison was still alive. Maybe in some other town, the décor might seem to be working a little too hard at maintaining its retro look; it might even seem like the owner has a serious problem with letting go of the past. But here, in Woodstock, it's just another hippie hostel, neither odd nor out of place at all.

Janet finds the harpsichord in the lamp-lit living room, positioned between tall windows that look out at the darkening woods. It's a pretty instrument with a case of light maple that is meant to look like it was constructed centuries ago, but Janet guesses that it's a modern reproduction. The materials, the handiwork; nothing about the instrument indicates that it's an antique as far as she can tell— and she's pleased that she can tell, that she's remembering so much of what she absorbed years ago, in the Guttenberg warehouse. Even the painting on the inside of the lid—a stag, an archer, a medieval lady in a long green dress peeping out from behind a flowering bush and beckoning to the stag to join her in her hiding place—is redemptive in a way that would not be seen in an antique instrument. The picture embodies a modern sensibility of finding safety from harm that would not appear in a hunting scene of this type.

Apart from admiring the painting—being a fake doesn't mean it isn't pretty to look at—Janet quickly figures out why some of the keys are silent: the strings have come lose from their tuning pins. They will have to be rewound on the pins and the instrument will have to be tuned. Janet has the wire at home and it will just be a matter of an hour or two to revoice the instrument. The job will also require a pitch pipe, which, of course, she has—one was packed in with every Guttenberg kit—but she knows already, that's not what she will use.

It so happens that, at one of the garage sales this summer, she found a tuning fork, and bought it. She didn't really need it, but she bought it anyway. Omens, Georgie always said, are everywhere. You just have to look for them. And you have to recognize them when they appear.

III

"I was waiting for you to call me."

Janet is listening to Georgie speaking to her on the phone. It is early morning, perhaps a week after she first saw him on Tinker Street. She is still in bed, but she was awake before the phone rang, and when it did, she knew before she answered who would be on the line.

Janet thinks that Georgie sounds aggrieved. She says, "I don't have your phone number."

"Nobody does," he replies. "Almost."

"So how could I call?"

"Janet Planet, Janet Planet, Janet Planet," Georgie intones softly. Now he is admonishing her, and she gets the message. She is clever—he always told her she was clever—so nothing should have stopped her if she wanted to speak to him. *If.*

"I thought that I would wait for you to call me," she tells him, and as soon as she says it, she realizes that in fact, that is exactly what she was doing. And now, maybe more: she is establishing ground rules, testing the next steps she takes in his direction. And yet, as she listens to his voice, all she wants is to console him. She wants him to console her. For what? For everything. For all the mistakes.

"Come have dinner with me, nena. I'll make Aji de Gallina," he says, naming a Peruvian dish of shredded chicken in a spiced milk sauce. "You always liked my cooking," he says. "Remember?"

She does remember. She always preferred it when he cooked because the food he made was delicious. The Fearless Guide never cooked, only the witches did, and they were both Midwestern girls at heart—what they served was what Janet thought of as standard diner food: meat, canned vegetables, potatoes. Georgie's meals were often miraculous blends of exotic, spicy tastes and he made desserts that tasted like clouds, puffy concoctions of fruit and cream with a hint of something peppery blended in.

"Alright," Janet says. "I will."

They agree on a time and say good-bye. Then, Janet gets out of bed and begins her day. She works zealously until noon, and after eating a sandwich in her kitchen, returns to the studio behind her house and plunges back into the tasks she's set herself. In addition to the two harpsichords she's salvaging for their owners, she has a new project in her workshop: a Guttenberg clavichord that she bought on eBay, very inexpensively. After her conversation with the monk in the bakery, it seemed like something more than coincidence when, while trolling for parts online, she came across the old kit instrument for sale, so she bought it. The instrument is made in what is called the King of Sweden style and is supposed to be a stark, severe-looking box with wooden keys, but somewhere in its past, some idiot had painted it gold and replaced the wooden keys with ebonized plastic. Janet's plan is to strip the clavichord down to the original wood, restain it, replace the keys and then resell it.

She quits around five-thirty, and then goes back to her house to shower and change. By the time she locks the front door behind her, only the edge of the horizon still holds a ragged ribbon of fading light; night has sailed across the sky and launched its stars. She is going to have to drive about twenty minutes on unlit roads to get to the address Georgie has given her, so she starts her car and turns on her high beams. She never listens to the radio in the car because she has to concentrate wholly and completely on driving along the narrow Catskill roads.

She stops along the way for one thing, a box of marzipan frogs, which she buys at a British-themed gourmet store that sits at a crossroads between several of the neighboring towns. Marzipan is something Georgie loves, and though Janet is still deciding, minute by minute, how much she wants to please him, this one thing seems neutral enough. It's simply a better version of Renna's housewarming gift.

A few minutes later, as the car is climbing higher into the foothills, she can see the house she's heading to above her, on a ridge, lit up like a beacon. It's a big house, modern and multileveled, with decks that in daylight must have spectacular views of the rolling hills and deep valleys sliced into the schist by glaciers on a million-year journey, a million years ago. When Janet arrives, she parks her car in the empty driveway in front of a garage big enough to hold several vehicles. She takes her box of candy and walks up a pathway edged with solar lamps cast in the shape of small rocks; even though the sun was hidden for most of what had been a gray, windy day, the lamps had stolen enough energy to do their job, beaming brightly as they outline the way to the front door.

She knocks, the door opens, and then there he is: Georgie. Jorge Castelan, looking, actually, better than he has ever looked, which Janet did not really notice when she saw him last week, briefly, on Tinker Street. He is lean, no longer pudgy, his features, always pleasant enough, now more defined; he is handsome almost, he looks strong and healthy. And though he must be, now, about sixty-five, he does not look it: even his hair is still only slightly silvered, and it is still thick, dark, a younger man's mop.

They embrace only lightly this time as he leads her into the house, which is all wood and stone and low furniture made of red and white oak bent by expensive processes into luxurious forms. In the living room, there is a huge fireplace with a hearth of pale gray slate flecked with gold. Fragrant logs are burning; the room is brightened by fire, track lights, candles on tables. Georgie gestures toward a couch where Janet seats herself, and he sits in a chair across from her, smiling, smiling, smiling. Janet waits, but no third person appears: no Carolee, no anybody. Apparently, for now at least, they are alone.

"This is a beautiful house," Janet says. She has other things to say—to ask—but isn't sure how to get started. Or if she even can.

Georgie shrugs. "It's rented," he says, disclaiming any interest in the comfort of his surroundings.

Janet suddenly realizes she's clutching the box of candy, so she hands it to Georgie. He opens it and laughs. "Frogs," he says. "There were frogs in the garden in Westwood, do you remember? In the koi pond, with no koi?"

Janet had forgotten, or thought she had: the marzipan came shaped as fruit or frogs, and she had chosen the frogs just because she liked them better. But as it turns out, what she had convinced herself was just a box of candy is, in fact, a box of time, of memory, because yes, of course, now she does recall, with great clarity, the huge koi pond in their garden, which, for years, held no koi, no pretty red and gold fish because Zella-Zed disliked them. Who knew why? Too big, too fat, too hard to keep alive, perhaps. The pond was empty until one day, the frogs moved in, tiny ones, bright green, with pebbled skin and blue spots on their hind legs. Everyone claimed they were a certain kind of frog that lived only in rain that sometimes pooled in the desert, in Sonora, frogs that ate cactus fruit and buried themselves in the sand. Therefore, they were sorceric signs, manifestations of *there* that had come *here*, energetically, to be near other powerful beings: Jorge Castelan and his women. The witches. The Fearless Guide.

And so the words just pop out of Janet's mouth; pop out, like the mysterious frogs. "Georgie," Janet says, "where are they? Where is Zella? Where are Lily and Namuria?"

Jorge Castelan puts the box of candy on the table and folds his hands in his lap. "I don't know," he says. He closes his eyes for a moment, takes a long breath.

Janet waits for more, but when he doesn't speak, she prods him. "I don't understand," Janet says. "What happened?" And then, softly, she asks, "Did it have something to do with me?"

She's amazed at herself, surprised that she can ask this question. But Jorge Castelan hardly seems fazed.

"Of course not," he says. "That was a very long time ago." He wags a finger at her, as if they are discussing something trivial, even silly. "But you should have come home."

"Yes," Janet says. "Maybe."

"Maybe?" Georgie says. "It would have been better if we'd had a fight. But you're so stubborn. You wouldn't fight with me. You just left."

"Is that what you wanted?" Janet says incredulously. "To fight?" She almost wonders if they are talking about the same thing. What happened between them, the night she walked away from him. From her father, her mother times three.

"Yes. Sometimes that's better," Jorge Castelan says, but he does not explain *better than what*. "But you probably would have beaten me to a pulp. Now, too. Do you want to see?" he says, suddenly playful. "Here." He balls his fists into a mock fighter's stance. "Put up your dukes."

This is a sorcerer's joke, a mocking ploy that Yamon would have pulled on him since, of course, he is not talking about a contest of strength, but of wills.

Janet smiles at him, she lets him know she gets it. But then she says, "Please. Tell me what happened."

"See?" Jorge Castelan says. "You won't let anything go. That's good. That's better than me. Even when there were things I desperately wanted to know, my mind would wander. Yamon would try to teach me and I couldn't pay attention. Maybe *that's* what happened," he says. "My attention wandered. You always have to be very focused, and I wasn't for a while. That's when I got into trouble. I had to leave the world for a period of time, and when I came back, they were gone. Lily. Namuria. Zella. They were all gone. The house was locked up, the electricity was turned off, everything was dark. I had no idea where they had gone. I still don't. I have looked for them, though, just as I keep looking for Yamon. But everyone has gone elsewhere."

Georgie grows quiet for a moment and Janet keeps still as she waits for him to continue. He seems to be looking inside himself, trying to explain what he has experienced. Finally, he says, "I think it was because I hadn't been writing. I had gotten lazy. I wasn't thinking. I wasn't paying attention," he repeats. And then he taps Janet on the forehead, his old gesture that is, itself, as attention getting as ringing a bell. "Listen to me," he says. "When you're young, you're ready for adventure. You'll go anywhere, do anything to be stimulated, to have things happen to you. It's like your skull is so thick that only big things get through—big ideas, big experiences—and so you have to go bang yourself up against as much as you can, as quickly as you can. *Bang, bang, bang,*" he says, smacking his hand against his knee for emphasis. "But then you go through a long stretch where things get dull. You work, you wander around, you eat and you dream, and it's okay, but your thick skull is getting thinner all the time. Soon—sooner than you can imagine—you wake up one morning and you're all mind; all thought, and everything is getting through. Everything! Too much! So you think, well, it's time for another adventure. But now the body is getting cranky. It carried you through all those deadly, dried-up years when nothing much happened and now it's tired. It's old! It just wants to lie down and rest! But the mind is still raring to go. That's what happened to me; I got caught up in arguing with my body and my focus weakened. My attention wandered, and so did the attention of the universe—if I wasn't interested, then it wasn't interested in me! That's when I was taken out of the world. I had to fight my way back."

"Where did you go?" Janet asks.

"There are good naguals and bad ones," says Jorge Castelan. "Yamon was—is—a good one. He's a trickster, and he can be dangerous, but that's not his intention in the world. However, going back ten thousand years, there have been some bad naguals, as you can imagine. The bad naguals pulled me out of the world and kept me imprisoned for a time. But even while I was incarcerated by them, I didn't stay still. I learned to fly through the walls they built around me—which is very important. You can't walk through walls, obviously, but you can fly through them. So that's what I did, and I went traveling. I even looked for Yamon, but he continues to elude me. Not forever though; I'll find him eventually. He burned up from inside when he left this world, but I can still smell him. Like a dog who knows his master—I can smell him. He's *somewhere*. So are Lily and Namuria and Zella. I just haven't had enough time to look."

As Janet listens to Jorge's story she realizes that something new has happened to her, that she is having an experience she would not have known before this moment how to describe, but she knows now: she is hearing Georgie's story on two levels at the same time. As a person who lives in the everyday world, she is well aware that what he's telling her sounds certifiably crazy. But there is also a part of her—the Janet Planet part, the girl who belonged to the last nagual and his witches and his Fearless Guide—who does not think that it is odd at all. Losing and finding the attention of the universe, being imprisoned between realities, looking for a sorcerer who has vanished into something other than death—for a good part of her life, this was normal dinner conversation. Night after night after night, she had listened to tales of power and magical otherness. Night after night, her companions agreed that yes, once we were in the desert and we crouched down, with our faces to the sand; and when we rose again we were different, we were savage, magical spirits who could roam the other side of reality, the dangerous realms where there is no god but only greater and lesser levels of the attention of the universe and the mind must be a cunning voyager. *Obviously, you can't walk through walls, but you can fly through them.* It still sounds almost logical to her. Maybe, she thinks, because she's getting older, too, and her skull is getting thin.

Janet laughs out loud. Hearing her, Georgie narrows his eyes. "You think this is funny?" he asks.

"I'm laughing at myself," Janet tells him. "Just at me." She taps herself on the forehead. "I may need a helmet soon. Especially if I ever have to go crashing through a wall."

"The older you get, the harder it is," says Jorge Castelan. "But all the more necessary."

He gets up then, telling Janet that he wants to check on the food he is cooking and is back in a few minutes with plates of chicken covered with a creamy sauce. Each plate is also decorated with slices of hard-boiled eggs, which Janet remembers as Georgie's favorite way of dressing up this dish.

From where she's sitting, Janet can see an open archway leading to a formal dining room, but Georgie seems to prefer that they sit and eat where they are, in front of the fireplace. He puts the dishes on a coffee table by the couch, and returns to the kitchen for cutlery and glasses of wine.

When he returns, he sits down again, eats a few forkfuls and smiles. "It's good," he says.

Janet agrees. "It's wonderful."

They are halfway through their meal when Jorge Castelan says, "I haven't written a book in a while, but I am going to write about this. About what happened to me. I think I'm going to call it *Flying Through Walls*."

There was a time when Jorge Castelan published a book once every two or three years. If you walked into a bookstore, there was a whole shelf of his works. But it has been, Janet thinks, almost a decade since his last book came out. "Me too," Janet says, to which Georgie replies with a puzzled look. "I'm doing something I haven't done in a long time," she tells him. "Actually, never before. I built a Guttenberg harpsichord. I found an old kit in someone's basement, put it together and sold it. And now I'm building a couple of others—I have two harpsichords and a clavichord in my shop."

Jorge Castelan puts down his fork and allows himself a long, theatrical sigh—one worthy of Renna, Janet thinks. "See?" he says. "Stubborn. We're back where all our problems started." But then he leans over and kisses her on the forehead, on her delicate, thin skull.

Just then, Janet hears the front door open, feels fingers of cold air reach into the room. "Well, hello," says Carolee Carter, coming into the living room with her coat over her arm. She is as attractive as Janet remembers from the brief glimpse she got of her on Tinker Street, but hard-looking also. Not just toned, but edgy, spare. *Spiky all over*, Janet thinks. *Not just her hair.*

"I'm so sorry I missed dinner," Carolee continues, tossing her coat on the couch. "I had business in the city and then the drive took longer than I expected tonight—an accident on the Thruway, I think. You know how it is—sometimes you can sail up here in two hours and other times, the traffic just kills you." Janet realizes that Carolee is talking to her, to Janet, because surely Georgie knows where she has been. And she is speaking to her with a sense of familiarity that Janet finds discomfiting, as if it is assumed, somehow, that they are friends, or are meant to be.

"I hope there's some of that great-looking stuff left," she says, turning now to Georgie. "I'm starved."

"It's in the kitchen," he tells her.

"Terrific," she says. "I'll be right back."

Janet had stood up when Carolee came in—she has learned some good manners over the years—but Georgie remained seated, which was to be expected; manners, good or bad, were gestures he had always deemed meaningless. But as Carolee passes by him on the way to the kitchen, she lightly brushes her hand across the top of his head, an action that can be read as either possessive or merely affectionate. Either way, it strikes Janet as just something else to feel put off by because it is not a gesture that either the witches or the Fearless Guide would ever have made in front of anyone. In the presence of other people, they were neither openly affectionate toward Jorge Castelan nor deferential. They just were; the four of them just *were*. The women were not his equals, but neither were they a harem—a word that had been used by a man named Arthur Rivers, the most vicious of the academics who had tried to debunk what Rivers had called "the Jorge Castelan myths." *Anything*, Rivers had written about the Castelan books, *can be made to seem mysterious if you want it to be.* He had not been content, though, to try to disprove the notion that Yamon had really existed, or that the stories Jorge Castelan told about his experiences were anything but what Rivers termed drug dreams, instead, he had taken particular aim at the nagual's private life. *Two witches and a Fearless Guide,* he had sneered in a review of one of Georgie's books that appeared in the *New York Review of Books,* though thankfully, he hadn't mentioned Janet. (*Because we were able to protect you,* Georgie had told her, speaking fiercely of having adjusted the attention of the universe away from her. *If he looked at you, he wouldn't even see your face.)* In the letter, Rivers had continued with his vitriol. *They were his students*, he revealed. *Three girls without a life, so he invented one for them.*

Janet remembers reading this and thinking, *So what's wrong with that?* She couldn't see how it mattered who the women had started out as; almost everyone she had run into in every commune and youth hostel and crash pad she had spent time in had reinvented themselves in some way; changed their name, their philosophy, grown their hair long, adopted a new mode of dress. So the women had decided that they were witches and a Fearless Guide, or Jorge Castelan had told them that's what they were. So what? Janet had met a lot of people who called themselves witches in the psychedelic days who were either busy trying to learn black magic or else spent a lot of time talking about communing with nature, who collected herbs, built bonfires and talked to crystals. Lily, Namuria and Zella-Zed were nothing like that—the image of any of them as flighty spell-casters was laughable—but so was the idea of this Carolee as their successor, if that was what was going on here. This spiky woman was hardly warrior material. *A hard body doesn't mean a hard mind*, thinks Janet Planet, a woman with a girl inside her who has unfinished business with a nagual and his women. *There is a reason that Zella was called the Fearless Guide*, she reminds herself. Georgie had always said that if Yamon had not met him, he probably would have done just as well with Zella, who Georgie said had more energy and discipline than all of them put together, who was the oldest of the women and, they all agreed, the smartest, who was so unquestionably trusted that she was given Jorge Castelan's finished manuscripts to copy edit before anyone else saw them. Janet can't imagine this Carolee—an exercise queen from L.A.?—fighting her way through the dangerous distractions of everyday consciousness to reach Yamon's spirit realms where, supposedly, the real battles began, the battle against death, the battle for power and the ability to see beyond the limitations of human understanding. The daughter inside Janet, who has now spoken to her father, who yearns for her lost mothers, grows wary on their behalf. Her heart twists and turns.

Carolee returns from the kitchen with a plate of food and then seats herself on a chair near Georgie. "I really am pleased to finally meet you," she says to Janet. "Last time…well. That wasn't exactly an introduction. I do know a little bit more about you now, because I made Georgie tell me. But I'm sure there's so much more."

"There's always more to know, right?" says Janet. She's being sly, which Georgie will find entertaining.

"I understand that I have a lot of catching up to do," Carolee says, giving just an inch.

"Yes," Janet says, finally looking over at Georgie, looking him in the eye. "Me too."

"You mean, me first," Georgie tells her. "You mean, whatever I need from you is less important than what you want from me."

"Why not?" Janet says, sparring with him, because isn't that what he told her he wanted her to do?

Georgie emits a big, barking laugh, which announces that not only is he highly amused, he also approves of Janet's taking him on—or rather, taking on his companion. "Bad girl," he says to Janet. "Bad, bad girl. But that's Janet Planet," he says, addressing Carolee. "Watch out. She only seems well behaved. When she feels like it, she bites."

But apparently, nothing fazes this Carolee—which, Janet has to admit, is probably a big plus in dealing with Georgie—because conversationally, she just sails on by. She seems to have her own agenda, and she's sticking to it.

"Well, things will unfold," she tells Janet, who thinks that perhaps Carolee is practicing sorcerer's language. "Or else I'll make them unfold—won't I Georgie? One thing I am very good at is making things happen."

When they have all finished eating, Carolee collects their dishes and carries them into the kitchen. After she returns, she says to Jorge Castelan, "What do you think? Would you like to show Janet what we're planning?"

"Of course," he says, nodding sagely and sounding quite serious. "That's exactly what we should do."

Georgie—who has switched into his courtly mode for the moment—finds both women's jackets and fusses over each, in turn, insisting that they both bundle up against the chilly night. When they have a moment out of Carolee's hearing, Janet tries to ask what all this is about, but he shushes her, whispering, "Be nice now, nena." Then he leads them outside and ushers everyone into a hefty Mercedes. The elaborate, fancifully furnished house, the expensive, showy car: for Janet, evidence is piling up that Georgie, in important ways—all centering around Carolee—is behaving in a very un-Georgie-like fashion.

Carolee says she'll drive, and Georgie insists on sitting in the back, leaving Janet up front to watch the person who is good at making things happen start the car and steer it down the driveway, into darkness.

Janet really, really hates driving along the unlit mountain roads at night—even being a passenger makes her nervous. And she doesn't like being in the big Mercedes because she keeps thinking that it's too wide for the road and any minute is going to slip off the side, into a ravine. Plus, after a few minutes, she has no idea where they are. She's familiar enough with the area between Woodstock and the larger town of Saugerties to the east, but they're driving west, along winding rural roads lined by dark fields and deep stands of pine. Just for effect, the cold landscape occasionally offers up a few dead trees, standing by the side of the road like huge black ghosts, threatening passers-by with their twisted branches that look like great burned arms. Carolee seems to be driving with confidence, following the beams of the car's headlights, which are turned on high, but Janet is not comforted.

Finally, they pull off the road and follow an even narrower path that eventually ends in front of a barn-like building situated with its back to a low, wooded hill; the area in front, however, looks newly cleared; with a rock-lined path leading to the front door and a clipped expanse of wintry grass all around that shows signs of having been recently tended by a landscaper.

Carolee kills the engine, and then turns to smile at Janet. "Well," she says, "we're here."

"What is this place?" Janet asks as they all get out of the car and begin walking toward the building.

"It's the old Phoenicia yoga institute," Carolee tells her. "But from now on, it's going to be the home of Centered Movement training."

"I'm sorry," Janet says. "I don't know what that is."

"Georgie told me you wouldn't," Carolee replies. "But that's why we're going to show you."

Carolee unlocks the front door of the building, snaps on the light and then enters, followed by Janet and Jorge Castelan, who has been silent since he got into the car. With quick steps, turning on more lights as she goes, Carolee leads them through a small reception area and then down a hallway lined with very old-fashioned looking doors, the kind with glass louvers at the top. In the hall itself, Janet sees evidence that repairs and improvements are underway: there are piles of lumber leaning against the wall, cans of paint stacked in a corner.

Gesturing toward the closed doors, Carolee says, "All of these are eventually going to be classrooms, or spaces for workshops." But she seems to feel no need to show off any of these rooms, walking past them all and keeping up her rapid pace as she heads toward the end of the hall. Here, there is a row of four metal doors, one beside the other, all painted a deep red and fitted with heavy brass handles.

Carolee pushes open the door furthest to the right and they enter an auditorium with about a hundred metal folding chairs facing a bare stage. The wooden floor looks battered and the gray paint on the walls is peeling off, but Carolee says, "This is all going to be fixed. We're not going to make it too fancy, of course—the point isn't to be comfortable, after all, and we'll have to get rid of all these chairs—but it's going to be perfect."

"Yes," Georgie says, his voice full of vigor, as if he hasn't said anything up to now because he was storing up energy for just this one statement. "Absolutely perfect."

Suddenly, Jorge Castelan leaps—leaps!—onto the stage. His agility is astonishing. For a moment, Janet really can imagine him flying through walls. Then, standing near the edge of the stage, facing the two women and the room of empty chairs, he begins to exercise a series of repetitive movements. Each movement is slow, precise, and accompanied by a deep groan. Carolee and Janet watch wordlessly as he goes through a cycle of ten movements, and then begins them again. It's a mesmerizing performance.

"You see?" Carolee whispers to Janet. "That's the first set of *attentions* in Centered Movement. There are six more sets, each progressively more difficult."

"Georgie is going to teach this here?"

"We'll train others," Carolee says, as onstage Jorge Castelan continues to flex his arms in specific patterns, lunge backwards and forwards and finish each cycle of movement with a loud clap of his hands. "But yes, Georgie will teach once in a while. The purpose…"

"I know what the purpose is," Janet says. "Control the flow of energy between the 'inside' and the 'outside.' Center your attention. Move into a meditative state where you are as alert as a warrior and yet as relaxed as a dreamer. I've read all his books. Only I don't remember anything about them exercising out in the desert."

Carolee regards Janet with narrowed eyes. "I'm trying to help him," she says.

"Oh?" Janet says. "Does he need help?"

"He hasn't written a book in ten years. Who even knows who he is anymore except a bunch of old hippies? Centered Movement will put him back on the map."

Janet is about to contradict Carolee—but something tells her to hold her tongue, to say nothing about the book that Jorge Castelan mentioned to her.

"There's a lot you don't know," Carolee adds.

"That's true," Janet says. And since she decides that she's just been insulted, she comes up with her own way of being confrontational. "For example, I don't know where Lily, Namuria and Zella are."

"Neither do I," says Carolee, without missing a beat. "And I hope they're alright. But they really weren't doing him any good. He needed to be pushed."

"Jorge Castelan?" Janet says. "He needed to be *pushed?*"

"Well, what do you think?" Carolee says. "They just all sat around that house and communed with the spirits or whatever they were doing."

"That *is* what they were doing," says Janet. "That's what they always did."

"Look," Carolee tells her, "I may not be going about this the way you like, but at least I've gotten him back to work."

"So do you think he can just pick up where he left off?" Janet says. "Maybe he doesn't want to. Or maybe he shouldn't."

"Well, we've discussed all this," Carolee informs Janet. "And he does want to."

"Then fine," Janet says. "He should certainly do what he wants. I've never known him to behave any other way."

It does occur to Janet, at this point—and probably before—that she is behaving badly. What has been left unspoken here, and what Carolee could justifiably say to her, is something along the lines of *Look sister, where the hell have you been all these years? Who says you get to have an opinion about any of this?* So she resolves, for the moment at least, to stop challenging Carolee. It's getting her nowhere and besides, it's making her feel bad. *Emo-o-o-tions, emo-o-o-o-tions,* she can remember Jorge Castelan jeering long ago and far away. *Emotions will kill us all.*

"Look," she says to Carolee, glancing up at the stage where Georgie is still cycling through his series of grunts and movements, seemingly oblivious to any conversation the women might be having, "Let me just tell you something. Let *me* try to be helpful." *So much for behaving yourself,* she thinks, but presses on. "He tried teaching once before, and it was a disaster. He sort of gets carried away. He'll say anything that comes into his mind. At least, that's what we—they—used to think was going on. I mean, sometimes Lily said maybe he was channeling Yamon, other times, she says that maybe he was just being a pain…"

"What does that mean?" Carolee asks, her voice arch, her expression decidedly unfriendly.

Struggling to explain, Janet says, "I guess if you live long enough, even with someone whom you think is a brilliant, maybe even magical person, you're allowed to think that maybe once in a while, he's just full of himself."

Carolee says nothing to this, so Janet continues. "The real problem with the classes was that he's…impatient. Seriously, seriously impatient. If someone doesn't immediately get what he's saying, or what he thinks they should understand, he can be pretty abusive. I mean, verbally. People used to run out of his workshops in tears."

"So he's tough," the exercise queen finally chimes in. "So what?"

"So it's not what people expect. If you only know him from his books, you think of Jorge Castelan as this vaguely awkward person who asks a lot of searching questions and is often taken to task by his teacher—Yamon—for being dense. But when Jorge Castelan is the teacher, he can be as mean to his students as Yamon was to him. Meaner. And confusing, contradictory."

"Only because he's so far ahead of where everyone else is," Carolee says. "Or don't you believe that?"

But their conversation ends there because, at that moment, as quickly as he had jumped up onto the stage, Jorge Castelan bounds off and strides over to where the two women are standing. "Centered Movement should be done for at least an hour," he says, "but even just a few minutes increases focus. However, the movements have to be done perfectly."

"I'll be the first one to take your class," Carolee says, looking pointedly at Janet.

"How are you going to get people here?" Janet asks. "Are you going to advertise?" Janet is having visions of Woodstock and its environs overrun by the die-hard followers of Jorge Castelan, along with the curious, the press and probably all the gossip shows. *Tonight on Access Hollywood: Secretive guru breaks his long silence, sets up shop in hippie haven.*

Georgie shudders. "That's the one problem with all this," he says. "People."

That makes Janet smile. Georgie's nature, in this respect at least, remains the same: he is, at heart, a deeply unsocial person. That was what the house in Westwood and the lives it sheltered was all about: keeping people—regular people, *human beings*—away. Away from them all. It was only Janet who slipped in and out of the protective boundaries they had all set up around themselves.

Solicitously, Carolee pats Jorge Castelan on the arm. "We won't worry about that for now," she says. "I'll just put the word out at first and the right people will hear about what we're doing. We'll be able to keep the classes small."

Carolee now links her arm through Jorge Castelan's and leads him out of the auditorium. Janet follows behind as they walk back down the hallway toward the front door. But as they reach the reception area and Carolee begins turning off lights, Georgie says to her, "You go on ahead for a few minutes. Let me walk with Janet Planet for a while."

"Of course," Carolee says, and steps off into the night, heading for the car.

Georgie follows for a few steps, but then stops Janet halfway along the rock pathway leading away from the nascent Centered Movement institute. "So tell me if I'm wrong," he says, "but I think you've already decided that I've brought you an evil stepmother."

"Me?" Janet says. "I'm too old now for anybody to be my mother. At least anybody new."

"Smart cookie," he says. "Always a smart cookie. Too smart for me."

"Hardly," Janet replies.

"Then tell me what you really think," he says.

"I will tell you what I remember," Janet answers slowly, thinking of a small, lithe woman in a black, full-skirted robe, deeply absorbed in the repetitive *kata* movements of kendo, one of the Japanese martial arts, which utilizes long wooden swords, called bokken, for practice. "That Namuria held the ranking of ninth Dan in kendo."

"Yes," Georgie agrees. "Like a black belt. She was very proud of that. And always practicing. But those sticks," he says, dismissively. "Who knows where they came from? Some bright bulb must have had the idea to add them later."

"Later?" Janet says. "Namuria always told us that kendo was ancient. The practice goes back a thousand years."

"A thousand years?" Georgie says, snapping his fingers. "How quickly does that go? What Yamon taught me was taught to him and his teacher was taught by the teacher who came before him—back, back, back. The sorcerers of Sonora have been around forever."

"So Centered Movement is older than Kendo."

Jorge Castelan smiles; a brilliant, loving smile directed only at Janet Planet. "Are you asking me which came first, the chicken or the egg?"

"No," says Janet, "because I know the answer to that question: it doesn't matter."

Her remark again brings out Georgie's barking laugh. "Too smart for me, too smart for your own good," he says.

They've almost reached the car, but while they're still out of Carolee's hearing, Janet tugs on Jorge Castelan's arm to stop him before he walks the last few steps.

"Georgie," she says. "You don't have to prove anything. Not at this point in your life. Not after everything you've done."

"Everybody," says Jorge Castelan, "has to prove everything, over and over again."

And then he brings out the mask that his face sometimes becomes and withdraws from her; she can feel it. He has this ability, to make curtains fall all around him, to raise walls of silence, slam doors.

So no one speaks as they drive back to the rented house. There are small good-nights all around—nothing more—as Janet gets out of the Mercedes and walks over to her own car. She slides into the front seat, starts the engine and drives away.

She concentrates totally, completely on what she's doing. It's a clear night, but dark, dark, dark—where has the moon gone? The twisting, two-lane road seems to swipe from side to side, as if it wants to run off into the trees. Janet turns on her brights, and as she does, she suddenly sees an animal up ahead, standing absolutely still in the middle of the road.

There's enough time so that she doesn't have to slam on her brakes, but can ease to a stop. The car rolls slowly to the end of its forward momentum, and then, deprived of power, sits on the edge of the rural road, its engine ticking as it cools down. Then there is silence, absolute silence, as Janet looks through the windshield at an old friend.

Well, maybe not *her* old friend, but one she's heard about. Standing in the cold, in the middle of the road between Phoenicia and Woodstock is an enormous coyote. It is motionless, but its breath flies from its open mouth as a thin cloud. There are certainly coyotes in upstate New York, but are they really, ever, this big? And this one knows her; she knows it does. Its stone-dark eyes are focused on her. It is waiting for her to acknowledge that at last, they have met.

So Janet gets out of the car. She stands behind the door, shielding herself, just in case she is wrong about what beast this is, but she doesn't think so. "Do you follow him everywhere?" she asks. "Do you never leave him alone?"

The coyote continues to stare at her, but makes no sound. It is even larger than she imagined at first, and silver-colored; sleek, streamlined, strong. A coyote among coyotes. A wraith, a guide, an elemental, a revenant, a killer, a dream. Janet addresses it again. She says, "Where are the witches? Where is the Fearless Guide?"

For a moment more the animal is silent. And then, closing its eyes and lifting its head to face the stars, it speaks. Its voice is a howl, a deep, resonant sound that rises from one note to another and then fades back again to nothing, a perfect, matched progression that journeys back and forth from here to there. And then, having fallen silent again, it turns to look at Janet once more—just a glance, just a briefest contact, eye to eye—and turns to walk off into the woods. On silvery feet, it pads away and disappears.

Janet waits for a moment, but she knows it is not coming back. And she has no more questions, anyway. So she gets back into her car, starts the engine again, and points herself toward home.

10

There came a time when Janet thought that the life she lived, and the way she lived it, was coming to an end. It seemed like it happened almost overnight. From the day she had left home, taken a bus from New Jersey to New York and ended up in Tompkins Square Park in the East Village, there was a counterculture that she could find just by looking for it. There were signs and signals everywhere: people dressed in beads and bandanas, shops selling incense and candles, whole neighborhoods centered around headshops, free clinics and alternative bookstores. The parks were places to get high and dance, to go to free concerts. Music played all the time, music sent messages about how to feel, how to live. And you could follow the music and the signs across the country, which Janet did; in California, as in New York, everybody was dancing, everybody was getting high and listening to the music and waiting for everything to burst wide open, to change, to die and be reborn.

But instead, it faded away. The counterculture was there one day and gone the next. And with it went a way of living on the margins that Janet had depended on. It had always been possible to get a job in the psychedelic days: you worked in a store or a stained glass factory or swept floors or joined the assembly line in a canning factory. You did anything that allowed you to dress the way you wanted to, that let you use your hands to do one thing while your mind drifted off, somewhere else. And you worked at something to make money, only: something you could walk away from when it was time to walk away, to travel, to leave and find something else.

The place Janet found was Guttenberg Harpsichords. Even before Jorge Castelan found her, Guttenberg was home. When she arrived in the morning, someone had already turned on the radio, cones of Nag Champa incense were burning in brass dishes on the shelves, and though every day, the necessary work got done, it never felt like work—the hours passed like the hours of life easily lived, the cool warehouse, streaked by shafts of sunlight and shadow, felt like a place one might have searched years for and then be happy to have found. The Guttenberg brothers came by once in a while to check on how things were going, to hand out orders to be filled and to do paperwork. In the afternoon, the REA Express driver, another long-haired freak earning his keep, showed up to take the boxes that had been packed and labeled, and once he was gone, that pretty much signaled the end of the day. It went on like that for years.

Until the older of the Guttenberg brothers died. At the warehouse, no one even knew he was sick; maybe they were all too young to even understand that you could get sick enough from anything to actually die. To die really, finally and forever. The younger one kept the business going for a while, but he didn't have the heart for it, or the head. And besides, Fekkenson had most of the market by then—selling harpsichord kits was hardly a growth industry; the instrument had experienced a period of popularity during the hippie days, but interest was dying out—and there wasn't really a need for two makers, one on each coast.

On the day that the younger brother handed out a share of what was left of the profits to his handful of workers and closed the doors of the warehouse, Janet sat, for a while, in the park where she and Jorge Castelan had eaten their lunches, with copies of the Los Angeles Free Press, looking through the want ads, wondering what she was going to do next. But there were no jobs; no hippie jobs, anyway. Suddenly people wanted secretaries and security guards, or they wanted women to work for escort services. They wanted tellers in banks. They wanted receptionists, nicely dressed ones, with dresses from department stores and manicured nails.

"You don't really need another job," Lily said to her that afternoon, when she got home to the quiet house, hidden behind its viney, flowering garden and its fruit trees. "There's so much to do around here." But Janet couldn't see what. She ordered their groceries; she made sure the cleaning woman who came once a week did a good job; she wrote checks to pay the household bills. AT&T. Los Angeles Department of Water and Light. Westwood Landscaping. Nordstrom's. All of that took about an hour, maybe two.

After she was unemployed, she often found herself alone in the house with Georgie. Noon was about when he finished working, and if the women were out, they would eat lunch together—their old habit, which he seemed to enjoy. But what he didn't like was to see the newspapers on the kitchen counter, because then he knew that she had been going through the want ads again. That bothered him. At first, Janet thought it was because he sympathized with her; he wished she could find something she'd like to do. Something she *could do*. How many other professions did working in a harpsichord kit factory qualify you for? But she began to realize that he really didn't want her to go back to work. None of them did. They began a campaign, subtle at first, but soon more open, to convince her to just stay home. With them.

One thing Georgie did suggest was that Janet go back to school. She hadn't finished high school—who needed a diploma when the revolution was coming?—but that was easy enough to fix. If she got her equivalency degree, he said, she could go to college. He'd send her to UCLA, introduce her to his old professors. After all, at heart, Georgie was an academic; he liked to study and to write. He had enjoyed school, he would have been enthusiastic about packing Janet off to classes every day. But it didn't interest her; what they would have taught her in school was not what she wanted to learn.

"Then fine," Georgie said. "Study with me. With us. There is so much we have to teach you. So much I haven't written about living the sorcerer's life, so much the witches know. The Fearless Guide will take you into the hills; she'll walk you through the canyons. You can unlearn ordinary reality; unlearn the everyday, undescribe what has been described to you and start all over again. There are alternatives, there is power, there are visions. There is a nonordinary reality in which we will meet you and begin the journey to infinity." That was the book he was writing then, The Journey to Infinity. *His editor in New York would call every week and say, when, when, when? People all over the country were walking into bookstores asking, when is Jorge Castelan's next book coming out? They wanted him to teach them more of what Yamon had taught him. They wanted to learn about the sorcerer's path.*

But the one pupil whose attention he really wanted was growing restless. She missed the bus ride every day; she missed the smoky smell of pinewood after it had been drilled to make a pin block; she missed the tools she had learned to use; she missed the daily routine, the comings and goings, listening to her friends talk about nothing; she missed the music on the radio. Even that had changed, and it didn't sound the same in her room above the garage. It had lost its meaning, its messages.

After lunch, Georgie took to reading her what he had written. First he'd read, then he'd explain, then he told her to practice. He sent her out into the garden, to sit under a lemon tree, to close her eyes and visualize the glowing road she could walk into a separate reality. He told her to find her spirit guides, to travel beyond the clouds. You found us, he said to her. You found me. There is a reason for that. There is work to be done.

But she didn't know if she wanted to do that work anymore. And besides, hadn't he found her? Whenever that subject came up, Jorge Castelan now said to Janet, "You are a searcher. To be a searcher has always been my way, too. That is one of the things that brought us together."

Perhaps he could choose to tell that story any one of a hundred ways, but Janet could not. In her reality, which resisted reinterpretation and remained linear, in which time was always moving forward, relentlessly forward, and which could not—would not—be adjusted to suit the whims of the last nagual, she still did not understand how to travel backwards and reverse their roles, or mingle them, as he so easily seemed to be able to. Jorge Castelan, the sorcerer to whom time was irrelevant and reality, malleable. And perhaps she did not want to do these things—or try to, or pretend to—just to please him. After all, she was growing older, she wasn't just his nena anymore, his girl, their baby. She was a person. And while she did want to work—she wanted to very much—she didn't think her vocation was to walk along the glowing road to infinity. She needed to find something else, something that wasn't his path, but hers. And most of all—the biggest secret of all—was that she didn't want to close her eyes. She didn't think she could ever say it to him, to any of them, but more and more, she wanted to live in a world that she could see.

☾

In her dream, Janet is walking along a red fence that divides a field in half. It's a summery day, mild and still. Nothing is happening in the dream, nothing good and nothing bad; Janet just keeps walking along one side of the fence, occasionally looking down at her hands. She is certainly asleep, but also aware that she is dreaming, that she is practicing a technique that Yamon taught Jorge Castelan and then he taught her: if you can find your hands in your dream and focus on them, that is how you can take control of the dream instead of letting your subconscious—which is a trickster, a distraction—take up your time with a lot of useless imagery and ridiculous symbols. In the dream, Janet is walking the fence in order to find the assemblage point, the place where whoever built this fence planted the first post. And what will she do when she finds it? Perhaps she will leave it alone. Perhaps she will move it to a point of greater advantage. *The assemblage point is adjustable—but only so far, and for only so long*, said Jorge Castelan to his daughter, repeating what he said that Yamon had told him. In other words, *Don't think you have all the time in the world to smarten up.*

Perhaps, Janet thinks, as she wakes up in darkness, she has already wasted too much time. Meaning what? In the dream, she was calm, purposeful, but in this pre-dawn hour, she is not. Last night, she worked past midnight and fell asleep exhausted, but has arisen just a few hours later, feeling compelled to go back to work again, so she pulls on a jacket over the long-sleeved tee shirt and flannel pajama bottoms she slept in, slips her feet, sockless, into a pair of rubber boots that she had left by the back door and pads out to her workshop through three inches of newly fallen snow. Overhead, Orion and his hunting dogs are low in the sky, but not ready, yet, to yield the starry field they prowl to the advent of morning. When Janet reaches the studio, it is night-cold, freezing, so she fires up the space heater as soon as she snaps on the lights.

In the center of the room is the clavichord she's been working on. Stripped of its garish gold paint, sanded down and stained a dark walnut, it's almost finished. She's been working on the two harpsichords in the shop as well, but the clavichord has become a kind of obsession. All that's left is to replace several of the key covers with cherrywood veneers that will add just the slightest hint of warmth to the stark lines of this medieval instrument. But she's going to have to wait a few minutes until the shop warms up because she's shivering from the cold—the temperature outside is in the single digits—and she can't trust herself with the glue pot she needs to use until her hands are steady.

So she sits down at her makeshift desk—a long plank of pine balanced on two sawhorses—and turns on her laptop to check her e-mail. A few inquiries have come in overnight, which she's too impatient to answer now. Then, as she scrolls down the list, she sees an address she recognizes, sort of, though she's never received anything from the sender before. She didn't even know there *was* a sender, and she still isn't sure of that once she opens the message, which is addressed to "unlisted recipients," meaning it could be something sent to a thousand people, or just to her. But because of where it's from—*peyotepalace@peyotepalace.com*—Janet has a feeling that someone has her, specifically, in mind.

The first thing she sees is a now-familiar image: the squat cactus and its companion, the distant, vee-shaped crow. Below the image is a simple two-line message: *Attached please find the first chapter of* Flying

Through Walls, *the new work in progress by Jorge Castelan. As a loyal reader, we thought you'd like to be among the first to read and review the latest teachings of this important, new-age master.*

Janet reads the two lines over again, trying to figure out what's wrong with them, because something definitely is. Jorge Castelan's books have been published by the same publishing house for over thirty years, and this kind of marketing technique—if that's what it is—is hardly their style: it's both too informal and too crude. Besides, this isn't how Georgie works; he doesn't allow his books to be read in pieces and he has certainly never invited the public, or even the most select group of friends, including the witches and the Fearless Guide, to "read and review" a work in progress. Listen, yes, as Janet had listened to him read, years ago; comment, no. Still, there is very definitely a file attached to the e-mail, a Word document, waiting to be opened and printed out. Half expecting her computer to be blown up by some alien virus, since she knows that you're never supposed to open an attachment that you aren't one hundred percent sure of, she takes the chance, opens the file and sends it to the printer that's sitting under the saw horses, on the floor.

And of course, once she has the chapter in her hand, she has to read it. The document, entitled, *Infinity for Grownups*, is not very long—only twenty-two pages. But for Janet, it is full of information. It is unlike anything else that Jorge Castelan has written, but it is completely his work, his mind, his thoughts, his way of expressing himself. And yet, in both subtle and not-so-subtle ways, each of these things has changed.

To begin with, gone is the bumbling boy persona that narrated every one of his previous books. And in this chapter, at least, almost gone is any mention of Yamon—he is referred to only once, referenced as a kind of mischievous friend who has skipped town and left his student, from here on out, to figure things out himself. And it seems the student has—or is trying to.

The boy, finally, is writing as a mature man, and in his writing Janet recognizes some of the things that Georgie said to her when they had dinner: how the mind is ready for adventure while the body, growing older, is busy shutting down. *The poor body,* writes Jorge Castelan, *spends half the day preparing to go to bed, while the mind, inside its thin skull, prepares to soar. Like a hatchling, the mind can't wait to break free from its egg of flesh and bone. The sorcerer's mind has been preparing for that journey all along; it aligns itself with infinity and growls at the universe to get its attention. This is a fierce time, thunderous and strange.*

By the time Janet finishes, dawn has cracked the sky. Thin twigs of light, pale as albumen, lie across the horizon; a flight of noisy starlings lands in the yard, looking for the birdseed Janet has taken to spreading near the studio door. She looks up, watches the birds for a while, and then reads the chapter again, deeply moved.

When she finally puts it down, she accidentally nudges her laptop, which has been displaying her screensaver—musical notes floating across a background of electric blue—and sees that she has left the Peyote Palace e-mail message on the screen. Even though there is a warning at the bottom of the text that says, *This is an automatic message. Do not reply,* impulsively, she does.

Where are the witches? she writes. *Where is the Fearless Guide?* And then she sends the message.

No sooner has she turned away from the computer than she hears the tinny ping that signals an e-mail being received on her end. To her great surprise, it's a reply from the Peyote Palace; apparently, there is someone behind the electronic curtain and he—or she—has been very quick about violating their own "do not reply" instructions. But when Janet opens the message and reads it, the information is disappointing, useless. It's the same thing that's posted on the Peyote Palace website: *They are traveling.*

What does that mean? Janet writes back in exasperation. *And who am I talking to?* In the hope that perhaps she is addressing someone she knows from her years with Jorge Castelan, she does something she never does: she signs the message with the name that Georgie gave her. *This is me,* she writes. *Janet Planet.*

She waits by the computer for fifteen minutes, then twenty, but there is no reply. So she leaves the computer on, but gets herself up off the stool she's been sitting on, sorts through the cherrywood veneers for the clavichord key covers and sets herself to work. She keeps waiting to hear the electronic signal of a new e-mail arriving, but none does.

For the next few hours, Janet works without stopping, but between the obsession about finishing the clavichord and the strange experience of receiving a chapter of Jorge Castelan's book literally out of nowhere and then having a mysterious e-mail conversation with some sort of electronic ghost, she's feeling like a year of highs and lows has gone by since she got up this morning.

Around eleven, when there's a knock on the workshop door, Janet is actually grateful to be interrupted. She knows who it is: Renna has taken to stopping by every morning on her way to the gallery, bringing coffee for both of them. The two women seem to have become friends, and though Janet remains reticent about revealing too much about her life, she's told Renna more than she's ever shared with anyone else about her years with Jorge Castelan. It was easy, in a way, because, looking back, as strange as that time might have seemed to someone who had lived a more normal life, Renna's life, though quite different, had taken an equally eccentric path. So wherever they've been before, here in Woodstock they have recognized each other with a clear eye. They are orphans, survivors, misfits. Women who sometimes still think that they are girls. Tough girls, though. And smart enough to know all this about themselves.

A few days ago, Janet had finally finished the repairs on Renna's harpsichord, which is now ready to be played, if only one of them had any affinity for it. Renna seems amused by the idea that Janet can build and tune these instruments to perfect pitch, but other than chopsticks—which sounds quite lovely, Renna thinks, on Robert Plant's faux antique—she really can't play very well.

Renna had been planning to complain about this again—what good is that beautiful thing sitting in her living room if no one can make it do what it's supposed to?—but she forgets about that when she sees the clavichord, which Janet had been keeping under a tarpaulin.

"I want that," Renna says.

"Why?" Janet asks. "You don't even know what it is."

"It's a miniature harpsichord,"

"No it's not. But if it was—so you'd have two instruments you can't play."

"I'd learn for this," Renna says. She gives Janet the coffee she's brought her and then pulls the stool away from the sawhorse desk and sits down in front of the clavichord "It's cute."

"God, I hope not," Janet says. "It's not meant to be."

She explains about the clavichord and taps the keys so Renna can hear how quietly it plays. "I still want it," Renna says. "How about I take it on consignment? I'll put it in the gallery—maybe someone will wander in and buy it. If not, I will—but you have to give me a discount."

"Okay," Janet says. "Sure."

Renna sips her coffee, and then looks over at Janet with the raised eyebrow that usually signals she's got something on her mind. "What's wrong with you?" she asks.

"Nothing."

"Now, now, now," coos Renna. "Your aura's gone all weird."

Janet laughs. "You know as much about auras as you do about clavichords," she says.

"So inform me."

Jorge Castelan was not very big on auras. Some people had them, some people didn't, but they weren't very important, he said: they were vestiges, remnants, some sort of evolutionary mistake that didn't know enough to just go extinct. All they signified was emotional leakage—feelings gone into overdrive that needed an outlet, so they kind of hung around the body for no reason at all. It was better not to have one, he thought. More evolved. Janet's, he had told her once, was water-colored, whatever that meant, and she shouldn't trouble herself about it. Like a layer of skin, he told her it would eventually just wear away.

Rather than go into all that, she says, "I did have a kind of weird morning." Though she wasn't planning to, she shows Renna the manuscript that was sent to her. "Georgie's writing another book," she says. "It might be a secret."

"Why?"

"I have a feeling Carolee doesn't know."

"But Jorge Castelan gave it to you?"

"I didn't think of that," Janet tells Renna. "Somebody sent it to me by e-mail."

"Who?"

"I don't know."

"Okay," Renna sighs, "I think I'm getting tired of this game." She plunks a few keys on the clavichord and listens to its muted sound. Then she gestures at the pages Janet is holding. "So what's in there that's so interesting? The secrets of the universe?"

Janet smiles. "Who knows?" she says.

"Well, maybe you'll let me read it sometime," Renna says. "I'd like to know what they are." She finishes her coffee, tosses the paper cup into a box Janet uses for trash, and starts to pull on the heavy shearling coat figured with Tibetan designs that she had draped over a chair when she walked in. She gives Janet a quick peck on the cheek and says, "I'll get somebody to come pick up the clavichord and bring it to the gallery. Stop by afterwards and you can help me find the best spot for it."

But before Renna can leave, Janet suddenly hears herself asking, "Have you seen them in town?"

"Who?"

"Georgie and Carolee."

"No," Renna says. "Why?" And then she pulls off her coat and sits down again. "Aha," she says. "Is *that* what's bothering you? Your dear Georgie and Carolee?"

"It's just that I've been leaving him messages on the answering machine at their house but he doesn't call back. It's been more than a week."

"Has it ever occurred to you," says Renna, who Janet has told the whole story of her visit to the Centered Movement Institute, leaving out only the part about the coyote on the road, "that maybe he's not getting your messages? Maybe Carolee doesn't give them to him? Or maybe she's read him the riot act about you and won't let him call you back."

"That's not Georgie," Janet says. "If he wanted to call, he would."

"People who are in love," says Renna, in a voice that telegraphs she is making a pronouncement, "usually do what the person they are in love with wants."

"Georgie?" Janet says incredulously. "You think Georgie is in love with Carolee?"

"Even gurus fall in love. Even at his age—or should I say *especially* at his age. Listen, he may be Mr. Magical Secrets to you and a whole bunch of other people, but he's still a man as far as I can tell. And he's not immune."

"But he hasn't even told her he's writing this book," Janet says. "I think."

"Where have you been most of your life?" Renna says. "Oh, I forgot. You were raised in fantasy land. Look, sweetie, just because you're in love with someone doesn't mean you trust them." She laughs out loud at herself, and says, "Boy, I think about nine guys I screwed wrote some version of that song."

The coat goes on again and Renna gets ready to go sailing out the door. But she's not finished, yet, with what she has to say to Janet. "Men, no matter how smart they are, or what they do—priests, princes, deep thinkers—they're all still boys. And they all think the world should stop in its tracks when they get a hard on. I think Einstein said that. Or maybe it was Mick Jagger. Of course if it was Mick and he was talking about himself, he was right. Believe me, I know."

Renna's idea of being philosophical is more breezy than profound, but she's left Janet with something to think about—an echo of what she had heard from the witches and the Fearless Guide more than once: *he's still a man*—but when the women said that about Georgie it was in the context of sex, not love. For Janet, the idea of Jorge Castelan being in love with that spiky woman, Carolee, seems impossible. *Lovey, dovey, wovey:* she can imagine how he would have sputtered those words in the past, full of ridicule if anyone had suggested such a thing; the Jorge Castelan Janet is familiar with is not all that big on troublesome romantic love with all its petty human complications.

And that, of course, was the heart of the matter: human complications. Good ones and bad ones. Wonderful, angry, strange, sad. And even unforgivable—maybe. After all this time, Janet still isn't sure.

☽

She was dreaming of the red fence; not for the first time and certainly not for the last. In the dream, she looked down at her hands, as she had been taught, so that she could center her attention, try to control the direction of the dream, and therefore, begin to look for the assemblage point. Instead, her attention was distracted by something in the distance; a shape on a hill she didn't see before in the otherwise flat landscape of dry fields. The shape took on a more distinct form as she walked along the fence, until she could see that it was a coyote, a big animal, silver colored, with eyes that could see everything. You would think, Janet told herself, that in a dream like this, that animal would have something to say. But it didn't, it just watched her, patiently. It had come from somewhere and eventually, it would have somewhere to go. But not yet. For the moment, it was her companion, hers alone.

And then she woke up, because someone was kissing her. The experience is pleasant at first: soft lips, breath on her neck—but then she realized that it shouldn't be happening. This was not another dream, definitely not: she was in her apartment above the garage attached to the house in Westwood, she had gone to bed alone, she had invited no one here. So she screamed, pushed away the man, creature, thing in the bed and ran for the door. Ran for her life, until the bedside lamp snapped on and a voice said, "Nena. Stop."

She didn't turn around because she didn't want to see him. If she didn't see him, then she could pretend this wasn't happening. He was a sorcerer, wasn't he? Then he could just fold himself up and vanish into some other realm, reappearing wherever he wanted to—as long as it wasn't in Janet's room. Reflexively, she looked down at her hands but reminded herself that she'd already decided this was not a dream.

"What are you doing?" she asked the wall.

"I want to be with you," said Jorge Castelan.

"Why?" his daughter asked, still speaking to the wall.

"Because it's time. Don't you think it's time?"

"No."

Jorge Castelan crossed the room. He stood beside Janet, touched her lightly on the arm, which finally made her turn around. But she still wouldn't look at him. He asked, "Why not?"

"I can't do that with you," Janet replied.

That brought the barking laugh from the last nagual. "But it's nothing," he told her.

"Then if it's nothing," Janet argued, "we don't have to do it."

"But we do, we do," Georgie said. He was being flirtatious now, which Janet found horrifying. It was like being confronted by a fake personality, some mode of being he had studied and was trying to reproduce. Some college boy, perhaps, someone he might have encountered long ago, on campus or in a class.

For a moment, she wondered if this was some sort of sorcerer's trick; something Yamon would have pulled on Jorge Castelan: break all the rules, all at once, upend every idea a person has ever had about you, turn their trust in you into something that can be used against them. And on top of that, appear in a new personality, something shallow and stupid and dense. A personality that cannot be reasoned with. That has concern only for itself.

"I love you," Janet said. It was her only defense.

"And I love you," said Janet's Georgie. "So come to bed with me. We'll see how much we love each other."

"Not like that," Janet said. "No." But inside, she was breaking down. She was beginning to bargain with herself: was it possible? Could she do this? She'd slept with boys, she'd slept with girls, she'd slept with more than one person at a time, more than one person in a night. Then why not this? Because if she did, she'd have to do it again, and again—she wouldn't be a daughter anymore, she'd be a wife. A witch. Every thought she had began to barrel into the next; she was resisting because she didn't want to be his wife. A child can pull away from a parent when she wants to, a child can even leave—but that's not so easy for a wife. And Jorge Castelan's wives, his women, had no life except the life that was part of his—that much had grown clearer to Janet as she'd grown older. And she couldn't do that; she just couldn't give herself up like that. But that's what he was after—she'd known it from the second she had felt his breath on her cheek. First she had lost her job, and then she would lose the rest of herself. That was why she'd panicked, why she'd screamed—because she knew what he wanted: everything. If she slept with him, she would become him; he would absorb her. That's what he did, that was the power that he had.

"Please Georgie," Janet said. "Go away."

But he was not to be deterred. He was smiling, almost purring, rubbing against her. "Janet Planet," he murmured to her. "Janet Planet, Janet Planet, Janet Planet."

"No!" she yelled at him, and then did something purely instinctive: she kicked him. Not where she should have, not where it would have done the most damage, but in the shin, which at least made him back away for a moment. He bent down to rub his leg and by the time he looked up to show her the puzzlement on his face, she was gone.

She ran downstairs, into the house, and knocked on every bedroom door, rousing Lily first, then Namuria and then Zella-Zed. They spun around her like satellites, they beamed soothing rays of love and concern at her, they patted her and embraced her and put expressions of deep, cleansing, loving attention on their faces—but their agitation, which was not for her but for what had gone wrong, which was what they kept asking—only showed her that they had all planned this together; the more the women clucked at her, the more she knew she was right. They never actually asked what was the matter because they knew. They loved her, but had agreed to this. They had always sworn they would protect her, but thought it was okay for their daughter to become their husband's wife. They loved her and they wanted to keep her, and Georgie had come to the conclusion that there was only one way to do that, the only way he knew. And because he thought it, they thought it was right.

While the women were still trying to calm Janet down, Georgie came walking through the front door. He had made himself into a being suffused with love; he was radiating love for all his women, all his children, his girls. But all Janet could think of was that if he was here, in the house, then it was safe for her to go back to the garage. Which she did, in full survival mode. The runaway still knew how to run away. She grabbed her shoulder bag, her favorite jacket, and an envelope from her dresser with some identification papers—and then she fled.

She walked through the night, through the empty streets of Westwood, California, and made all her thoughts go away—he had taught her that, too, how to move forward on nothing but forward momentum—until she found a diner, and used the phone there to call a cab. When the cab driver asked her where she wanted to go, she said the bus station, where she waited until 7 a.m. for a bus that would take her to Portland. A friend who had worked at Guttenberg had moved to Portland; Janet had talked to her recently and had been invited for a visit. So she would go visiting. That's how she thought of it, that morning, in downtown L.A., in the grungy bus station with a departure board that said there were buses leaving for everywhere, at all hours, on any day. Visiting. People who went visiting usually planned on returning home.

And maybe she did. Maybe she was rebelling again, maybe she was testing them, him, herself. Maybe she was seeing how far she could stretch the ties that bind, how much freedom she could stand, how much uncertainty. Or maybe she had just been staring at a wall for much longer than just that few minutes tonight, and had found a way to go flying through it. She fell asleep on the bus and dreamt about nothing. She dreamt about nothing. It was a relief.

☾

She had bought a one-way ticket to Portland, but not because she wasn't planning to go back after her visit. All the time she was at her friend's apartment, and even later, when she'd moved on, she kept expecting them to show up: two witches, a Fearless Guide and the last nagual—surely they could find one human girl, with or without a trail of crumbs behind her, wandering around the confines of one continent on one luckless planet rolling around on the ordinariest level of reality. But they did not, and Janet never once even called to tell them where she was. Did not even call to hear them breathe before she hung up. But then, that was also part of what Georgie had taught her: be where you are, do what you're doing. Be hard and smart, tricky when you need to, invisible when it suits your purposes. Walk through the world without regret, because sorcerers regret nothing. They give up everything they have, when they have to. And they go on.

Still—not one phone call, just to hear them breathe? That was hard-hearted, cruel—a penalty she had imposed on herself as well as her adopted family—but behavior she had probably learned from Georgie, too. She thinks of that now, in her workshop, after Renna has gone, as she picks up her cell phone and dials the number at the house in Phoenicia, only to hear what she has been hearing for days: Carolee's voice saying that no one is home. Janet leaves another message for Georgie, but she knows he won't call back because she has figured out what's going on. She is in what the women used to call an icy period, something they all went through at one time or another when they had done something to annoy Jorge Castelan, or displease him. Janet should have expected this, she imagines, as a repercussion of the night at the Centered Movement Institute when she had compared Centered Movement to kendo. Jorge Castelan resented that, and this is his way of letting her know.

Well, Janet tells herself, she put him through an icy period for years, decades. She can pay the price for that by giving him a few more days to call her back.

Then she glances over at her computer to see if any e-mail has arrived from her mysterious correspondent, but none has. Silence has descended everywhere. Like a wall, a fence, a curtain, silence stands before her. It will not yield.

"Someone is interested in buying the clavichord." That's what Renna calls to tell Janet a few days after a very handsome boy had come by with his father's pickup truck and an armful of blankets to transport the clavichord to Renna's gallery. The boy had been wearing a vintage Grateful Dead tee shirt, which he'd told Janet was his payment from Renna for transporting the instrument, but from the way he talked about her, it was clear that she had made another conquest and he would have gladly carried out her errand for free.

"Really?" Janet says. She had expected it to be decorating the front room in Renna's gallery for a while. It actually looked like it had made itself at home there, among the photos of long-haired boys and girls in miniskirts and beads. "Who?"

"I don't know," Renna says. "Some guy called, said he'd been passing by last weekend, saw it in the window and decided he wanted it, but he had a couple of questions. He's going to be here around six. Why don't you come by a little before then?"

Janet works in her shop all day, making good progress on the harpsichord that needs its interior rebuilt. A new project—apparently a very early Guttenberg, perhaps one of the first kits that came off the brothers' quirky assembly line of handmade parts—is on its way by truck from North Carolina; its owner had told Janet on the phone that it needs some refurbishing. But before she gets to that, Janet will have to tackle the other project that has been waiting for her, the kit that came in a jumble of pieces packed into crates. At the moment, it is standing in a corner, seeming to take up more than just the physical space it occupies as it waits to be assembled. When Janet thinks about how long it has waited to be created—the parts of the whole knowing what they are meant to be but not yet joined together to form a completed entity—she can feel the thing yearning for her attention. Each time she passes by, as she looks for a tool or goes to her sawhorse desk to work at her computer, she gives the crates a tap and sends them a message to be patient; their time is coming. She'll get to them soon.

By late afternoon, though, she's decided that she's done enough work for one day. After locking up the shop and returning to the house, she showers, changes, and, with a little time to spare, pours herself a glass of wine and sits in her living room, looking out the window, watching winter's thin daylight retreating from the world. She drifts off somewhere for a few minutes, and when she focuses again, she finds herself wondering, *Where am I now?* In Woodstock, she reminds herself. You're in Woodstock, New York.

It's cold outside, but Janet bundles up and walks into town, rather than drive. By now, this walk has become so familiar to her that she doesn't even have to think about where she's going; her feet just follow the road and take her toward Tinker Street, past the tannery brook and up a few blocks, to Renna's gallery.

There is sitar music playing in the gallery, old tapes Renna has had from some long-ago time when that was the background music to everything. The gallery is cozy, warmly lit, and Renna has been burning incense, so it's a pleasant place to while away half an hour or so while they wait for the man who wants to buy the clavichord, but when the time stretches to an hour, Renna suggests that he's probably changed his mind and they shouldn't hang around anymore. By seven-thirty, Renna is ready to close the gallery and go home, but Janet says no, let's wait a while.

"For what?" Renna asks, impatiently lighting a cigarette.

"For him," Janet says, gesturing toward the door, where a tinkling bell announces that someone is walking in.

She's known it from the minute Renna called. She's known it all day. Jorge Castelan would say of course she knew because it was his *intent* to end the icy period today—tonight—or rather, it was the intent of the universe for their period of estrangement to be ended, because that is a sorcerer's function, or one of them at least: to serve as a conduit for what the universe intends. And so he is here, bundled into a hooded parka. The hood also has an intent, although it is somewhat more mundane: not to stave off the cold but to keep the wearer's face hidden until the last minute, because Georgie is also playing a game. Or maybe, Janet thinks, what he's doing is reenacting a scene, trying to take them both into a dream that needs reworking; it needs thinking through. On his part *and* hers? Perhaps.

Pointing at the clavichord, Janet says. "You don't really want this, do you? I could have just brought another tuning fork."

"Ha, ha," says Jorge Castelan as he unzips his parka and pulls it off. He places the garment on a chair and then, addressing Renna—who makes no pretense of disguising her astonishment when she realizes who has just walked into her gallery—he says "Never underestimate Janet Planet. So smart, so quick! Immediately, she jumps right into the moment and whizzes right by me, into the past. A shared past—even better. That's an important technique, a weapon, if you use it correctly. It can put a person off-balance, if the person being spoken to does not expect such a tactic. But did I expect it? What do you think?"

Recovering quickly, Renna gestures at the photographs arranged around the gallery and says, "I would. My past is all over the walls here. It's hard to hide from."

"All these are you?" Jorge Castelan asks.

"Most of them."

Georgie walks around the room, hands clasped behind his back in a studious pose. Janet watches him, watches him playing. He is the center of attention, and is enjoying it as he makes a full circuit of the gallery's front room.

"But you're not this woman now," he says, referencing the photos on the walls.

"No," Renna says with a wide smile. "I'm better."

Janet turns from Georgie to Renna, and narrows her eyes. *She is flirting with him*, Janet thinks. And thinks, *well, that's not the smartest thing to do*.

But Jorge Castelan encourages her by continuing the conversation. "I was taught that the past should be erasable," he says, looking directly at Renna. "You should change your name, change your history, change your trajectory, when it suits you. Be brave, start again." Then he finally turns to face Janet. He grins at her. "That one," he says. "She's better at it than me. Maybe it's time I took some more lessons."

He walks over to the clavichord then and presses some of the padded keys; the strings vibrate, but so softly that they seem to release only imaginary notes to float around the room. "This is quite nice," he says to Janet. "But such a strange thing. The only one who can really hear it is the person who plays it, or someone standing right next to it." Again, he taps the keys, and the instrument sighs.

"I didn't really mean to fool you," he says, now addressing both Janet and Renna. "I do want to buy this lovely thing. This *thing*," he repeats, as if he's suddenly discovered that the word has two meanings. And then he shrugs. "Those monks up on the hill—they don't think any of us should have *things*, do they? But I'd like this one." The expression on his face now is one of delight, as if he's made an important decision. "Janet," he says, "I think there's a restaurant around here that sells tacos, right? Let's go eat tacos together. Let's seal the deal. Yes?"

"Alright," Janet agrees. "Let's go eat tacos."

"You don't mind, do you?" Jorge Castelan says to Renna, making it clear that she's not invited.

"No," Renna says, though certainly, she does.

Janet goes to the back of the gallery to get her coat, and Renna follows her. Out of Jorge Castelan's hearing, she whispers to Janet, "He really is interesting looking—even at his age. What is he? Around sixty-five? Maybe older?"

"I knew it," Janet says. "Renna, don't start with him. It's really not a good idea."

"Of course it's not a good idea," Renna replies. "But he has an effect."

"Yes," Janet says. "He does. He always does. That's the point."

But as she leaves the restaurant with Jorge Castelan, Janet has more to think about than Renna's flirtatiousness: she has to decode all the mixed messages that were flying around the gallery. Janet even suspects that the symbolism was intentional: Jorge Castelan surely knows what a clavichord is, how it sounds. In Janet's experience, he knows everything he needs to know.

Which he confirms with his reply to what she says to him as they leave the gallery. "You could have just called me, you know, instead of engineering that scene."

"And what fun would that have been?" he asks.

He takes her arm and leads her down Tinker Street, which has become a snow-bound lane, lit by streetlights for only a few blocks until it vanishes into the country darkness. Janet points out where they have to go—there's a Mexican restaurant just a few steps down the street—but Georgie stands still for a moment, seeming to relish the night air.

"I thought I would never like the cold," he says to Janet. "It's surprising, yes? But I do. It's a challenge. Every time you leave the house, you have to have a plan. Boots, hats, gloves: where are we going? How long will we be outside? It's not like California—remember? In California, you could just open the door, walk outside and wander around."

Janet does not reply that she cannot ever remember an instance of Jorge Castelan just wandering around. But here, now—yes, they do have a plan. The restaurant is close by: a welcoming place, decorated with flickering candles and strings of colored lights. And there are a fair number of diners for a midweek winter evening: the locals like to patronize the local restaurants, and this one is a particular favorite.

They are shown to a booth and almost immediately provided with chips and salsa. Jorge Castelan happily digs in, while Janet takes a minute to look around. Either nobody here knows who Georgie is, or, because it's Woodstock, everybody does but no one is going to make a big deal out of it.

"You're still mad at me," Georgie says, after they've ordered.

"A little, yes," she agrees.

"But I told you it was just a game."

"It's not that. I called you," Janet says. "I left messages. You didn't call back."

Waving his hand dismissively, Jorge Castelan says, "Oh, Janet Planet, you don't want to be mad at me because of *messages*. How important are *messages*? Words on scraps of paper."

"I was trying to tell you how much I liked your book."

He does not respond, choosing, instead, to concentrate on the food that is now being brought to the table.

"Did you send it to me?" Janet persists.

"No."

"Then who did?"

"I don't know," Jorge Castelan says, though Janet suspects that he may be lying. Sorcerers can lie with impunity; he has said as much. But then he makes an unexpected admission. "Do you know who would be angry that you've read it? The princess. I finally told her that I'm writing another book, but I haven't let her see it."

He actually sounds pleased about the idea of upsetting Carolee, and that's interesting to Janet: apparently Georgie is not so enamored of Carolee—the princess? So she's got her name now—that he can't enjoy antagonizing her. That's vintage Georgie, too: throw a wrench into the universal works, just to see what happens.

Still, Janet can't keep herself from prying, just a little. "Why won't you show it to her?"

"Oh," he says airily, "the princess has lots of plans. And most of the time, they suit me. But the book…well. That is not something I need help with. Or an opinion."

After that, they eat in silence for a while. Then, finally, Georgie says, "What do you think? These are better than the tacos in the park, no?"

"So you remember those days, too." Janet says. "They are not erasable?"

Jorge Castelan stiffens. He puts down his knife and fork. "Alright," he says. "At last. You have declared yourself."

Taken aback, Janet says, "What do you mean? This is just a conversation."

"No, it's not. We have never had *just a conversation.*"

Perhaps that's true. And perhaps now she is the one who has woven a secret message into the fabric of the evening. Did she mean to? *Yes,* she tells herself. *No.*

But whatever is happening between them now continues to happen. Georgie says, "I did look for you, you know. But you hid yourself very well."

"What?" Janet says. "Is that what we're talking about?"

"If we're not careful," Jorge Castelan answers her, "that is all we will be talking about, forever."

"I just meant…"

"I know what you meant. You meant to blame me for your own strength. Your own decisions."

"Is that what I'm doing?" Janet says quietly.

"Yes, that is what you are doing," Jorge Castelan says to her. "What you all did."

Again, Janet has the experience of hearing Jorge Castelan on two levels at once—or maybe, three, maybe ten. There are the words he says to her and then there is the *intent* inside them, the layers of experience that fill up each word, stuff each syllable with time, pressure, memory, anger, confusion, regret. Stuff them to bursting.

"You're right," Janet says. "I made my own decisions. But that made you mad. I couldn't stand it when you were mad at me," she says, and feels, suddenly, that she may start crying. She has never admitted this to herself before, how hard it was for her to disappoint him. It was a feeling so big, so overwhelming—still; *still!*—that it swallowed up anything she felt about what he had done to her.

But Jorge Castelan seems not to be in the mood, now, to offer Janet any comfort. "No one understands how difficult all this is for me," he says fiercely. "Only the Yaqui shamans have tried to comprehend what has been given to me to comprehend, and I have had to learn it all myself, with no background, with no choice in the matter. *No choice.* Unlike you. Unlike…them."

Lily. Namuria. Zella. He can barely say their names. But he can go on…what? What is he doing? Janet wonders, concentrating on him instead of how she feels as a way of keeping herself from bursting into tears. *Is he defending himself? Georgie?*

"They should have just waited for me," he mutters. "I always came back. *Always.* They should have trusted me. The problem," he says to Janet—and he sounds much calmer all of a sudden, as if they have transitioned back into some sort of normal conversation—"was that they didn't like the princess. But they didn't have to—they just had to wait. I shouldn't have had to tell them that. I," he says, "shouldn't have had to tell them anything."

Now what are they talking about? Janet is getting lost. All she can figure out is that he's just told her that the witches and the Fearless Guide knew Carolee and something seems to have happened between them all. But she's not about to ask what—she's not about to ask anything right now that might set him off again—and apparently, Jorge Castelan is not going to tell her. Not because he doesn't want to—it seems, at the moment, that he is ready to say anything he feels like—but because his conversation has veered far from any linear storyline. His thoughts seem to be flying, and only some of them are turning into words.

"Women squabble," he says to Janet. "The drama is beyond me. *I don't understand it,*" he tells her, and now he's growling again. "Human things. Human. Weak, silly, stupid. I don't have time."

Abruptly, he puts some money on the table and then stands up. "I am going to call a cab," he says to Janet.

"I'll do that for you," Janet offers—perhaps out of habit, trying to make things easier for him, even when he's making everything harder. "I have the number programmed into my phone." As she dials, she thinks, *Here is one weak, stupid human thing we share*: neither of them likes to drive.

Jorge Castelan bundles himself back into his parka and stalks out. Janet follows him, being brave, she thinks, since he's in a mean mood. But he keeps his silence, and she keeps hers for the few minutes that it takes a car from the local cab service to show up. As he climbs into the back seat, Georgie says to Janet, "I'm not as angry as you think. Don't stay up all night and worry."

She's so astonished that she can't think of what to say in reply, and then he's gone. He's irritable, he's lying about things, he's pushing and pulling and being sly—and then, all of a sudden, he decides to be kind, or, at least, kind for him. But he had often been that way with her; on his crankiest days—*crabby* was the word Lily would use at those times when his work wasn't going well, or something else was making him feel out of sorts—he would still pat her on the head, or tap her forehead. It was his sign that he was still there, still saw her, even if his attention was elsewhere. Even if he was distracted or his mood was dark.

And again, Janet feels like crying. Something is wrong with him, she thinks. Something is wrong with her. Every conversation they've had starts out one way and ends up another. Their connections are all crossed. Maybe it's because there are just the two of them now, when there should be five.

She should call a cab herself, since it's late, and probably too dark to be walking the roads. But when she phones, the cab service tells her it will be at least half an hour until they can get another car to Woodstock, so she decides that she might as well walk after all. Starting down Tinker Street, she passes Renna's gallery, and sees that the lights are still on inside. Of course. Renna is probably waiting for her. She's an incurable gossip; probably she's just boiling over with anticipation, wanting every detail of what Janet and Georgie had to say to each other.

Janet doesn't think she can face that right now, so she walks past the door, but immediately hears it sweep open behind her. Renna must have been watching through the window, hoping to catch Janet on her way home.

Ushering Janet into the gallery she says, "So? How did it go?"

"Not well," Janet replies.

"Why? What's wrong?"

"It's too complicated to explain. If I even can."

"Do you want to try?" Renna says.

Maybe she's just being friendly, Janet thinks. Maybe she's just being nice. But maybe not. "I don't think I can, right now. My head is kind of spinning."

"Well, I could see how he would do that to you," Renna says.

Okay, Janet thinks. *Maybe not* was right. There's something else going on here—and immediately, Renna makes clear what that is. "I bet I could take that Carolee," she says. "I don't think I told you this—once in a while I do keep a tiny secret here and there—but back in the good old days, in L.A., she moved in on me with a guy. What he saw in her I don't know, but then, I didn't care so much that time—it was just the bass player in some grunge band you probably never even heard of—but Jorge Castelan? That could be interesting."

"Are you crazy?" Janet says. "He isn't just some guy you can fuck and then hang his picture on the wall."

Renna, who has been flitting around behind the paper-strewn desk in the corner of the gallery, suddenly freezes. "I don't think you know me well enough to talk to me like that," she tells Janet.

And Janet decides to agree with her. "You're right," says. "And you don't know me."

As upset as she was watching Jorge Castelan being driven away, now Janet is even more unstrung. She hadn't meant to explode at Renna, but now that it's done she doesn't know how to take it back. And doesn't know if she even wants to. She marches out of the gallery, slamming the door behind her. Out in the cold night again, she slips and slides her way down the street because she's not being careful and the sidewalk, between Renna's gallery and the lane around the corner that parallels the tannery brook, has been neither shoveled nor salted. Even when she reaches the road and walks along the side, in the snowy grass, the going is unsteady, each step unsure. And though there's little traffic, she has to keep watch for cars since she's sure that she would be invisible to any driver coming by.

When she finally reaches her house and steps inside, she hears the phone ringing before she even snaps on the lights. She doesn't remember where she left the handset, so she stalks into the kitchen, where there is an extension, attached to the wall by a coiled cord.

She expects it to be...well, who? Anybody? But of the cast of characters that Janet imagines might be calling her at this hour, after the night she's had, it's one person she didn't bet on: the voice on the other end of the telephone brings her the icy tones of Carolee Carter.

"What did you do to him?" Carolee says, as if they are already in the middle of a conversation.

Janet thinks of using Renna's line—*I don't think you know me well enough to talk to me like that*—but it sounds too movie star-ish for her. Instead, exasperated, she tries the truth. "Nobody can *do* anything to him," she says.

"Are you serious? He's the most sensitive man I've ever met. He needs to be taken care of and instead, after a couple of hours with you, he comes back here acting angry and upset..."

"Be careful," Janet says to Carolee. "He might hear you. Then there's no telling what might happen."

After a moment of silence—Janet can hear static buzzing in the phone—Carolee says, "What are you talking about?"

"He doesn't like it when women squabble," Janet says. And hangs up the telephone. That, at least, makes her feel a little better. It's not enough to make up for how she feels—angry, resentful, put upon; aggrieved by all—but it's something.

01

If Janet had ever performed an act of sorcery, it was leaving Westwood with nothing but what she had grabbed in a few hasty minutes. It's ironic to think of it now, but in a way, she was simply carrying on what is apparently the family tradition—to go traveling—though she, of course, was limited to human-built conveyances, to the realms of the natural world. Probably, somewhere in her mind she was expecting to cool off after a few days, to let the anger slowly fade and then find a way to deal with what had happened because, no matter how wrong they were—all of them— it was unrealistic to expect them to understand that. After all, everything they did involved channeling the intent of the universe. So how could they make mistakes? And even if someone, judging their behavior from what they would have considered to be a damaged perspective, thought that they had done something wrong, still—how could anyone want to leave them? How could anyone not want to spend their days with the special, powerful, chosen few who knew that they had moved beyond the limits of what mere people—mere men and women—could see and experience?

And what, exactly, did they experience? There were so many times after Janet's energetic leap that they tried to show her. And in many different ways. One evening, after work, she bought a bag of Turkey pistachios—one of Georgie's favorite treats—and brought them home with her. Instead of going to her apartment, she went straight to the main house, but Lily told her that Georgie wasn't there. They were standing in the entranceway to the house and Janet could clearly see Georgie sitting on the couch in the living room, eyes closed, feet on the floor, his hands folded in his lap. When Lily saw Janet looking in Georgie's direction, she smiled, took Janet's hand, and led her into the living room, where she solemnly told her to sit at Georgie's feet. "That's not him," Lily said, "that's just what's left when he is doing the work of building the energy to approach infinity." "What does that mean?" Janet asked. And Lily said, "it takes years and years—maybe even decades—to develop the strength to fight through the barriers that block the sorcerer's path to the infinite. Jorge Castelan is there now, beyond, above, far away from us—gathering energy, making himself ready. It's energizing just to sit with this shadow of him." Lily finished, and left Janet alone with the nagual. Could she touch him? Speak to him? Tentatively,

Janet leaned her head against his leg. She thought she could hear the blood moving slowly through his veins; she thought she could feel his breath in parts of his body that did not breathe. She thought he had reached down to touch her hair, but when she looked up at his hands, they had not moved. "Come away now," Lily said, returning to the room after a while. "If you spend too much time with him when he is not here, it can be dangerous," she told Janet. "You might be tempted to try to follow him and none of us can do that, not yet. We would be lost in an instant."

Lost. Never to be found. Later, there were times Janet thought that was exactly what had happened to her, but for the opposite reason—because she hadn't followed him. In Portland, a human girl working in a factory that made window blinds (horrible work, a horrible job), she kept thinking that beyond the simplest things (buying food, doing her mindless job, turning the television on and off), she didn't know how to live without a sorcerer to guide her. She had to unlearn his magical ideas, stop expecting every step she took, every conversation she had, to be fraught with meaning, infused by signs and portents. Life, she began to remember, was not something lived at the edge of a cliff while you waited for the instruction to jump off. Crows were not likely to gather around you at lunchtime, bringing secret messages. And you couldn't spend your days waiting for something mysterious to happen, nor could you adjust the past or manipulate the future, no matter how hard you tried. Dealing with the present was hard and confusing enough.

With the counterculture gone and the hippie trail leading nowhere anymore, Janet was mostly alone at the margins of a world she was unsure of how to relate to. And she had no skills, no way to progress. The only thing she knew how to do, besides make harpsichord parts, was to type, something she had learned long ago, in school. So in the evenings, she found herself in secretarial school, in a class full of welfare moms and other startled looking ex-hippie chicks, wondering where the revolution had gone wrong. She saw her first word processor. She learned to use a fax machine.

And she learned to keep to herself. Jorge Castelan had taught her to dissolve her boundaries, but now she had to resurrect them; there was no other way to get by. She had lost a lot of time, a lot of training for how to live in what passed for normal society, and she made too many mistakes, among them, talking about who she had lived with, what her life had been like with Jorge Castelan and his women. People who knew who he was, knew his books, either wanted Janet to take them to meet him or else quickly gravitated away from her, accusing her of having been a member of a cult. (Can a cult, Janet wondered, be just five people? Wouldn't some minimum number be required to reach that status? A dozen brainwashed people? Twenty? Twenty-five?) There was no in-between reaction to Jorge Castelan's name: he was either a guru or a faker who had created his own fake history, a fake belief system, who had fabricated all his experiences in the Sonoran desert with an imaginary Yamon.

Over and over again she was asked: What do you believe about him? And the answer she came up with—Nothing that he says happened to him and nothing he writes about is a lie, which doesn't mean it's true—*was not good enough for anyone. Probably not even for her. So she started telling people she met that she had lived on a commune for almost a decade. Then she'd shrug, and laugh at herself, at the poor, stupid hippie life she'd led. And go back to typing up someone's insurance form. While inside her head, black clouds rolled around. Coyotes howled.*

"Let's start over again," Renna says, standing on Janet's doorstep, with a cake box in her hand. Janet, who was sleeping, isn't sure that she's awake; she may be dreaming of Georgie, of the time that they were in the restaurant—isn't that what she said to him? Or thought of saying to him? But that was last week. And that was at night; this is morning, a gray day, clouds pinned to flat sky above the line of pine trees across the road.

"Don't tell me you were still in bed," Renna says. "It's nine o'clock. Are you depressed or something?"

"Just tired," Janet replies. "I was up late last night, working."

"That's a sign of depression, too," Renna tells her. "Or is it mania? I forget."

She hands Janet the cake and heads down the now-familiar hallway to the kitchen. "Won't you come in?" Janet says to the back of Renna's head.

In the kitchen, as Janet shuffles around making coffee, she stops for a moment to gesture at the cake box. "What happened to you in your life that you think cake makes up for everything?"

"You mean it doesn't?" Renna says, sitting down at the table and then opening the box to reveal a fancy, fondant-covered concoction topped with sugary flowers. "I actually bought this from Meggie's," Renna says. "*Bought* it. That place is expensive and I'm cheap, so this is a serious apology."

"You don't have to apologize. I should. I said something stupid and you weren't really who I was mad at."

"So have you made up with the great sorcerer?" Renna asks as she slices the cakes into slabs.

Janet brings over mugs of coffee and sets them down beside the plates. "Who says we had an argument?"

Renna's eyebrow lifts, which Janet has come to know as her trademark expression signaling everything from doubt to ridicule. "You sure had something," she says. "That was obvious as soon as you came back to the gallery."

"Isn't this where you and I got into trouble?" Janet reminds her.

"Yes," Renna says sweetly, "but now we're friends again."

Janet stabs her fork into her slice of the cake, which looks like a great deal of work has gone into making it. The fondant is lavender and smooth as glass; the cake inside is white and the edible flowers are yellow entwined with purple buds. It's a beautiful concoction, but overdone, Janet thinks. Her first bite tastes heavy, much too rich.

"He's gone so far past the human," Janet says, "and I've slid so far back. Maybe that's why we can barely talk to each other anymore."

"To be honest with you," Renna says, "I never understood much of what he was getting at in those books. But is that the idea—to stop being human?"

"Not to stop," Janet replies. "To be more than."

"And you think he is?"

Janet answers carefully, unable, still, to deny him. Still not sure that she should. "I think that's what most of his life has been about. And he's still trying."

"Well, now that you've explained it to me," says Renna, "maybe I should try? Apparently, all I need is to clear my mind and practice some focused magical passes, which are the very core of the ancient Centered Movement techniques that will enable me to reflow the energy of the universe through my own energy fields and thus better understand the intent of infinity for my personal path through this godforsaken world." She shows Janet a broad smile. "How do you like that? I added the last part myself. I mean, about the godforsaken world."

Surprised, Janet asks, "Where did you come up with all that?"

Renna reaches into the suede shoulder bag that she's draped over the back of her chair and pulls out a stiff, gold-edged square of paper. "From this," she says.

It's an invitation, which she hands over to Janet, who scans it quickly. "So they've started the workshops," Janet says. "And you got invited to attend?"

"Well, not exactly. You know who lives down the road from me?" She names a television actress Janet is familiar with. "She doesn't actually live there, of course—she has a weekend house, but she's never there, so I get her mail for her. Not much comes to that address, and what does I usually just forward to her manager."

"Do you read her mail, too?" Janet asks.

"Of course not." Renna sniffs. "I mean, almost never. But when I saw Carolee's return address on this, I couldn't resist."

"Alright," Janet says. "So?"

"So I want to go!" Renna says. "It came with a pamphlet that explains all about Centered Movement. It actually sounds like fun."

"Fun?"

"Sure. Like the sixties. You know, expand your mind, open new doors of perception, groove with Jorge Castelan. I mean, we're here in Woodstock—why not give all that a try again?"

"I don't think you'll exactly find the experience groovy," Janet says, "but go ahead. Enjoy yourself."

"I want you to come with me."

"Oh, no," Janet says. "That's the last thing I need right now. Besides, Georgie is very likely to just throw me out."

"He wouldn't do that."

I'm not as angry as you think. That could be a lie, too. "Yes," Janet says, "he might."

"Oh, so what if he does?" Renna replies. "I'll walk out with you and it'll be very dramatic. Either way, that Carolee will be so pissed off when she sees me there. You know what I think she's doing? She's trolling for celebs. I'll bet she sent these things out to the high and mighty up and down the east coast and on the west coast, too, just in case anybody's in town and wants to fly, drive or swim upriver in order to meet the great Jorge Castelan. What better way to get yourself back into the spotlight? I suppose she could have gotten her hooks into some actor, or another musician…but a real, live sorcerer? How do you top that?"

"I still don't want to go," Janet tells Renna. "Besides, she'll be twice as pissed off to see me."

"Oh, I get it: she's the one you had a little tiff with. See, I was right. I knew there was something up."

"I'm not going," Janet repeats.

"Oh yes you are," Renna says, "because I don't want to go by myself. What if I actually get caught up in all this Centered Movement stuff? A psychic once told me that I was very vulnerable to spiritual influences. If I start going off the deep end or something, you pull me back."

"You're assuming a lot," Janet says. "You're assuming that I would know how."

☽

The first Centered Movement class starts at 8 pm on a Friday night, and Renna has called Janet at least three times during the day to ask what she should wear. Each time, Janet has had the same answer: anything you want, though she knows that her answer is not making it any easier for Renna to decide how one should dress when attending sorcerer's school. But when she finally comes to pick Janet up, she is wearing an outfit that, for Renna, looks remarkably subdued: a long, silky shirt over a pair of loose, cotton aviator pants, and relatively modest jewelry. Janet had been envisioning scarves and beads; something suitable for an audience with the Beatles' Maharishi.

"How do I look?" Renna asks.

"Ready to be enlightened," Janet tells her.

"You never know," Renna says. "It could happen."

It takes about twenty minutes to drive to the Centered Movement Institute. Somehow, all the repairs and reconstruction seem to have been accomplished. The outside of the building has been freshly painted a kind of dark maroon—a color that Janet remembers has spiritual significance: in reading a human aura, maroon signifies stamina, strength of purpose and a fighting spirit. Georgie, Janet decides, must have chosen the paint. He may not be an enthusiastic believer in auras, but apparently, he is also not opposed to hedging his bets—unless, as it occurs to Janet, this is Carolee's contribution. Perhaps, Janet thinks spitefully, she has been studying some new-age handbooks.

An area near the building has been cordoned off for parking, and there are already dozens of cars stabled there, in the darkness. Renna maneuvers her car into a spot at the back of this crowd of vehicles, and the two women head toward the front door of the Centered Movement Institute, where they encounter a brace of security guards who are checking invitations. There is no list of names, apparently, so just the gold-edged square of paper gets them inside.

And who do they encounter first but Carolee, who is greeting the stream of arriving guests. "Here we go," Renna whispers to Janet, readying herself for the expected unpleasant encounter, but something worse happens: Carolee either does not remember who Renna is, or has decided not to. In any case, she simply smiles at Renna, but directs a deep frown at Janet.

"I'm not sure he wants you here tonight," Carolee says.

"I'm not sure I want to be here," Janet replies. "So we'll just see what happens, okay?"

Without waiting to hear if Carolee has anything else to say, Janet takes Renna's arm and leads her down the corridor toward the auditorium. "That bitch," Renna says. "Did you see her pretend that we've never even met?"

"So go punch her in the nose or something," Janet says. "That'll get the evening off to an interesting start."

"She might turn me into a toad," Renna says, shooting a glance over her shoulder at Carolee's back.

"You're thinking of the wrong kind of witch," Janet replies as she pulls Renna along. "This isn't that kind of fairytale."

In the auditorium, as promised, all the chairs have been removed and dozens of mats are scattered around the floor. Some of the fifty or so people who have assembled for the class have staked out a spot near the stage; others have taken a mat and plopped themselves down on the floor, in the middle of the room, or off to the side. Janet picks up two of the mats and, followed by Renna, puts them back down on the floor near the back, not far from the door. And then, like everyone else in the room, they wait.

Looking around, Janet does not see many familiar faces, though she does recognize one or two old rockers who still have houses in the hills and a few other local notables. Other than that, she and Renna are in a room full of strangers who are remarkably quiet, even tense.

But then Janet also notices something completely unexpected, something she would have thought would be absolutely forbidden—in fact, it was even mentioned on the invitation: no cameras allowed. And yet, while they are trying to look unobtrusive, there are two people—one man, one woman, both, Janet notes, wearing maroon-colored tee shirts—standing on either side of the auditorium, holding what look like very high-end camcorders. Janet is genuinely amazed: Jorge Castelan, who has never even permitted a photograph of himself to appear on a book jacket, is actually going to allow himself to be videotaped?

Finally, after what seems like forever, there is some movement onstage. The first person to appear is Carolee, who is greeted with a smattering of applause—Janet guesses that many in this room are her friends, but they don't know the protocol for this kind of thing. Do you applaud? Do you bow? Should you arrange your face so that it displays an appearance of rapt attention?

Most opt for looking attentive. Carolee welcomes everyone and makes some brief remarks that focus mostly on how carefully those in the room have been chosen to attend this first class in Centered Movement, which will be taught by the great nagual himself, Jorge Castelan. Shortly, she continues, the nagual will explain more about the genesis of Centered Movement but first, she wants to present everyone with one condition they will have to agree to before the class begins.

"In a moment," she explains, "other friends of ours will be passing among you with release forms. Signing the release is your promise that you will not discuss what you learn here today, you will not share what Jorge Castelan teaches you, and by yourself, you will not try to teach it to others. Doing so could be dangerous for yourself and for anyone who you try to demonstrate Centered Movement to until you have truly mastered the techniques."

The "friends" turn out to be a pair of young women wearing the same type of maroon tee shirts as the people operating the video cameras. One concession she has to make to this Carolee Carter,

Janet thinks, is that as she had said herself, she clearly knows how to organize, how to create a plan and carry through with it. Certainly, Jorge Castelan's money is paying for all this, but he wouldn't have had the slightest idea of how to pull all this together—the building, the equipment, the coordinated tee shirts. There is marketing expertise at work here, and that, despite the past failure of her own enterprise, has to be attributed to Carolee.

The young women pass among the assembled proto-students of Centered Movement, getting them to sign photocopied forms that no one seems to bother reading very closely. Signing the forms, though, seems to add to the sense that something very serious is taking place, which now permeates the silent group of men and women staring up at the stage.

"Thank you," Carolee says gravely as the maroon-shirted women collect the forms and carry them out the doors to the auditorium, which are then closed. "And now your teacher will join you."

With that, Carolee steps to the side and Jorge Castelan strides onto the stage, followed by yet another young woman in a maroon tee shirt, also holding a camera—this one clearly meant for close-up shots, as the woman positions herself nearby, at the edge of the stage. Carolee keeps her gaze trained on Georgie as he walks forward, and catching a glimpse of her face, Janet sees a look that seems, to her, completely familiar. Whatever Carolee may have thought of Georgie's other women—or even how well she knew them; all that remains unclear to Janet—when it comes to Jorge Castelan, she shares at least one trait with them: utter fascination with the last nagual. While the witches and the Fearless Guide may have grumbled about his behavior now and then, even complained about him among themselves, they remained devoted to him and to the life he had decided they all should lead. He was their whole world, and everything he told them about the world was what they believed.

But who is Jorge Castelan to the first class of Centered Movement students? The old hippies, new celebs and nouveau riche owners of vacation houses, mountain retreats and ski chalets that have been drawn here by the promise of seeing the last nagual in the flesh? Do they still think they're going to learn something from him? Probably, Janet thinks, Jorge Castelan is an idea that has floated in their minds for decades, a dream about gathering strength and developing power, a guide to the other side of reality who had faded from their attention when the days that promised there would be a new reality also disappeared. But he has come back and is standing before them—above them, really, elevated on a stage, no longer just the drawing of a figure striding through the clouds but real, flesh, a man who aspires to be not wholly a man but has decided to appear as himself, here, now. Dark haired, dark eyed, compact, strong: who can tell how old he is? Who wants to remember how long ago they read his first book, if they are now old enough to have read that book when it was first published? Even to Janet, he looks younger than she knows he is, or must be, since it is one of those irrelevant facts that he has always been impatient with. He stands at the edge of the stage for a moment, looking at the crowd, taking the time, it seems, to note every face—including Janet's. He sees her, she knows he sees her, and then he looks away, which signals that the icy period has resumed. *Fine*, she thinks. *Back and forth, back and forth*—has there ever really been a time when the relationship between them has been settled? Because of his willfulness. And hers.

Jorge Castelan has now begun to speak. He is firm, brief, exuding the kind of impatience that Janet has expected: the role of group leader is unnatural for him, and it shows in his body language—he stands with feet apart, his hands on his hips, like a military man addressing his troops—and in his clipped, accented speech.

"The way you perceive the world we live in, you live in," he says, "is all wrong. You see it as real, when in fact, it is a shell. It is a screen of data, false symbols and garbled information that is meaningless; it is a veil that conceals the energy fields that are the real pathways of the universe which *will not pay attention to you*," he emphasizes, his voice, for a moment, edging toward a guttural growl, "unless you crack the shell. Centered Movement is a way to crack that shell. Long ago, many, many thousands of years ago, Centered Movement was practiced by the shamans of the Yaqui people in Mexico, a secret technique that they passed down from lifetime to lifetime, but carefully, to only one or two practitioners in a generation. Now, I am going to share the techniques with you. But you must follow them exactly, and exactingly. There can be no variations, not a single change or deviation from the movements as they are meant to be executed. Over time, if you begin to master Centered Movement, you will make tiny cracks in your own shell, and perhaps those cracks will get bigger and bigger. Perhaps the energy of the universe will begin to seep in to your mind, your body, your bones. Then, the next levels of Centered Movement will help you to control that energy, use it to attract and deploy the attention of the universe to aid your spiritual development and move into other, more advanced realms of the realities that are now unknown to you. But that will all come later. For now, let us begin with the simplest movements. You will learn them here, practice at home and then return. As you leave tonight, you will be given a schedule to follow. If you don't follow it, please don't come back."

With that, Jorge Castelan begins to demonstrate the first, then the second, third and fourth in what he explains are the first series of Centered Movements. He then instructs the now silent crowd to do the movements with him and then repeat them. Janet, like everyone else, does as she is told; glancing over at Renna, Janet sees that she, too, is concentrating on repeating the muscle tensing and stretching movements that Jorge Castelan has demonstrated.

He has refined the techniques since Janet last saw them; they are less like Kendo kata now and more like yoga, but not quite, because they are not poses but constant, repetitive movements that first require stretches that pull at the muscles and tendons and then demand almost complete stillness while trying to flex "inner muscles" that Jorge Castelan says will first seem like they don't exist, but do; the student, with practice, will begin to feel these muscles and be able to control them, which is the first sign of mastering the techniques.

As Janet goes through the repetitions again and again, she begins to think of how she's been here before, how this feels, in many ways, like she's living some part of her life over again. She's stood in rooms like this before, in the time on her own, before Jorge Castelan, and then even afterwards—though afterwards, for just a little while—because nothing, no one, ever came close to Georgie. In halls and rented lofts, in unheated buildings, in basements and converted storefronts, she was watching, looking, listening, searching for whatever someone smarter, more spiritual, more magical, more powerful, more thoughtful, stranger, older, odder, born far away or supposedly much longer ago said there was to search for. And now she's doing it again, open to it again, the possibility that maybe there is something else, something important she could find if someone would show her where it is; she is feeling it again, that lost sense—a youngster's yearning that Georgie said returns as you grow older—of wanting to be taught, to be told secrets, to be initiated into whatever there is to be initiated into, to be pushed through a door, a passage, to see a light, a sign, a spark, to find that inner muscle, that hidden heart, second sight, third eye, lost chakra, past life, that will explain who she is and why she is and what it is that she is supposed to be doing with her spirit, her soul, her life.

Are they good or bad, these thoughts? Helpful? Painful? Ridiculous? Should she know better? Should she give in? Perhaps she can't even if she wants to because she's getting tired of doing the movements. She's in decent physical shape but there's something about all this stretching and stopping and turning again and again that's exhausting—a reaction that she can see others in the group are having as they try to sneak an unauthorized break from the repetitions to catch their breath or simply sit down on their mats, giving up for the time being, which Jorge Castelan does not like. "Get up," he insists, "keep going, keep going," and some do, some don't.

Renna is one of those who chooses not to go on. Turning to Janet, she whispers, "Do you think we can slip out of here? I'm going to need a chiropractor if I keep this up much longer," which helps Janet to decide that she also has had enough. What was she thinking, a moment ago—that maybe all this made sense? Only because it is Georgie up there on the stage, commanding, cajoling once again. *I know amazing things, I have had amazing experiences and you will too, if you do what I tell you to.*

Since they are already near the back of the room, with plenty of people in front of them to hide behind, Janet and Renna are able to make an unobtrusive exit. But just as they are easing themselves out one of the auditorium doors, someone breezes past them, heading into the room they've just left. Renna barely notices, so intent is she on making an escape, but Janet grabs her by the arm and pulls her back inside.

"Hold on a minute," she says.

"What?" Renna complains. "Why?"

Janet doesn't think she can explain—she just has a feeling. Something more than just a person has just brushed past her; something that roused the attention of Janet Planet.

"Just wait," Janet says, so forcefully that Renna simply stops in her tracks and turns around.

What they both see is a young woman—a girl, really—walking a straight path down the center of the auditorium, toward the stage. Thin, long brown hair, wearing a sweater and jeans, she looks like just another kid brought up in Woodstock by hippie parents, a product of communal schools and a relaxed outlook on life. But there's something unexpectedly purposeful about her stride, her demeanor. This is a girl on a mission, laid-back attitude or not.

She stops just before she reaches the stage, standing close enough to be heard, and seen. "Excuse me," she says.

She has to say it three times before anybody responds to her. Jorge Castelan goes on with his stretches, seeming not to hear her, but Carolee soon appears at the edge of the stage, kneels down and says, angrily, "You can't interrupt the nagual in the middle of a demonstration."

The girl doesn't even acknowledge Carolee. "Mr. Castelan," she says, "I want to ask you about Nina Acheson."

Janet stiffens. She inhales, deeply; thinks she sees Georgie do the same. Or maybe she just feels it, hears the sound of his pulse quickening inside her head.

But he still does not respond to the question. Carolee is hurrying down the stairs at the edge of the stage, heading toward the girl, probably with the intent of ushering her out. But before she can intervene, the girl says, "Nina Acheson, Mr. Castelan. She lived with you, didn't she? Well, there are reports today on the Internet that her remains have been found—out in California, in Death Valley. I mean, she's dead. Did you know about that?"

Carolee, who is now standing beside the girl, looks like she has been struck by lightning. Her face goes ashen, her hands clench into fists. "Who are you?" she hisses.

"My name is Ashlee," she tells Carolee. "I'm with the New Age Times, over in Saugerties." She's smiling so sweetly that it's impossible to tell if she's being clever or is really oblivious to the trouble she's causing.

Turning back to the stage, the girl says, "Mr. Castelan? Would you like to comment? We don't actually publish the paper until next week, but we're doing the story on our website this afternoon."

Jorge Castelan still does not acknowledge her. Instead, he simply stops, like a machine that has been unplugged. He stands motionless on the stage for what seems like a few very long moments, and then simply turns around and walks off without a word. Everyone in the auditorium has also stopped doing the movements and is standing absolutely still, unsure of what to do next.

Renna touches Janet on the arm. "Honey?" she says. "Did you know her? Nina Acheson?"

Janet nods. "Yes," she says. "I knew her."

Thinking that Janet looks as dazed as everyone else in the room—maybe more so—Renna decides to take her in hand. "Alright," she says, pushing the auditorium door open again and gesturing to Janet to follow her out. "Let's get out of here. We'll talk about it at my house."

Leaving behind the auditorium full of confused people staring at a now empty stage, they walk down the hall and out the door of the Centered Movement Institute, find their car, and then drive in silence all the way to Renna's house. Once inside, Janet seems to emerge from the fog that descended on her when she heard the name Nina Acheson. "Can I use your computer?" she asks Renna, who says sure.

The computer is on a desk in a room in the back of the house that Renna uses as an office. Janet gets online, while Renna stands behind her, watching.

"What are you doing?" Renna asks.

"I'm getting my e-mail," Janet tells her, then asks, "How much do you know about me? I mean, really?"

"Just what you've told me. Which isn't all that much, actually. Not that I haven't tried to get more out of you…"

"I lived with him for a long time," Janet says. "Almost ten years."

Renna answers her with a gentle voice, "I gathered something like that."

"I remember you told me that you Googled me."

"But nothing much comes up. Just the rumor that he adopted a daughter."

"I know. Because of what he wrote: 'You would not think that three women and one man can give birth to a daughter.' Well, the three women were named Lily, Zella and Namuria. Namuria's real name was Nina Acheson."

"Oh my," Renna says, genuinely shocked. "I'm so sorry."

Janet has opened her e-mail inbox now and there it is: the message she knew would be waiting as surely as she knew that girl at the Centered Movement Institute was going to have something to say that she didn't want to hear. *peyotepalace@peyotepalace.com*. She clicks the mouse and the message opens. The first thing she sees is the same image that accompanied the announcement about Jorge Castelan's book: a graphic of a squat-looking, spiny cactus with a crow flying above it. Below that is a scanned image—a clipping from something called the *Romeo Flats Times-Express*, which is apparently a local newspaper published in a town called Romeo Flats, near Death Valley, in California. The clipping is headed: "Remains of Castelan Follower Identified."

Janet closes her eyes for a moment and practices something Jorge Castelan would probably laugh at: a moment of simple, silent meditation, meant to do nothing but grasp at the possibility of inner peace. What is she remembering? Some Buddhist philosophy, some hatha yoga breathing someone showed her once? She knows enough bits and pieces of spiritual techniques that she should be able to calm down an army, but she can't seem to make her heart stop pounding in her chest. So she opens her eyes again, blinks, and starts to read. She couldn't quite believe the news coming from the mouth of that girl from the hippie paper, but there's no ignoring this article—or the fact that someone has deliberately sent it to her.

The scanned clipping attached to the e-mail explains that nearly a year ago, a pair of hikers on an extended trek into an area of Death Valley National Park called Natural Bridge Canyon, which features an arching stone bridge, came upon the badly rusted remains of a blue Volvo, tipped over in a remote gully. They took a picture of it, meaning to drop the photo off with the park rangers when they ended their trek, but as they continued to walk, they began to come upon scattered bones and fragments of clothing that they decided looked like human remains. As soon as they could get a cell phone signal, they called the rangers, who eventually came out to investigate. The car was hauled out of the canyon and the bones were sent for DNA identification, which had finally produced results. There was now conclusive evidence that the remains were those of a woman named Nina Acheson, who preferred to be called Namuria Beek—and Namuria Beek, the paper reported, was one of two women, known as the witches, along with a third, known as the Fearless Guide, who had lived with and were devotees of the author-cum-guru Jorge Castelan. Acheson's family, who hadn't heard from her in years, confirmed those few facts. No one had offered any information about where the other two women might be, and efforts to reach Castelan—who was now living in Woodstock, New York, following a reported rift with the three women that had led him to be absent from his California home for an unknown period of time—had been rebuffed. Reached yesterday, his spokesperson, the fitness trainer Carolee Carter, said that Castelan would have no comment.

"Lily's out there too, somewhere," Janet says aloud, though she's really talking to herself. As soon as she read the description of the abandoned car, she realized that the blue Volvo must have belonged to Lily—that was the only kind of car she ever bought. Time would not have altered her choice. So perhaps DNA tests had produced the identity of one person, but Janet knows that in the California desert, there must be at least two. And it is likely, she concludes, that really, somewhere out there, are the remains of three.

"What happened to them?" Renna murmurs, reading over Janet's shoulder.

"I don't know," Janet says.

Hesitantly, Renna asks, "Do you think Georgie does?"

"He says he doesn't. But this..." Janet gestures helplessly at the screen.

"Who sent that to you?"

"I don't know that either. But the same person who sent me the book chapter, I suppose. Someone who knows Georgie. And who knows me."

"Who?"

"Renna," Janet replies, "if I could answer these questions, believe me, I would." She turns back to the computer and closes her e-mail. "I think I'm going to go home," she says.

"Why don't you stay here for a while? Maybe it's not a good idea for you to be alone right now."

"Why? Do you think something is going to happen to me, too?"

"I wasn't implying…"

"I know. But I'll be fine. I just need to go home."

In the hallway, Janet pulls on her coat and slips through the door that Renna opens for her, forgetting to say good-bye. Outside, it's a late winter afternoon; there are grim clouds overhead, an empty sky. The gray road she's walking, bordered by dense stands of bare trees, could be leading anywhere. It certainly doesn't seem like it's leading home. She walks and walks, but each time she looks around, it seems like she's in the same spot. Feeling suddenly tired—more than that, genuinely exhausted—Janet veers off the road and sits down on a fallen log.

This is a lonely landscape, Janet thinks: mountains, trees, clouds, a road. It's like the cover of one of Jorge Castelan's books. She watches the desolate scenery, alert for anything that may be hidden in the shadows. She listens for something that may or may not come. Then she puts her head down, buries her face in her hands and closes her eyes.

Georgie, Georgie, she thinks. *What did you do?*

VII

"I know where he was."

Listening to Renna's breathless voice in the phone, Janet can barely make sense of what she's saying. *He?* Surely, she means Georgie—what other "he" would Renna be so anxious to share information about with Janet? But—*where he was?* What is she talking about?

"I don't understand." Janet tells her.

"The missing time they keep talking about in all those vile stories. Between the time he was in California and then turned up here. I know where he was," Renna repeats.

"He was elsewhere," Janet says automatically. This old habit—saying what Jorge Castelan would want you to say—simply will not be banished.

"Honey," Renna says gently. "Do you want to know?"

"Yes," Janet says, though her voice sounds dull, even to herself. "I want to know."

"Then are you going to be around for a while? I could come over."

"You're home?"

"I'm home. I got in a couple of hours ago. It was a nightmare flight, but aren't they all nowadays? I missed my connection; they still haven't found one of my bags and…oh, tell me to shut up, will you? You don't want to hear any of this."

"I completely forgot that you were coming back today."

"Missed me that much, did you?" Renna says, but then eases into a more soothing tone. "Well, I imagine you've had a lot on your mind." She waits a moment, waits to hear anything Janet might say, but she listens to silence. "Janet?"

"I'm here."

"I don't know if this is going to make it any easier."

"It's that bad?"

"It's complicated."

"Alright," Janet says. What other reply is there to make? "I'll be in the workshop."

Janet can only imagine what kinds of gossip she's going to be hearing in a little while when Renna appears. She's been in California for almost a week, attending the funeral of a friend's husband, an actor famous for playing brawny action types. All kinds of rumors must run rampant in those circles, and Janet isn't surprised by the idea that maybe one of the subjects of speculation was Jorge Castelan. Why not? The story about discovering the remains of one of Jorge Castelan's "followers"—which seems to be the term of choice—has spread across the Internet and into the tabloids and gossip magazines. Even *Rolling Stone* has done a story. As Janet expected, the blue Volvo has been traced to Lily (whose real name, it turns out, was Barbara Anderson) and now speculation about the fate of the other women abounds: did all three commit suicide? Did Jorge Castelan murder them? Where are the other two who were known to live with him? Also out in the desert somewhere, bones bleaching under the sun? Since Jorge Castelan has lived a secretive life, the details of the story—one man, three women, the house in Westwood hidden behind gardens and fruit trees and oh, yes, it seems the man hadn't been home in two years, though no one seems to know where he had taken off to—are all the more fascinating for being so sketchy.

Arthur Rivers, who years ago had brought himself some brief notoriety by trying to debunk Georgie's teachings, is heard from again and is invited onto a number of television programs to discuss the pervasiveness of cults in American society. Janet sees him on one of the morning news-and-chat shows. She thinks he looks fat and evil and concentrates so much on what he looks like that she manages to hardly hear what he has to say. But she remembers it afterwards and seethes, because it isn't true. At least some of it isn't; perhaps she's angry because some of it may be: Rivers suggests that a cult is exactly what Georgie had created in the house in Westwood and accuses him of trying to replenish the ranks of his followers by setting up shop in Woodstock and promulgating a new version of the teachings in his books which, Rivers contends, are pure fiction. There was no Yamon, no visions in the desert, no revelations about ancient secrets of the Sonoran sorcerers.

Then it gets worse. A woman sends a comment to a widely read blog, and posts video testimony on YouTube, alleging that her sister's death, a decade ago—a leap from a cliff in the Blue Ridge

Mountains—which had been ruled a suicide, was actually an attempt to recreate the story of Jorge Castelan's energetic leap into the infinite that, as a young man, had marked his initiation as a sorcerer. But many others, none of whom have ever even met the last nagual, come forward to say that Jorge Castelan's books, his stories, have enriched their lives, taught them to try to reach beyond the everyday for mystical meanings, deeper realities.

Grainy photos appear online: is that Jorge Castelan, circa 1969, leaving a restaurant, slipping into a car? An old picture from a UCLA yearbook turns up: Jorge Castelan, looking almost heartbreakingly young in a sporty pullover, smiling at the camera. There are new photos too: Georgie and Carolee outside the Centered Movement Institute, which is temporarily shuttered; Carolee—the fitness-trainer/spokesperson—shopping in a market in Phoenicia.

But the spokesperson keeps silent—at Georgie's instruction, Janet assumes—and Jorge Castelan himself continues to have nothing to say. He won't give interviews. He has no comments; he will explain nothing. Janet keeps expecting someone to track her down—identify her as Janet Planet, the missing daughter of this strange family—and hound her about what she thinks happened. But whatever magic Georgie witched up years ago when, as he claimed, he had kept Arthur Rivers from dragging her into the Jorge Castelan truth-or-fiction controversy, still seems to be holding, and she is left in peace. Well, not peace, exactly—she has no idea what happened to the women, but she is haunted by the image of Lily's beloved car abandoned in the desert. More even, than by the idea of "human remains," which sounds like something actors with edgy haircuts would be discussing in a TV crime show, the car seems emblematic of some deeper, personal mystery. What were they thinking? What were they trying to do? And how can Georgie not know? While she turns these questions over and over in her mind, Janet skirts the edges of the question she knows she should be asking herself: how could she have let a lifetime pass—their lifetime—without getting back in touch with them? These women she loved, who loved her. Like all angry children who expect, someday, to reconcile with parents they left behind, Janet is appalled that time has now run out on her. She wakes up at night overwhelmed with grief. And sometimes, fury. At herself, at Georgie, at the witches and the Fearless Guide.

She's glad then, that Renna is back. Her company has become a reliable distraction for Janet, along with her fits of dramatics. The past week has actually been more difficult for Janet because of her absence. Used to having people around, but not necessarily close friends, it's been a surprise to find that she's censoring herself less and less around Renna who, from the beginning, has seemed to have no trouble opening up to her.

Less than half an hour later, Renna pushes open the door to Janet's workshop, seeming like she can barely contain herself. She gives Janet a quick hug, perches herself on a stool and says, "I can't stay long. I talked to that kid I hired to work at the gallery while I was away and it sounds like he's just about run the place into the ground, so I want to get over there as soon as I can." She watches impatiently as Janet continues to stand at her work table, making jacks for the harpsichord sitting in the middle of the shop—yet another project that she's taken on. "Sit somewhere, Janet," Renna tells her. "You can't keep working while I talk to you."

"It's that bad?"

"Well, it's not only about Jorge Castelan. It's about Jack Jackson, too."

"Your friend's husband?"

"Yes, my friend's husband. My friend's husband the great, big macho movie star."

"So?" Janet says impatiently.

"So this is the kind of information we could make a lot of money with—if we were that kind of people. I mean, the kind of people who call the tabs and sell them dirt." And then Renna adds, "Or the kind of people who betray our friends' confidences."

"Which we aren't," Janet says in a warning tone, though she still has no idea of what she might be cautioning against.

"Of course not." Renna is wearing jeans, a filmy blouse and ropes of pearls; she grabs the strands of her long necklace and holds onto them as she leans forward. "I have to be serious about this," she says. "It is all really kind of awful."

"Jesus, Renna," Janet says "What is it?"

"Cancer," Renna says. "Jorge Castelan has cancer."

Janet's reaction is immediate, vehement. "That's impossible. I mean, you just have to look at him. He looks great. You said yourself…"

Renna interrupts her. "He was at the Ivinger Institute. Do you know what that is?" Janet shakes her head, no, so Renna rushes on. "It's an alternative medicine center in the Bahamas, on a private island. They use treatments you can't get in the United States—or anywhere else, for that matter. Herbal things, diet, purges, different drugs—things that are supposed to be toxic, but not if you administer them in certain dosages or combinations or something like that. Anyway, they're very expensive and very exclusive. They treat millionaires and celebs, and they know how to keep secrets. You will never see a photo of one of their clients walking through the front door or wandering the grounds. Never. Well, apparently, that's where your Georgie was for about a year—and supposedly, they helped him. He went into remission. But then he and Carolee spent another nine or ten months in a private villa on the property, just to make sure he was alright. And he was for a while—but I hear that now, he's not. Angela told me. That woman finds out everything. *Everything.*"

Renna's admiration for her friend's ability to ferret out secrets is lost on Janet, who keeps shaking her head. "Impossible," she says, but can't stop herself from asking a question. "What kind of cancer?"

"Pancreas. It's one of the really bad ones."

"And you know all this how?"

"Because while they mainly treat cancer patients, they also treat people with AIDS. Not just HIV positive but the next stage. The bad stage: drug-resistant AIDS."

"And?" Janet prompts.

"And Jack Jackson had AIDS. He'd been HIV positive for a very long time and then, a couple of years ago, nothing his doctors prescribed worked anymore, and he was desperate. He wanted to go on working as long as he could, I mean, you can be an HIV-positive actor and play all the sensitive roles, but Jack was an action guy, a hunk. Nobody wants their he-men to be bisexual, which is what would have come out if his HIV status leaked to the tabs. He and his wife, my friend Angela, had kind of an open marriage—I guess what we used to call an open marriage. Who knows what the p.c. term for it is now? Anyway, once the regular meds stopped working, he and Angie went to Ivinger and that's where they saw Jorge Castelan and Carolee Carter. They couldn't help but recognize Carolee—she was all over the place for a while: TV, magazines, everywhere—but they didn't know who the man with her was. Everybody's very private there—they don't exactly sit around having dinner with each other or anything like that—but they overheard her talking to him, heard his name and they figured it out."

"I can't believe this," Janet says. "You're sure? Your friend couldn't have made a mistake? Maybe it wasn't Carolee and Jorge."

"It was them."

"My God," Janet says. "I just can't imagine this is real." Her mind is racing; it's like she doesn't know which part of the story to try to absorb first. She begins with the part that involves Georgie more indirectly. "Well, I guess if Carolee has been going through this with him, she can't be the total bitch she always seems to be. I mean, she must actually care for him."

"See, this is probably one of your big failings as a human being," Renna tells her. "You think you're so tough but really, you're a softie. I bet anybody can pull the wool over your eyes just like that." She snaps her fingers for emphasis. "Don't fool yourself," she continues. "I know who she is. I don't know how she got involved with Jorge Castelan, but she must have smelled money. She seems to have somehow separated him from his…um, longtime companions, so she was probably babysitting his assets. Maybe she thought he'd leave her some money if he died. Or a lot of money. He's got tons, right?"

"Yes." Janet says. "There's lots of money."

"Believe me, I know all about this because I was bad at it. Desperately bad—getting money from men, I mean. The term used to be palimony. I'll have to give Carolee some grudge points for being so much better. Where do you think this whole Centered Movement thing came from?"

"I thought you were interested in it."

"I was, until it turned out that it will kill you if you're not ready to participate in a triathlon—*and* until it occurred to me on the plane coming home that Carolee's probably the one who came up with it, not him, no matter what he says. Think about it: a live Jorge Castelan fronting some mystical exercise system might be just as lucrative as glomming onto a dead guru's estate. I just don't quite get why he would do it. Do you?"

"I'm not sure I understand any of this," Janet says.

"Any more communiqués?" Renna asks, glancing at Janet's computer, where the musical notes of her screensaver float in their pixilated sky of electric blue.

"No," Janet replies. "Nothing."

"That doesn't give you the creeps? Someone apparently knows exactly who you are and how to get in touch with you, but you have no idea who that is or why he—or she—is doing this?"

"I don't think it's anything bad," Janet tells her.

Renna begins to gather up her things—her Tibetan coat, her leather shoulder bag—preparing to be on her way. Then, suddenly, she reaches over and taps Janet on the forehead. "Too much magical thinking still going on in there."

Georgie's gesture. Janet feels it in her heart. To Renna, she says, "You know, it's like this is how I started my life: harpsichords and tuning forks. And Jorge Castelan. And here it all is, back again."

"And that surprises you."

Janet nods, yes. "Unless you're going to tell me that this is just my karma at work."

"You know what I believe?" Renna says. "You are who you are. You want what you want. And after a certain point, you can make yourself crazy trying to change." And then she's out the door.

In the psychedelic days, everyone of a certain age was ready for the world to split open and the mind-bending truth to spill out. For many, The Peyote Palace *was the first expression of that truth, of which more and more was revealed with the publication of every subsequent Jorge Castelan book. And what was the truth? That surely, there was more to life than school and work and marriage and a house in the suburbs? Surely whoever, or whatever, had created all of existence had more in mind than this brief slog between the poles of birth and extinction that alternated between bland and painful with one or two spikes of joy—joy as a sop, as a distraction—in between? Perhaps humanity had been living on the surface of reality for so long that human beings had forgotten what the ancients must have known: that there was magic, power, mystery and meaning to be found if you just looked deeper. If you looked harder. If you were brave.*

And one of the things it meant to be brave was to face down death. To encounter its skeletal visage and shatter it; to break down the door it guards—the door to the next place, the next phase—and walk through.

Death, Jorge Castelan taught, was pointless, a fantasy that no one had to believe in. "What a ridiculous concept!" he wrote. "Why do we believe it? Because everyone else says it's so? How do they know? Sorcerers," he explained, "and those with sorceric knowledge—never die; what a waste that would be! To spend a human lifetime developing a deep understanding of alternative realities, the strength to access them and the ability to adjust the attention of the universe to allow you to move with and, as necessary, manipulate your passage into infinity through the energetic flow of time and existence only to have all that concentrated power vanish in an instant because a sack of flesh had wasted away, or had been irreparably damaged by accident or perhaps by some idiotic act of violence?"

In trying to understand what he meant about not dying, ever, Janet had once asked if he was talking about reincarnation, which had annoyed him. "No," he had told her forcefully, "that was another ridiculous idea—that some little spiritual bundle keeps getting repackaged inside new shells of flesh and bone time after time. You would have to be truly ignorant," he barked, "to buy into that idea." Then did he mean something that she translated through her very limited understanding of Buddhism and Hindu beliefs (limited indeed; it was rooted in having read a few books and listened to a lot of stoned conversation among the workers in the harpsichord factory) as reflecting some loose amalgam of ideas surrounding the core concept of "being one with the universe," along with a little high-school-level Einstein ("matter never dies, it just changes form"), or maybe his ideas were closer to what Jung was getting at when he explained what the alchemists were after, which Janet presented to Georgie as, they weren't trying to literally turn lead into gold, they were trying to accomplish the transmogrification of their souls? As Janet unfurled this patchwork of what he undoubtedly considered a lot of new-age nonsense, Jorge Castelan became more and more irritated. "No, no, no," he told her: "don't compare the sorcerer's way with anything else! What the Yaqui shamans knew, what Yamon taught me, is different than anything anyone else has ever tried to explain. If you don't understand, just say so. Don't guess. This is too important."

"Okay," Janet said. "I don't understand. Sorcerers don't die."

"No," said Jorge Castelan.

"Then what happens to them?" Janet asked.

"They burn up from within," Jorge Castelan explained. "It's a remarkable sight. And then they go elsewhere. But it takes a long time—a very long time—to understand how to do that. Very few people really can."

"But you can."

"Not yet. But someday I will be able to. And then I will be able to follow Yamon to wherever he's gone."

"And Lily? Zella? Namuria?" Janet asked Georgie.

"Yes," he told her. "They are learning, too. I'm teaching them. But I can't teach you this—yet. You're too young. At your age, you don't believe you're going to die anyway, so how can I teach you to alter an experience you don't believe you're going to have?"

Well, of course she didn't believe she was going to die. How could anyone who was part of the bright, dancing, love-filled, revolutionary, mind-bending generation of hippie wanderers ever die? But they did, they do. In fact, Janet can remember the first time it occurred to her that death—the real deal, lights out and good-bye—was coming for her, someday, just like everybody (almost everybody) else. It was when she was packing up to move to Woodstock. Janet did not think of herself as being attached to keepsakes—when she moved from place to place there were very few things besides clothes and other necessities that she bothered to take with her—but in a drawer, wrapped in a sweater, she came across one memento that she had been carrying around for years: the moonstone ring that Lily had once given her. She had not worn it for more than a decade but impulsively, now, slipped it back on her finger. It was a weighty piece of jewelry, a white stone with an icy blue sheen to it, set in a silver band that had been meant to convey the bonds of love, of family. But all that was long gone: beautiful as it was, comforting as it was to have it back on her finger again, its symbolism, now was all sentiment and little else. Subtract the fond memories and the ring was just another object now, a thing, *a human contrivance for pretending that human vows and gestures, words uttered, pledges made, and plans, had the power to outlast time. To create a barrier against change and shifting circumstance. They did not. The past faded, the present consumed itself with busyness; the future had intentions of its own. And it would leave you behind, soon enough, just as you discarded your own days as they trailed away behind you.*

And so the final protective membrane disintegrated; the protective cocoon fell apart. So many years removed from Jorge Castelan, Janet still, immediately, thought of him and knew that he was right, about this, at least: it was *ridiculous, all this struggling and striving and planning for a future that at some point, was not going to include you. Time and age, inevitably, would see to that: there was no human magic that could frighten them away.* Still, it was impossible to stop behaving as if being alive was a permanent *condition and to be shocked when you had to confront the idea that it was not. Unless, of course, you were a sorcerer, or a witch, or a Fearless Guide, ready, when the time came, to burn up from within. Which would somehow take you elsewhere. Not just up the New York State Thruway to Woodstock, though that was certainly a kind of elsewhere. Incense, candles, peace signs and hash pipes: a last outpost, perhaps, but hardly what one would think of as the final stopping off point for the last nagual.*

☾

"Georgie?"

"Yes, nena, it's me. What are you doing? Can you come for a visit?"

Janet is in the middle of working; she is fitting the sound board into the case of one of the harpsichords and is having difficulty. It has to be glued in quickly, and then have rails attached with no room for error, but the sound board that came with this particular kit was either badly cut to begin with or it's warped over time, because it doesn't sit correctly in the case. If she tries to force it, the instrument will never sound right, and she's beginning to think that she's going to have to make an entirely new one. That's going to be an adventure—she has plans to follow, but she's never made this particular, critical part before, so figures she's going to have to try a few times until she gets it right. She was considering the idea of going to the lumber yard this afternoon, but it's been weeks since she's seen Jorge Castelan—once again, he hasn't been answering phone messages—and, though she thinks of refusing, the impulse to exact some childish revenge passes quickly.

He tells her that he's at the Centered Movement Institute and asks that she meet him there. Janet goes back to the house, changes her clothes and then checks her watch: it's early afternoon, on a day clear and just warm enough to think about spring. The trees are still bare but the creeks are beginning to run with meltwater; there has even been an evening thunderstorm, the kind of weather system that usually doesn't travel over the mountains until the days are longer and the winds more changeable and crackling with energy.

It's a weekday and there's little traffic on the road between the two small towns, so Janet actually find herself enjoying the drive, which pleases her. She's not ready to imagine herself as someone who actually likes to drive, but this is a big improvement over her usual white-knuckle trips, even on short runs to the supermarket in Saugerties.

When she reaches the Institute at the end of the narrow road that takes her up into the hills, she's not surprised that the place seems deserted: she's heard from Renna, who knows everything that goes on in Woodstock, that the Centered Movement classes have been temporarily suspended. Jorge Castelan isn't making appearances where reporters or anyone else can hound him about Nina Acheson. But what is unexpected is to find Georgie sitting on the front steps. It's an odd sight, she thinks: outside, alone, he looks like just anybody—just a guy, casually dressed in chinos and a windbreaker—hanging out, waiting for a friend to show up. Someone you might run into by accident and make small talk with.

He waves when he sees her car. She gets out, goes toward him, and he gives her a long hug. Then he takes her hand and says, "Let's walk for a while."

She has a hundred questions for him—during her drive to the Centered Movement Institute she has, in fact, planned an interrogation for him—but as soon as he touches her, holds her in what is unmistakably a loving embrace, she can't quite begin. The embrace has disarmed her *intent*. It has caught her off-guard, since she expected—well, what did she expect? A man bowed by grief or wearing the defeated face of contrition? If so, she was mistaken. Whatever he is feeling is unknowable for the moment because, when he chooses, Jorge Castelan can make himself into a cipher, turn his usually expressive face into an unreadable mask. So Janet decides that she will have to be cautious. She will observe the protocols that in the past had always been in place: the last nagual will have to be the one to bring up the subject of Nina Acheson and her sisters if any conversation about the women is going to take place. Jorge Castelan will have to declare the rules, define the boundaries of what can or cannot be said because otherwise, he is perfectly capable of refusing to say anything at all. And Janet can't let that happen. There are things, now, that she needs to know.

And so she waits. She lets him lead her through a stand of pines that opens onto a stony field. Here and there, patches of early wildflowers, purple buds on thin stalks, have laced themselves into the cold grass. As they walk through the fields, Janet steals a glance at Georgie now and then, slowly letting herself accept that his new leanness, the definition in his face, his frame, is probably etched by illness as much as by whatever wellspring of energy he is calling on to deny that he is anything but fit, strong, an antic warrior still, strange and mystifying as he has always been.

Overhead, a flock of Canada geese suddenly cuts through the sky, honking to each other as they cross from west to east. Jorge Castelan looks up and smiles.

"Not crows," he says.

"No," Janet agrees, "definitely not crows."

He squeezes her hand. "There was a time when you were… content," he says to her.

Janet understands that this is actually a question, and she knows what part of her life he is wondering about—the only part that matters to him.

She answers him honestly. "Yes," she says. "For a long time, I was. Everything was easier when I was with you."

"Until it was harder."

"Yes," Janet agrees. "Until it was harder."

They walk on a little farther. The grassy plan has given way to bare ground; gritty soil shifts beneath their feet. The afternoon light has deepened; there is a sheen of gold behind the blue.

"I miss the house," Janet tells him, honestly. "And the garden. I dream about it, sometimes, that I'm still there."

"Me, too." But when Jorge Castelan says that he dreams, it may mean much more than those few simple words imply. And perhaps that's what he wants Janet to understand, because he suddenly begins speaking about something else. "Do you know that I recognized you from the first day?"

And she does understand: he is approaching the question she had always wanted to ask him but thought he would never address: *why me?*

"Did you?" she prompts.

"Not the way Yamon recognized me, of course—that kind of *wham* is too intense for anybody, really." He smacks his free hand against his leg for emphasis. "But when I walked into the warehouse that first day we met, I could see a line of stillness that went from about twenty feet over your head, right through you, down into the ground. And when you walked, it went with you. The air would change color around you: it got more silvery."

"That doesn't sound like me at all," Janet says. "Sometimes I feel pretty crazy."

"Then you should stop, because it's wrong. You're making yourself feel that way."

"It's still there, you think? This...stillness?"

"Oh yes," Jorge Castelan says breezily. "You haven't changed as much as you think."

Since he's volunteered all this, Janet is emboldened to ask one more question. "Why did you come to the warehouse? I mean...you couldn't possibly have actually needed a tuning fork."

"I used to work in an office near there, a long time before, when I was a graduate student. I'm sure I told you that."

He hasn't really explained what Janet would like to know, but he sounds tired of the subject now, so she understands to let it go. Accident or *intent*—why did he come to the warehouse in the first place? That meeting, the event that changed her life. She has never known the answer. Perhaps she never will.

They have been wandering for more than half an hour. The Centered Movement Institute is somewhere behind them, too far to be seen. Ahead, in the distance, are the soft brown peaks of the Catskills, ridged with pines. A blue sky, gold clouds, shafts of sunlight streaming into the valleys. They are walking on the footprints of the glaciers, now, on a flat plain of bald rock where the earth has been scraped down to its granite bones. Finally, they come to an overlook, the rocky edge of a gorge protected by a low stone wall that is meant only as a warning; if you wanted, Janet thinks, you could step around it and walk off into the air.

Here, finally, Jorge Castelan stops and lets go of Janet's hand. He turns to her and says, "We have to ask them to stop. I know they're angry with me, but enough is enough. It's not like them to cause me so much trouble."

Janet is relieved that he has finally raised the subject of the witches' fate, but surprised by the turn it has immediately taken— though of course, she tells herself, she shouldn't be. If he really didn't know where the women had gone, and doesn't believe that dead means *dead*, at least for him, for them, then he is not going to mourn them, he is going to be angry. And how much there is for him to be angry about: he is a private man who has now been forced into the position of being a public figure—and one not receiving the reverence he is used to. Opinions, in fact, remain decidedly mixed. Day after day now, new references to the work of Jorge Castelan keep appearing online. It seems that every new-age site—and conversely, every website run by skeptics and debunkers of the same fields, from the paranormal to alien encounters—features some excerpt from his writings along with the story of Nina Acheson, Barbara Anderson and Victoria Gordon, which, it turns out, is the given name of Zella-Zed. Sometimes he is blamed for their deaths, sometimes he is not. In the past, Georgie had managed to avoid most direct contact with his own notoriety. He enjoyed it, surely—when it was almost solely adoring—and surely he fed it, contributed to it; probably the time had come when he could not live without it, but it also seemed to be something that he preferred to visit—to check on when he felt moved to, when he needed to be reminded that he was still a powerful force, that he was admired, important, even revered, by some—rather than live with his fame all the time. And now, he seems to be famous as much for something awful as for a lifetime of teaching the Yaqui way.

Alright then, Janet thinks: he has his reasons to be angry—but at the women? This kind of trouble is the last thing they would have wished for him, or ever tried to bring about. Jorge Castelan may have decided to blame his long-time companions for his current problems, but for Janet, this is an appalling conclusion. The contemplative mood she had allowed herself to fall into as they walked through the fields vanishes in an instant, and now she is getting upset at him.

"I know about Ivinger," she says, letting the words spit themselves out as immediately as her anger brings them to mind.

The last nagual reacts to this revelation with a shrug. "Yes? So? I'm fine now. That's just an old sorcerer's trick: when the body is ill, the sorcerer sends it to a place where it can get well. But in the meantime, the sorcerer goes elsewhere. And now I am back, I am well, as I told you. You don't need to worry about me."

"How could I ever worry about you?" Janet asks, though she is speaking untruthfully. "You told me that sorcerers don't die."

With a slight tilt of his head, Jorge Castelan signals that he hears a disturbing note in Janet's voice. He says, "You are asking me something else, I think. What is it?"

"I need to know what happened."

"Need?"

"Yes. Lily, Namuria and Zella. They were my friends. I need to know why they ended up...where they did."

Now it is Jorge Castelan's turn to offer a rebuke. He says, "Your friends? They were more than that. They suffered when you left."

Janet is stung by this—enough to want to defend herself. She says, "I suffered, too."

But again, the only response Janet gets is a shrug; the sorcerer's disinterested response to human tribulations.

"I see," Jorge Castelan says. "You may leave but I may not."

"It's hardly the same thing," Janet answers.

"Of course not. I knew what I was doing, and why. I told you before, all they had to do was be patient. To wait for me to come back."

"And then what was going to happen?" Janet asks. "Did you think Carolee was going to move into the house and become one of the girls? The head witch?"

"That is a horrible thing to say," Jorge Castelan tells her.

"I know, it is," Janet admits. "But I feel horrible, and I'm very confused. I mean, Georgie, what were you thinking? Help me understand."

He does not help her. Instead, he says, "This is interesting. You continue to question me."

"Who else can I ask?" Janet says. "Who else have I ever asked anything important?"

"Well, perhaps I have run out of answers for you. Perhaps you should just go find them yourself." The last nagual waves his hand dismissively. "Get on a bus," he says. "Go to Este Muralla. That's what I did. Perhaps Yamon will answer your questions."

It takes Janet a moment to realize what Jorge Castelan has actually just told her, and when she does, she's shocked: he has let slip one of his most carefully guarded secrets. Or more likely, it was not an accident: the last nagual is not careless; he would not have told her the name of the town where he met Yamon—because that must be what Este Muralla is—unless he meant to do so. But why? This greatest of way stations of the counterculture was never identified in any of his books because, said Jorge Castelan, he did not want a horde of hippies and searchers descending on the town to look for Yamon. Even today, the exact location of the bus station where he met the old Indian remains a mystery to those who remain devoted to the work of Jorge Castelan. The women knew, certainly, but they never shared it with Janet Planet, and so it remained unknown to her, too—until now.

Unsure how to respond, Janet simply goes on asking questions, though it occurs to her that what she is doing mimics some of the more exasperating dialogues that Jorge Castelan had with his teacher, and which he reported in his books. She says, "What would I find in Este Muralla? You told me that Yamon is gone from this world."

"That doesn't mean he couldn't come back in some other form. I remind you that he is a trickster—I have explained that before."

"But you said you can't find him. You said you've looked."

"In one sense, yes, I have looked in many places—in one reality, then another and another. But there are many more, and Yamon is a great sorcerer." Jorge Castelan fixes Janet with an odd gaze, as if he's seeing something about her that he had not noticed before. He says, "You think I haven't looked hard enough? Is that it? Do you think that because the body was weak, so was I?"

Again, Janet is at a loss about how to reply. She has asked him about the fate of human beings and instead, has been drawn into a conversation about his travels through the sorceric realms. But what else should she have expected? She reminds herself that this is still Georgie she is talking to and for him, that *is* where fate operates: in the elsewhere, in the other reality—the multiplicity of other realities—in the places that belong to the sorcerers, which humans are separated from by their blindness and their fear. Now, however, Janet seems to have disturbed *him*, perhaps by implying that he is vulnerable—which would imply that he may still be human, after all.

And so Janet does not have to reply because the last nagual decides to answer his own question—at least, that is how Janet perceives what happens next. In an instant, it seems to her, Jorge Castelan moves his body from *here* to *there*: first, he is standing beside her and then—*snap*, just like that—he is on the other side of the stone barrier at the edge of the gorge, with nothing between him and infinity but the clouds, the wind, the air.

Janet is aware that she should be startled by this sudden, even bizarre turn of events, but she is not. The moment seems highly unreal and at the same time, completely inevitable because this is what he knows, Georgie, this is what he believes: confronted with an impasse, a problem without a solution—or a human being who doubts him in any way—the sorcerer sees these obstacles only as walls that he must fly through. A sorcerer does not walk: he has to jump.

And so, Janet wonders, is that what she is going to see next? The energetic leap that will prove the power of the last nagual? Then, later, will she find him home in bed? That, as he wrote in *The Other Side of Reality*, is what followed his leap into the infinite when he was with Yamon; he woke up the next day in the old Indian's shack, naked but without even a single mark on his body. Years ago, no matter what he believed, he wouldn't let Janet take the same risk. So does that mean what he says happened to him didn't, really? Or that it did, but that flying in and out of infinity is a feat that only he can accomplish—though perhaps not all the time, perhaps not at will?

And are these even useful questions for Janet to be asking herself? Because it occurs to her that what might be happening right now is something else entirely: perhaps this is another test that Jorge Castelan has devised for her. Or for both of them. Does he actually expect to wake up in bed once he steps off into the air—which is exactly what Janet is sure he's contemplating—or not to wake up at all? What *is* the intent here: action or metaphor? It is impossible to know, impossible to understand or even guess what is going through the sorcerer's mind. What he sees or what he intends, just as it is impossible for Janet to guess what he expects her to do. Follow him into the void?

That is not her wish for either of them. It never was; it is not now. So she offers an alternative, a path to follow that will lead her where she is probably going anyway. That will satisfy him, she thinks, and spare them both. Let there be no test—neither of wills nor of the spirit. Let things go back the way they were. For the moment, she has demanded enough of the last nagual.

"Georgie," Janet says. "Let me do it."

"What?" he murmurs. "Do what?"

"Let me talk to them. Lily, Namuria. Zella. I have things to say to them, too." Clouds pass across the mountains; the sun continues its slow descent toward the horizon, sliding shadows around in the valley below. Jorge Castelan is silent; he and Janet have switched roles, somehow, and now he is the one with no response.

Eventually, Janet continues. "Wherever they've gone—are going—I'm sure they'll turn back and see me. And listen to me. Mothers can never resist when their daughters need them. Never."

Jorge Castelan looks up at the sky. He is thinking, or he is watching for something, but Janet simply waits. She watches him.

"Alright," he says finally. He takes a few steps back and in the space of a few moments, he's standing beside Janet again. "You try."

And then he strides away. Which is also not a surprise; he has left her, probably, the way Yamon often left him abruptly to complete some sorcerer's task he had been assigned. After Jorge Castelan has gone, Janet sits down on the ground and closes her eyes. She thinks about the women; she calls them near—but this is not magic. There is no sorcery, she knows, in having a conversation with human beings who have gone elsewhere; people do it all the time, in different ways. Besides, in what she has read recently about Jorge Castelan, she has also discovered small parcels of information about the witches and the Fearless Guide—Nina Acheson, Barbara Anderson and Victoria Gordon—that have made her feel close to them once again. Some of this information was already known to Janet, as was the fact that Nina was from Ohio, Barbara from Delaware and Victoria from Illinois; but their long-estranged families have added some additional bits and pieces: all three women did go to UCLA, though Victoria was there long before the other two. Victoria had graduated but the two women who would later be known as Lily and Namuria had not. Nina had lived in New York at one point and had called herself a beatnik; Barbara had gone to a Catholic high school, she had been a Girl Scout who turned into an unhappy teenager and thought, in California, she would find a more meaningful life. Victoria Gordon had worked in a bookstore after school. She was quiet, introverted; people seemed to recall that she wanted to be a writer. Her parents didn't want her to go to college at all; she had gotten scholarships and had worked to support herself at UCLA.

Janet thinks that she understands the women from these brief sketches perhaps more clearly than she ever had when she saw them every day. They were lost girls, as she had been, runaways of a sort—just a decade or so older than Janet, a decade too old to be hippies, but not to feel the need to change themselves, to transform, to be something other than their upbringing and their surroundings and the middling expectations of their families and friends had led them to think was possible. And Janet, now—Janet at this moment in time, sitting cross-legged on the earth's granite bones, on a bare, bald hump of its billion-year-old skeleton—is older than either of them had been when they had "adopted" her. Which makes her the child of changeling children, of strange girls, witch girls, living an odd and intentionally unconventional life.

The facts about Victoria Gordon—Zella-Zed—are perhaps most interesting to Janet, because they contain one extraordinary piece of information. True, it turns out that she is older than the other two women and was, in fact, not one of Jorge Castelan's students during his brief teaching career but a contemporary, a fellow undergraduate, which means that she would now be in her late sixties—somewhere around Georgie's age. But those pieces of information are not so startling: what is, is that Victoria Gordon is apparently Jorge Castelan's legal wife. They had married when both were still in college; seemingly, then, she would have known him during the years when he was traveling regularly to Mexico to learn from Yamon.

To address her old friends, Janet has no rituals to perform, no ceremonies. She simply moves her breath from the inside of her body to the outside to join the breezes, the clouds scattered like scarves above the mountains, and with each breath she says. *I'm so sorry. Everything ended the wrong way.* And she pictures the women, moving through the cool rooms of the house in Westwood with its roof of red tiles, its fruit trees, its shady garden, and can hear them say, each in turn, *I'm sorry, too.*

Then let it be my turn, Janet tells them. *Leave Georgie to me. He's sick; I think he's doing crazy things. But I think I can deal with him now. I think you should let me try.*

Janet opens her eyes and sees that the moon has been launched into the blue fields of the sky. It is a mild presence, just one more element that has appeared in a changeable landscape that is busy transforming itself from daylight into evening, from light to darkness, from this hour to whatever will happen in the next and the next and the next.

VIII

I have probably allowed myself to get too involved already. But I have received a letter that I don't know how to answer, or even if I should. Perhaps you do.

Janet, in her workshop, is staring at the words in the e-mail; black letters on a white background, all made out of electricity. Bits and bytes, coming through underground cables, passing across glass fibers, transported by routers through the air. Coming to her straight from *peyotepalace@peyotepalace.com* again, and again the message is unsigned and labeled, "Do not reply." But, as she has before, she writes back anyway, trying a different tack. *Do I know you?* she asks, hoping for but not expecting a reply.

She is so mesmerized by the three brief sentences onscreen that it takes her a moment, after she sends her unwanted query, to even think of opening the attachment. When she does, she realizes that she's looking at the scanned image of a handwritten note, which reads:

Dear Eli: I am writing to you because I don't know who else to get in touch with. Is it true, what I've been reading? Georgie has come back? He must be furious with us, just furious. We did search for him, but he must have been so far away! Or maybe he didn't want to be found? I don't know what to do now. He has always trusted you, so I thought you might have some advice. My sisters are still traveling, so there's no use trying to ask them. Will he want to see me? I don't even know how to get in touch with him; he's put up a very energetic wall and I can't even get close. What do you think? Please write back. I'm at Harmony Road Farm. I didn't know where else to go.

—Z

Janet's immediate reaction to this note is shock, and then anger. Somebody, she tells herself, is carrying out an elaborate hoax; somebody has finally tracked her down, identified her as Georgie's Janet Planet, and has decided to do something really cruel. But the e-mail has come from the same address as the earlier messages, the first of which was a chapter of Jorge Castelan's book. So this must be the same person—someone named Eli? Who is he? And why would he want to fool her in this horrible way? For what? To what end?

She checks, but of course there is no answer to her question—*Do I know you?*—so she goes back to the scanned image of the note. If this is not a trick, then the letter could only have been written by Zella; she often signed her name as simply, "Z." And besides, the content of the message sounds like her. Who else would be worried about the things that the letter writer is clearly frantic about: that Georgie has "come back"? That he must be angry? Janet has no reason to doubt that everything she's read about Nina Acheson and Barbara Anderson—Namuria and Lily—is true. Namuria is dead and it's likely that Lily is, as well. But apparently, amazingly, the Fearless Guide is alive.

If that really is true, the revelation is as eerie as it is welcome. It's as if somehow, Zella had heard Janet's silent meditations at the edge of the precipice where Jorge Castelan had left her not so long ago. As if the Fearless Guide has answered—indirectly, though, through a third party.

That's a thought that gives Janet a jolt, mirroring, as it does, the unanswered question that she has already dispatched through cyberspace: who is Eli? *He has always trusted you.* That must mean Eli is someone Jorge Castelan has known for quite a while. Wouldn't that suggest that somewhere, long ago, Janet would have met him, too? Or at least heard his name? But she simply doesn't remember an Eli, neither as someone's real name or as one of the "re-names" that Georgie was so fond of giving people.

Deep in thought, Janet gradually becomes aware that her hand hurts. She looks down and realizes that she's gripping a pliers she doesn't even remember picking up, and holding on to it so hard that her hand is growing achy and stiff. Letting go of the tool—carefully placing it down next to her laptop—seems to release her from the exercise of searching her memory. But then, standing up, she feels dazed; not dizzy, not sick, just at a remove from herself. She's operating her body but doesn't quite feel integrated into it. It's like she's experienced a blow that knocked her psyche off-kilter, and she can't quite find a way to clear her vision, both inside and out.

She walks out of the studio into a young season that is finally getting warmer. The morning air has a cold edge but the temperature has risen enough for Janet, just in shirtsleeves, to feel comfortable doing nothing but stand still for a few moments, eyes closed, and absorb the sunlight. Around her, the yard between the house and her workshop has overspread itself with dandelions; the patchy grass, infused with early spring rain, is trying to turn green.

Her intention is to cross the yard, go into the house and have something to eat, but that's not where her footsteps take her. Instead, she walks down her driveway and turns toward town. It is only when she reaches the tannery brook that marks the edge of the few short blocks of stores and restaurants that she identifies, for herself, what her destination is: she's headed for Meggie Duncan's bakery.

Late morning, mid-week, the bakery isn't very busy. Meggie is standing behind the counter, leafing through the *Woodstock Times* and drinking a cup of coffee. "Hey there," she says, looking up as Janet walks in.

"Hi," Janet replies. "Mind if I ask you something? Remember how we've talked about Harmony Road Farm?"

"Sure," Meggie agrees. "That blast from the past."

"Didn't it close down?"

"Gosh, I thought so. It was kind of a wreck even when I was there, and that was a zillion years ago. Everybody was too stoned to do much work in the fields and we never really got anything to grow very well. Except pumpkins. I don't even remember *why* we planted pumpkins—if we did. Maybe Ontario just sprouts pumpkins in the fall. It was pretty though; one October, we had a whole field of bright orange pumpkins covered with snow. They looked like big, fat, frosted muffins." Meggie gives Janet a quizzical look. "Why are you asking?"

"Someone forwarded a letter to me from a person who says she's living at Harmony Road Farm. I was just wondering if you thought it could be the same place."

Meggie looks thoughtful. Finally, she says, "Well, it was where everybody showed up at sooner or later. We had all kinds drifting through, I remember: draft dodgers, stoners, people heading further up north or out west, to Alberta or Vancouver. I suppose somebody could have bought the land, refurbished the buildings and put the word out that Harmony Road was open again. Maybe someone thought it would make a good old age home for lost hippies."

Janet smiles and feels like she's beginning to reconnect with herself. "I thought that's what Woodstock was."

"Now, now," Meggie says. "We are a vital community with thriving businesses and a busy tourist trade."

Janet points at the *Woodstock Times*. "Is that what it says in the paper?"

"Absolutely," Meggie says. "And that we should vote against rezoning for any more developers to come in and build ski runs."

Janet buys a pound of cookies decorated to look like psychedelic daisies, which Meggie puts in a box and ties up with twine. As she hands the box to Janet she says, "You know, you could look it up online. Everybody has a website nowadays. If the commune is open again, maybe they do, too."

Janet leaves the store and, carrying her box, continues down Tinker Street to Renna's gallery. There's a cluster of small brass temple bells tied to the gallery door that clink melodically as Janet walks in and finds Renna, in a black outfit—a Chinese shirt and silky pants—sweeping the floor. She's changed her hair color recently to make it more silvery blonde, the tint emphasized by the fact that she's got half a dozen silver bracelets on each wrist. Janet has the fond thought that Renna looks like a glam-rock Maoist.

"Brought you some of Meggie's cookies," Janet says. "So good morning. Can I use your computer?"

"Sure," Renna tells her. She gestures toward the back of the gallery, to the office space where she has her desk and her computer.

She takes the box of cookies, opens it and says, "Cute." Then she puts aside the broom and follows Janet, who has seated herself at the desk and turned on the computer. "What's up?"

"Well, I have a story to tell you," Janet says. "But give me a minute. Just let me get online." She watches the tiny hourglass displayed onscreen while the computer loads up its programs.

Munching on a pink and purple daisy, Renna says, "So I hear that the Centered Movement Institute is back in business."

"Apparently," Janet says. She's a little reticent about the subject because she hasn't shared everything she knows about it with Renna. In fact, Janet has actually told Renna very little. She's kept to herself, for instance, almost all the details about the day that she and Georgie took that long walk through the fields and across the rocky plain because it seemed something too private—too much of what Janet could only express as a family matter—to try to explain even to Renna. And though Renna knows that Janet has been talking to Georgie, she does not know much of what they've been saying, because Janet has mentioned only very edited versions of the conversations.

Janet has not seen Jorge Castelan in person for weeks, but he does call now and then; mostly late at night, which is vintage Georgie. He likes to talk on the phone in the hours when most other people would be asleep. It may also be, Janet suspects, that one of the people who must be asleep when he calls is Carolee, but she doesn't ask. Actually, she doesn't ask him much at all, she just listens. He seems to her to be almost hyper alert, like his mind is racing, like his heart is pumping wildly. Words rush from his mouth; thoughts, ideas, all coming at her through the thin wire of the telephone in her kitchen. She sits on a stool in the dark, chilly room with its moonlit window, with the dim image of the night-blackened trees and the blacker barrier of the distant mountains leaning in, and listens.

One thing she listens for is mention of the witches and the Fearless Guide, but Georgie seems to have been freed from them; from their memory, their presence, their putative death. He has moved away from addressing the problem of where, in their travels, they may be after having left this reality, because he is not constantly reminded that it is a problem to be solved, or even addressed, unless he wants to. That's because the twenty-four-hours-a-day, seven-days-a-week news cycle that is a constant feature of life in the new century has also moved on, away from Jorge Castelan; the coroner out in the desert corner of California where the remains of Nina Acheson were identified has officially ruled the death a suicide and declared that Barbara Anderson—Lily—was a probable suicide as well. There is no hint of foul play involved, no murder, and no one seems to be able to milk any further details out of the story, such as Jorge Castelan's stay at the Ivinger Institute, which remains his—and Janet's—secret. Without any new revelations to keep it interesting, the story of the last nagual and his witches soon disappears from the pages of the gossip magazines and the message boards of the blogs.

And for all this—for quieting the notion that his name should be attached more to a scandal than to a lifetime's work of helping to reveal the many other levels of reality that can be accessed through the practices of the Sonoran shamans—Jorge Castelan thanks Janet Planet. The fact that their conversation at the overlook began with a confrontation is forgotten: he is focused only on what happened after he left her and that, he has decided, has worked in his favor. *See, nena,* he says to her on the phone, *you have become a powerful witch, even without trying. So powerful that even you didn't know what you could do.* Janet barely even argues with him about this; it seems to please him, now, to praise her, and so she lets him say what he likes. *Your mothers love you,* he insists. *They are helping you even as they continue their travels.*

He continues to talk about how long he was gone from the world as if his time at Ivinger was only one possible reality—one level of many accessible to a sorcerer who can leave his body in one place, while he is elsewhere. Presumably, he has begun to suggest to Janet, the women have done the same. And he has added a new coda to the story that is both the life he lives and the books he writes: how he must begin preparing for the work of leaving again, of planning his own journey into the infinite, though this time, on his own terms. And late at night, in her chilly kitchen, Janet closes her eyes and listens to his voice with the part of her that he opened, long ago, that has no boundaries, that stays awake forever, even when she dreams. She thinks that it is impossible to explain this to Renna. It would be impossible to explain it to anyone who does not know Jorge Castelan.

But to Renna, human nature is explanation enough for almost anything, so she's content enough to just stand behind Janet, now, as she Googles "Harmony Road Farm" and to wait for an explanation.

There are hundreds of mentions of Harmony Road Farm, particularly in the published memoirs and online blogs of people who had lived there for a while, years ago. From ex-radicals to wandering flower children, the writings and even blurry old photos of those who had once sojourned at the commune just on the northern side of the U.S.–Canadian border tell the story of trying to keep body and soul together during the cold winters, of staring out of the windows of the dormitory-like rooms at bare, bitter fields, and trying to scrounge enough wood to feed the pot-bellied stoves that were usually the only source of heat. But there are also many people who have better memories: they describe golden summers that were like a return to childhood—swimming in the creeks and ponds on the property, sleeping in an outdoor hammock on warm nights ablaze with northern constellations. And always there is the memory of conversation; talk of revolution and spirituality, of planning a new world or of finding a way to live differently in the one that already existed.

Janet also does find a few more contemporary references to the farm: apparently, it had been a derelict property for more than two decades, but in the late 1990s, an ice cream mogul who had camped out there for a few months when he was a teenager had bought the property and revived the old commune as a kind of combination youth hostel and tour destination for graying baby boomers looking to revisit the days they had spent wandering the roads of North America in Volkswagen vans and old school buses dandied up with psychedelic paint jobs. There are also, it seems, some permanent residents; anyone, in fact, who is willing to pitch in and contribute to the small community of ex-hippies who had come back to try living off the grudging land again is welcome to give it a try. What is not listed, however, is any kind of phone number, which is more or less in keeping with the anarchistic arrangements that always prevailed at Harmony Road: there was never anyone to call because no one was in charge. Apparently, that is still the case: if you want to go there—or find someone who's living at the farm—the only way to do that is to show up.

"How long do you think it would take to drive there?" Janet asks Renna, who suggests putting the information into a mapping program, which quickly serves up driving directions and a time frame of about five hours from Woodstock to the Ontario town of Downey, which is near Harmony Road.

"I guess that's doable," Janet says.

"You actually want to go there?" Renna asks. "To a *commune*?" She says the word as if Janet has suggested climbing into a time machine.

Janet laughs at her, but says, "Yes."

"Alone? In your car? You must be kidding yourself." Renna says. "The way you drive, you'll never make it an hour out of town before you smack into a tree or get squashed by a truck or…"

"Okay, okay, I get it," Janet says. "Maybe I can take a bus or something."

"Or maybe you could get someone to drive you." Renna smiles playfully. "Hint, hint."

"Really?"

"I could be persuaded," Renna tells Janet. "I've actually never set foot on a commune before. It might be interesting. But why do you want to go? Who's there that you want so badly to see?"

Who had first told her about Harmony Road Farm? It's impossible to remember; it was too long ago. It was back in the time when what mattered was the sense of community, of belonging, of being part of a tribe whose members were recognizable to you wherever you went. Long hair, fringed jackets, tie-dyed tee shirts, beads, sandals, bangles, beards: these were your people, from the east coast to the west. So you got on the road and found your people on their communes, in their shacks and squats; you ate lentils with them, helped with the chores—new-age pioneers!—and then went on your way. San Francisco was the main destination, but if you were feeling a little paranoid, then Canada was the refuge; that's where you went to escape the draft or to hang with those who said that life in the States was getting too crazy, too weird. Canada was where you went to wait.

For what? For something to happen, because surely, it had to. Who could go on living in the dull, materialistic world, run by fascists and morons? Run by Nixon the monster. Canada was a good place to wait for the revolution to start, for the third eye to open wide and see the truth, for the day when the world would crack open, too, and magic would pour out, love, oneness, whatever. For things to stop simply going on the way they always had. Everything had to change.

When all this went down, Janet had expected to be one person in a crowd of many. Millions. For a while, that group was centered around Harmony Road, a commune where more than a hundred people lived at any one time. Janet had spent only one winter there, though, and that was enough—she couldn't believe how cold it could get on the flat plains of Ontario, scoured by the Arctic wind—and in the spring, when a couple of people said they were heading back to the States, to the west coast, Janet went along with them.

When she was at Harmony Road Farm, she had been the youngest person living there. It was easy enough, after that, to be the youngest in a much smaller family—the one that lived in the house in Westwood—and to try to adapt to the way they lived, to give credence to the things they believed. It was another way of waiting, though where the last nagual and his women were headed it did not seem possible for Janet to follow. At least, later, when she thought back on the years she lived with them, it was hard for her to believe that even they ever entertained the idea that she could. Jorge Castelan was on a great journey that had started in a bus station in Mexico, and to be his companion required a deep, unquestioning commitment that Janet was not prepared to make. But the witches were; they had. So had the Fearless Guide. It had never occurred to Janet, not once, not ever, that anywhere along the way any one of these people would require help from her. The sorcerer's daughter had always thought her parents were stronger than that.

Janet Planet, Janet Planet. Having shed her name, she thought she had also shed her obligations. Or perhaps, all along, she was still just waiting. For what? For the world to crack open, for the attention of the universe to turn her way again. For whatever she is supposed to do—though following the lead of the last nagual, she is determined that whatever it is, she will do it on her own terms.

IX

"How do you think she knew to go to…what's this place called again?"

"Harmony Road Farm. And I couldn't tell you how she knew. Maybe she looked it up, like I did. Maybe someone told her about it. Georgie was gone a long time—I suppose she, Lily, and Namuria might have been trying to figure out what they would do if he didn't come back."

"They could have just stayed in the house, no?"

"I guess it depends on what they thought had happened to him. I just don't know."

Janet and Renna have been on the road for almost five hours, making better time than they had expected. They had left at dawn; it is now just after eleven in the morning and they have already crossed over from the northern edge of New York into the province of Ontario and are on a road leading out of a suburb of boxy houses into a landscape of seemingly endless grasslands. Except for regular route markers, there are no road signs to tell them where they are, but by relying on the GPS system in Renna's car, they are fairly sure that they are heading in the right direction. Every now and then, Janet's gaze wanders to the GPS screen, watching as the little car avatar that represents their progress gobbles up the electronic miles. When she turns back to look out the window, she keeps asking herself if anything looks familiar, but she hasn't been here in decades and there are no landmarks, nothing to see except the rippling plains of grass, yellow when the sun is bright, greener when clouds float across the bowl of the sky. Long and flat, like shredded sheets, these northern clouds seem to bump against the sky's rim, lingering on the horizon until they drift away.

Finally, at a place where the road bends and splits into smaller rural routes, there is a signpost for a town called Downey. Thirty years ago, the town was just a small collection of grocery and farm supply stores gathered around a crossroads a few miles down from Harmony Road. Now, as she and Renna drive through the town, time finally opens itself up to Janet and winds backwards. This, she remembers, this little cluster of stores at the road's edge, looks much the same as it did the last time she saw it. Just a few minutes pass by before the electronic car on the GPS screen and its real-life counterpart leave the town behind and are on the road that leads back out into the country.

"There," Janet says, pointing to a hand-painted sign on a stake that has been planted in brown earth, near a grove of waving cattails. *Harmony Road Farm* has been lettered in bright poster colors on a wooden board decorated with a smiling sun and an equally cheery moon wearing what looks like a jaunty crown of stars.

Though the sign looks new, probably someone has just recently refreshed the paint, because Janet remembers the sun and the moon with their welcoming greeting. Their familiarity hits Janet with an unexpected suddenness: it feels like she just saw them yesterday, just turned down this road, heading home.

Glancing over at Janet's face, Renna says, "Are you alright?"

"I think so," Janet tells her. "But boy, am I having déjà vu."

"I think you can only have déjà vu about a place if you think you've been there before but you really haven't," Renna points out.

"Well, I'm sure having something," Janet says as Renna turns the car onto the unpaved path that angles off the roadway just beyond the painted sign.

About a quarter of a mile later they begin to see buildings, many more than Janet remembers. Her guess is that a number of the structures are residences; some are small, perhaps for a single group or family, some are larger to accommodate more communal living, but most have a kind of knocked-together quality, as if they were hammered together when they were needed without a lot of concern about aesthetics. All are painted bright colors, or are decorated with murals: the happy sun and moon are a repeated motif, but there are also a variety of other images ranging from flowers and rainbows to a pretty decent rendering of Che Guevara.

Renna slows down as a pair of brown dogs wearing bandanas around their necks come running up to the car, barking happily and scattering a flock of chickens pecking in the grass at the side of the road. "My God," she remarks, as they continue past a large, barn-like building that Janet remembers as the communal eating hall, "this place looks a little like hippie Disneyland. And is that a VW mini-bus over there? That thing with the swirls painted all over it? I haven't seen an actual one of those in a million years."

Janet sighs. "It all looks different," she says, "but the same. I guess that's the point."

"Is there an office or something like that?" Renna asks. "I mean, this is a big place. How are we going to find her?"

"If there is an office, that would be something new," Janet says. "I think we're just going to have to ask around."

The first people they spot are a couple, a bearded young man and a woman in a sun dress and sweater, walking out of the building that Janet remembers as housing a kiln; if the commune members are still operating the old Harmony Farm businesses, then this is where they make and fire pottery and stained glass panels. As she rolls down the window, Janet realizes that she's not sure who to ask for—Zella-Zed or Victoria Gordon—so she tries both names.

The young man seems to think for a moment and then says, "Sure, Zella. I think she's living in one of the cottages out by the creek. Do you know your way around?"

"I think so," Janet tells him. She says thanks to the couple, who wave good-bye and continue on their way. Janet directs Renna down another side road, which eventually winds through a grove of water oaks that have rooted themselves in the rich soil beside a rocky creek. Where the road ends, the trees also give way to a clearing where a row of wooden cottages stands along the edge of a field laid out in small plots: these are the commune's kitchen gardens, planted with herbs and flowers.

Renna parks the car at the edge of the road, and follows Janet toward the cottages. In their common yard, beach chairs and an old grill look like they have recently been dusted off and set out to do service for the warmer season to come.

It's very quiet here, and there seems to be no one around until the door of one of the cottages opens and a woman carrying a watering can starts slowly down the stairs. She's dressed in jeans and a blue work shirt, and she's very thin, sprite-like in her movements. Janet stops short to study her for the moment before she notices them. Her hair is different—she had been blonde and now has a cap of choppy gray hair—and she looks much older. But Janet knows who she is. She is sure she would know if she were blindfolded; there is something in the air around her, something in the molecules of the light, the wind, that is completely familiar to Janet Planet.

"Zella," she says softly. There is no need to speak even a decibel louder.

The woman stops, mirroring Janet's deliberate pause before the next moment is upon her. And then she turns her head. "Janet," she murmurs. "It's you, isn't it? It's you."

She puts down the watering can and walks toward Janet, who holds out her arms. Embracing, she feels, to Janet, like her bones are the latticework of a bird's skeleton; tiny, light, easily breakable. And it is Zella who holds onto Janet; she is without tears but seems not to want to let go.

Finally, she takes a step back, but reaches out to hold Janet's hand.

"You look like you," she says. "Just like you."

Janet smiles at her. "I am me," she says. "Still." She squeezes Zella's hand. "And I am so glad to see you again."

Zella nods, as if she almost can't bring herself to speak anymore. But she does, because she has something important to ask. "You've seen him, haven't you?"

"Yes," Janet tells her. "I've seen him."

"Then he really is back?"

"Yes," Janet assures her. "He is."

"I've read what they've been saying about him in the papers, but I didn't know if any of it was true," Zella continues. "I thought it might be Carolee Carter trying to get at me in some way."

Soothingly, Janet reaches out to stroke Zella's arm. "Oh, no. Not you."

"But you do know Carolee though, don't you? She's bad potatoes," Zella says emphatically. "I don't know why Georgie could never see that."

Bad potatoes is an expression Zella often used; Janet has no idea what its origin is but she certainly knows what it means. A bad potato is something—or someone—cursed. Rotten to the core.

Suddenly, Zella seems to notice Renna for the first time. "Who are you?" she asks. She sounds disturbed, almost frightened.

Janet answers for her. "This is my friend Renna," Janet says. "She drove me here."

"We can't talk in front of her."

"You can trust Renna," Janet says comfortingly. "I promise."

"I'm good potatoes," Renna chimes in. "Honest."

The severe expression that Zella had adopted relaxes. "Alright. If Janet says so, I believe her." She turns back to Janet then, and regards her with an intense look. "But don't try to fool me about anything."

"Zella. We've been driving for hours. I came here because I wanted to see you, not for any other reason. It's been much, much, much too long."

"Oh it has been. It has been," Zella says. Now, she's almost wailing. "I'm sorry, I'm sorry. I've just been so...alone. Everyone here is very nice but they don't understand a thing."

Still holding Janet's hand, she leads the three of them toward her cottage where they all sit, arranging themselves on the steps. The air is still, and moving into afternoon, the daylight has taken on an odd yellow cast that seems to bring the flat landscape of trees and planted fields into sharp relief. The silence around them makes Janet feel watchful, edgy, like a storm might be building somewhere out on the vast plains beyond her line of sight.

"How did you end up here?" Janet asks Zella.

"You told me about it," Zella replies. "Don't you remember? It was a long time ago, but I always liked the name: Harmony Road."

"I don't remember. But it was a good place to come."

"I didn't know what else to do. I couldn't go home."

Gently, carefully, Janet starts to ask the real questions she wants answers to. *Still* wants. Her efforts to have this conversation with Georgie have failed, but perhaps Zella will speak more plainly and not veer off into magical language. "Why?" Janet prods.

"It was all Carolee's fault," Zella begins. "A couple of years ago, she started writing to Georgie. She had some crazy idea about exercises, I think it was."

Janet steals a glance at Renna, who nods, almost imperceptibly. "Centered Movement," Janet says.

"That's what it was called," Zella agrees. "She said she had done some research into Yaqui shaman practices and found that back before Yamon's time, they had incorporated certain movements into their rituals that maybe even he didn't know about. She sent Georgie photographs of glyphs that she said were scratched on some rocks in the desert showing the pattern of these movements. I didn't see anything in the photos except some squiggly lines but Georgie thought it was some kind of breakthrough. He began telling us that Yamon had mentioned these movements before he'd gone elsewhere, and this was his way of directing Georgie to figure them out."

"Why did he think Carolee Carter knew anything about the Yaqui way?" Janet asks.

"I don't know," Zella says. "But after she started writing to him, he used to watch that TV program she had." The frown on Zella's face reminds Janet of the joke the three women used to share about men and how they think with their peyote buttons. "Finally," Zella says, "he invited her to the house to talk about the photographs she'd sent him. He said she had an idea about making tapes of Georgie doing this Centered Movement stuff and selling them. Can you imagine?" Zella looks off into the hazy distance. "I'm afraid we weren't very nice to her when she came around—and she came around a lot. Georgie used to get angry at us for that." She turns back to Janet, her face now looking parched, pale. "He's still angry, isn't he? Because of her, because of…everything."

"You know how he is," Janet replies, hoping this is an answer but knowing that it isn't. "There's not a lot Georgie will explain to me and so I don't understand. Can you help me?" Janet asks. "Can you tell me what happened?"

"He just said he was leaving one day. He said he had to go dream traveling and that he would be back. He said he couldn't do it in Westwood anymore because the old naguals—the bad ones—were putting up walls around the house that even he couldn't get through, so he had to go away. He said we should wait, that he'd be back. But he never came back."

Renna, who has kept silent, finally ventures a question. "How long did you wait?"

Zella tells her, "More than a year, I think."

"How could you possibly…"

Janet silences her with a look, but Zella doesn't even seem to have heard her. She simply goes on with her story. "One morning, I was walking past his room and I smelled fire. I called Lily and Namuria and they smelled it too. Then we really got scared because we knew what had happened: he wasn't traveling anymore—he had left the world. That's what he always told us would happen some day: he would burn up from within, like Yamon, and then he would be free to travel even further, to infinity. We were very upset—I mean, we were happy for him, that he had finally found a way to do what he was always supposed to, what Yamon wanted him to—but we were so alone without him! And then when we got the eviction notice…"

"What?" Janet says. "Who could evict you? Georgie owned the house, didn't he?"

"He gave it to Carolee. He gave everything to Carolee, I think. We called the bank, and they said he had signed power of attorney over to her. The only thing we still had were our own bank accounts, the ones in our names. There was plenty of money left but…we didn't know where to go. What could we do without him? How could we live?"

Again, Janet glances at Renna and warns her, with a look, not to jump into the conversation. She can just imagine what her friend thinks about all this: the women had money, they had each other, what was so hard about just picking themselves up and moving on? The answer, of course, is that it was impossible, unimaginable, as Zella goes on to say. There was only one thing they could think of to do.

"Lily said we should follow him. She thought that's why he'd sent the smell of fire to me. To the Guide. She said it was the blue streak we were waiting for."

"Oh, God," Janet says. "I'd forgotten about that."

Zella nods her head and goes on. "Georgie always said that if we were separated, and we knew he was gone, then we should wait for a blue streak to tell us what to do. When he was in the desert with Yamon, he often saw blue lightning on those nights when he was going to have an important lesson, so he knew that blue was an important color in shamanic practices. That's why he always wanted Lily to have a blue car: she was the best driver, and he said that if we ever needed to we could all get in the car, and she should drive as fast as she could—drive like a blue streak—and eventually, we'd slip into infinity where we could find him."

"The desert," Janet says.

Zella nods. "We thought it had to be the desert, but Mexico was too far. Death Valley was closer." Now, Zella's eyes begin to tear up. She rubs her face on her sleeve, and then continues. "It didn't work, though. We drove and drove as fast as we could—the engine was screaming—but nothing happened. Finally, we ran out of gas. Lily and Namuria got out of the car and just started walking, in the same direction we were driving—which was nowhere. There was nothing around but rocks and brush. And it was so hot! It must have been a hundred degrees. I tried to stop them—I said we'd have to go home, go somewhere, but they wouldn't listen. Lily got so mad at me! She said that if I didn't believe what Georgie had told us for years and years, then she and Namuria would just go on without me. It wasn't that I didn't believe, it's just that I knew it was useless. At least it was for me."

Zella has been able to stop herself from crying, but her eyes remain red-rimmed. To Janet, she seems to be shrinking inside her clothes, as if she is becoming more fragile by the moment. And that's almost what Zella says next, reinforcing Janet's sense, from the moment she saw Zella again, that some living connection between them had been rearranged or reinforced, that she could almost read the Guide's mind.

Zella says, "I feel like I was so much stronger when I was younger, Janet. Georgie, Lily and Namuria always seemed to be gathering strength over the years but me...I don't know. I tried to keep up with them but maybe I just wasn't smart enough, or...witchy enough. Maybe a guide just plods along."

Janet is trying to think how to respond to this terribly sad idea—what could possibly constitute *witchy* enough?—but Zella doesn't expect to be contradicted, and certainly not with kind words. She rushes on. "When we were younger, Georgie and I, we always used to go hiking in the hills, up past Laurel Canyon. Then, I was the stronger one, if you can believe that. That's why he started calling me the Fearless Guide, because I could hike for miles. We used to go on the most amazing hikes, back when we were students, before he met Yamon. Later, he told me that the hikes we took had prepared him for what Yamon made him go through; Yamon used to take him for walks in the desert that went on for hours to see if Georgie would fall apart, but he didn't because I'd taught him how to hike in the heat, how to stay strong."

"I never realized that you and Georgie were married," Janet says, wondering if it is alright to even mention this. But Zella seems not to mind.

Zella waves her hand, as if this is old news, and unimportant. But she does explain. "We got married when we were in college," she says. "Then I worked in an office for a while when he went to graduate school." She closes her eyes for a moment, remembering a past that must seem barely recognizable to the wife of the last nagual. "He had such trouble with his dissertation. They kept rejecting it. That's when he started going down to Mexico."

"Did you ever go with him?" Janet asks.

"Oh no," Zella says. "I had to work. But after he met Yamon, I always felt like I was studying with him, too, because Georgie would come home and tell me everything he'd learned. We used to talk all through the night, and then I'd just change my clothes and go to work. And Georgie would write. That's what I mean," Zella says. "I used to have such energy."

Energy, to the Fearless Guide, probably has layers and layers of meaning. Janet tries to address just one. "You hiked out of the desert didn't you? When Lily and Namuria left you? That must have taken an enormous amount of courage—and strength."

"Do you think so?" she says to Janet, seeming eager to believe her. "I thought that I was just lucky. I only had to walk for a couple of hours until I found a park ranger. I lied to him: I told him I'd been camping by myself and left my equipment behind because I was too tired to try to carry it out. He gave me quite a lecture; he said it was an amazing coincidence that he was driving in that area and found me, otherwise, he said I'd never have made it out. I would have died."

Now, Janet also knows what Zella is going to say next; but that hardly takes any special connection. The story is becoming almost pitiful, painful to listen to. "I should have died," Zella says. "Just a regular human death. I failed them. I failed my sisters, and I failed Georgie." Finally, she begins to sob. She leans against Janet's shoulder and cries with real pain. "He must be so mad at me! So mad. I bet that's why he came back; Namuria and Lily probably found him and now he wants to tell me how horrible it was that I ran away."

"No," Janet says firmly. "That's not it, that's not why he came back."

"You're sure?"

"I'm positive."

"You've asked him?"

"Yes," Janet tells Zella, which is only partly a lie. "He wanted to write another book. That's what he's doing now." Another half-lie, but Janet has made up her mind not to worry how she will untangle all these confused motives and perceptions. In fact, it has occurred to her that doing so is not her job, not at all.

Then something else pops up in her mind. She asks the Fearless Guide, "Who is Eli? You wrote him a letter."

"I don't really know," Zella says as she tries to stop weeping. "He's some old friend of Georgie's—somebody he met in Mexico a long time ago, but I've never seen him in person. I know he built that website for Georgie. When Lily and Namuria and I left the house—when we knew we weren't coming back—we asked him to post the information that we were traveling. Just in case anyone was looking for us. Lily's sister was always calling; we didn't want her to know where we'd gone. Or anybody else, until we found Georgie and he told us what to say."

"You don't have to say anything," Janet says, stroking Zella's hand. "It's alright. Everything's going to be alright." She knows that what she's offering is comfort without meaning, but it's all she's got right now.

When Zella has calmed down enough, she brings Janet and Renna into her cottage, which she tells them that she shares with several other women who are off somewhere at the moment: working in the pottery shed, Zella says vaguely, or maybe they're making quilts in one of the dormitory residences. Zella gives her guests something to eat—some terrible concoction she spoons out of a pot on the stove. It's barely palatable, but Renna, with a grace that Janet silently thanks her for, remarks that it's just lovely.

Renna and Janet had discussed the possibility of spending the night at Harmony Road, but while Zella is distracted cleaning up, Janet whispers to Renna that she wants to go home, if Renna thinks she's up to driving all the way back to Woodstock. Renna says sure, she can do it, she's had enough of the commune anyway. It's a little weird; too much of a time trip in a way that strikes her as much too serious. Woodstock, she says, at least has a bit of a sense of humor about itself.

So Janet tells Zella they're going to leave, but promises to come back. She writes down her address, her cell phone number and the number of the land line phone in her house, and repeats, again, that everything is going to be alright. She says this emphatically and, she hopes, *energetically.*

Once they've left the commune behind and are on the road, Renna says, "So do I have to tell you how crazy that conversation was? I mean—blue lightning? Blue streaks? Jorge Castelan took a little too much peyote down Mexico way, I think. And what was that babble about slipping into infinity? Those poor women committed suicide, pure and simple."

"They weren't always like that," Janet says. "And he wasn't...like he is now."

"Why didn't you tell her where he really was? That he was at the cancer clinic?"

"Because it's not my place to tell her that what the witches did, what she's torturing herself over not doing, was for nothing. Georgie's going to have to work that out with her in a way she'll accept."

"And who's going to make him do that? You?"

"Maybe," Janet replies. She looks out the window, letting the miles pass as the afternoon fades away. Finally, she says, "He saved me, you know. He probably saved all of us in some way or another. The witches, the Fearless Guide and Janet Planet. Four lost girls. He was magical to us—you just can't imagine. Or maybe you can: remember how it was? When we were a million years younger than now? How much we wanted there to be something else to believe in besides being materialistic and making war and obeying some God with a beard and a bad disposition? I think everybody who read Georgie's books and decided he was a guru helped make him into one. And Lily, Namuria, Zella—and me, me too—we made it worse by dealing with him that way at home. Maybe without all of us he would have just been a guy who ran into an old Indian in a bus station and wrote an interesting dissertation about spirits and shamans."

"You know what I think?" Renna says. "Even after everything—I think you still kind of believe in him."

"What I'd like is to believe in what he believes. It helps when you think you know secrets that make your life special."

"Janet," Renna says, "two people you cared about apparently killed themselves because of him."

"Yes. Trying to drive like a blue streak." Janet pictures the blue Volvo racing across the desert flats toward a pale horizon that never comes any closer. Red rock cliffs cut into the sky, crumble inch by inch, century by century, under a pale, burning sun. With these images in mind she says, "I sometimes wonder if all Yamon really wanted was to talk to Jorge Castelan. I mean *only* Jorge Castelan. He saw this young man standing in the bus station and decided, *That's the one I'll tell everything to.* Maybe he just didn't mean for Georgie to tell anyone else. Maybe it doesn't work that way."

"Maybe *what* doesn't work that way?" Renna asks.

"Finding out what's on the other side of reality," Janet tells her. "If there *is* anything."

"Well, let's hope there's a gas station," Renna says. "Or our reality is going to be that we're going to have to push this car home."

It's after midnight when Renna drops Janet off at her house, and she goes straight to bed. Closing her eyes, she falls asleep feeling like she's dozing in a movie theater, watching a film of the night highway, the white lines that mark the lanes rolling by in an endless procession, like chalk marks being scratched one after another on a blank surface of slate.

She wakes up late. Startled, nearly falling out of bed, she thinks she's been dreaming about something bad, but can't remember what. Not finding her hands, this time, no controlling her dream: it had knocked her around and then pushed her back into the tail end of morning.

The first thing on her mind is to talk to Georgie; she wants to tell him about Zella. She calls the house but gets the answering machine. She calls the Centered Movement Institute and is told he isn't there. She calls his cell phone, which is not connecting at all; there are days the signal seems to travel around the mountains and days it doesn't even seem to be able to jump across a creek. Frustrated, she walks out to her studio but is too restless to work, which makes her angry. Usually, her workshop is the place where she can clear her mind and just function, be a tool herself, a human machine with a simple purpose, a set of specific skills. That level of immersion, of distraction, seems impossible today, so she goes through the round of phone calls again, with the same result. That bothers her too: Jorge Castelan has to be somewhere, and she's determined to find him. She's not in the mood, today, for his moody behavior.

So she gets in her car and surprises herself by driving with a sense of determination, even abandon. She hears her tires squeal as she goes around a wide bend in the road, and it doesn't bother her in the slightest. In fact, she's pleased.

She arrives at Carolee's house, parks outside and rings the bell. Janet is ready to barrel right past Carolee if she has to, but no one answers the door. She rings and rings, listening to the bell chiming behind the locked door, echoing through the empty rooms. If they are empty. Janet is feeling so much like she's on a mission that she actually walks around the house, trying to look through the windows to see if somehow, Jorge Castelan is inside, hiding from her. But she doesn't think so. As with Zella, she is certain, now, that she would feel the very air around her change, vibrate, if he was somewhere nearby.

Convinced there's no one at the house, her next stop is the Centered Movement Institute. There, she finds one of the young women she remembers from that first session she attended sitting at a desk near the front door, wearing the same kind of magenta tee shirt that she had on last time Janet saw her. The girl doesn't look up at first, her attention riveted on the screen of a television that's bolted to the wall, something new since Janet was here last. She glances at the TV and sees Jorge Castelan, on the stage in the auditorium, grunting his way through the movements that are supposedly the legacy of the old Yaqui shamans.

"Is he inside?" Janet asks the girl, who finally turns to look at her.

"No," the girl tells her. "That's a DVD. There's no one here right now."

Janet's not sure she believes her. She's not sure of anything right now. "Okay," she says, but means something opposite, because instead of leaving, Janet walks past the desk and down the hall.

Knowing who she is, or recognizing her as someone she's seen with Jorge Castelan, the girl doesn't try to stop her but goes back to watching the taped performance of the last nagual.

Janet walks down the hallways, randomly opening doors, but finds no one. The auditorium, too, is empty, though there are mats on the floor—evidence that classes are indeed in full swing again—and a video camera on a tripod waiting on the empty stage.

Janet walks around to the side of the stage and opens a door that she thinks must lead outside, but instead, she finds herself in a windowless space that seems to be serving as some sort of video control room. There is a console bristling with switches and a bank of monitors along the far wall. On a desk below the row of monitors is an open log book where someone seems to have been keeping track of tape segments, and on a shelf above the desk, there are about two dozen squat black boxes. Each box has a label on it, hand-lettered with a name—*Beta Master Session 1*, *Beta Master Session 2*, and so on—and a date; one of the dates Janet recognizes as the night that she and Renna attended the first Centered Movement class.

Janet knows what "Beta Master" means, so she can easily figure out what the boxes are: the original video recordings of Jorge Castelan's Centered Movement series, probably what DVD copies are, or will be made from, like the one that the girl is watching in the building's reception area. Suddenly, Janet decides that they don't belong on the shelf in this room; she has a better idea of where they should be.

She is able to stuff a few of them into her shoulder bag; the rest she tosses into an oversize plastic tote bag she retrieves from a store room she had passed earlier. Then, she walks back through the auditorium, down the hall and past the girl at the reception desk, who is still absorbed in watching the DVD. Janet says a pleasant good-bye, and the girl replies without even looking in her direction.

She gets back in her car and drives away. The road she's on twists and turns as it runs along the edge of a dense wood. Janet travels only about half a mile before she pulls off onto the shoulder, parking her car under a canopy of leafy branches. She's very proud of herself; she's driving, carrying out maneuvers that seem tricky to her—she's never parallel parked next to a tree before—as if she had all the confidence in the world.

With her purse slung over her shoulder and the tote bag in her hand, she cuts through the woods, following her feet as if she knows exactly what direction to go in, where to take a short cut through a place she's never been before. This is exactly the kind of journey, short or long, awake or in dreams, that Jorge Castelan has always said was possible: your *intent*, your ability to see ahead without being able to see with your eyes, will carry you along.

Eventually, she reaches the stony field that she remembers from her walk with Georgie, and now she can retrace the route they took before they arrived at the scenic overlook. But this is a very different kind of day; she feels different. The weather is different, too: the sky seems more brightly lit, the air is warmer and swirling with breezes. Overhead, starlings are letting themselves be swept around the sky by these flighty winds.

At the overlook, leaning against the stone wall, she has no thought of repeating Jorge Castelan's feat of stepping around the barrier and tempting the rocky void below. She's not here to attempt sorcery—at least not Georgie's kind. All she's thinking about, really, is what she said to Renna: that she, the witches, and the Fearless Guide had helped Georgie—Victoria Gordon's Georgie—turn himself into Jorge Castelan, for better or worse. Some of it better, much of it worse, if the evidence of two suicides and whatever other tragedies could be laid at his doorstep was to be believed. And Janet can't help but believe it. Now Carolee was just making all that worse with these tapes, the lunacy of those grunting exercises she had persuaded him to adopt as his own. Maybe Renna was right and his behavior could simply be blamed on the fact that when men get old, their brains get soft in the presence of women they desire. If so, it was time he sharpened up again, time he sorted out his desires once and for all.

One by one, Janet pulls the tapes out of the tote bag and throws them into the gorge. They are quickly followed by the ones in her shoulder bag, tumbling such a distance that Janet hears nothing when they crash on the rocky glacial scar tissue below. Or else, she thinks, some crack in the world has opened up and that's where they've gone. She wouldn't be surprised: she threw them with great energy and unmistakable *intent*.

It helps, but it also doesn't. The act of throwing the tapes into the void feels absolutely right; it feels like an act of great defiance, like a message that somebody better receive really soon. But it also feels crazy, and Janet feels crazy; she usually has herself under control, but not today; today she is a person with no boundaries again, a person whose thoughts and feelings are morphing into actions without the censor in her brain saying, *Hold on a minute baby, what do you think you're doing?* She marches back across the stony fields to her car and drives like a mad person, blasting the radio and honking her horn at every bend along the lonely country roads.

At home, she tries once more to do some work, but still can't. So she sits in her living room—an old couch, a rescued lamp, shelves of books—listening to music on a boom box she bought at some long-ago yard sale. She's playing CDs, anything she's got that's loud: reissued albums of long-haired boy bands from the decade of psychedelic dreams. Cream seems to fit her mood the best: *In the white room with black curtains near the station.* Whatever that means, it's very close to how she feels.

She's expecting something to happen and isn't surprised when it does: the police arrive in a few hours, knocking at her front door. Two young, serious-looking men in uniforms bristling with what look like small appliances: guns, of course, but also walkie-talkies, batons, metal-edged notebooks, weapon-sized pens. Woodstock may bill itself as "The Colony of the Arts" but the police are the police, even in this supposed bastion of free thinking; maybe they even have to appear extra serious because of that.

They ask if she knows anything about a set of tapes being stolen from Carolee Carter Enterprises, which, or who, is apparently the owner of the property that Janet is accused of having walked off with. Yes, Janet admits immediately, explaining not only did she steal them but has also disposed of them. Irrevocably and forever.

She is quickly placed under arrest and driven to the local police station where she is seated in a chair by the desk of a female officer, a woman with a bored, blank face, who asks Janet questions and taps the answers into a computer. The questions, Janet thinks, sound like they have been composed for the interrogation of illegal aliens: *Where were you born? How long have you lived in Ulster County? What form of identification do you have?*

Once all the questions are answered, Janet is fingerprinted (which leads her to wonder if she will turn up in some nationwide search of miscreants, since she was arrested some thirty-odd years ago at an antiwar demonstration in Manhattan, at Union Square, but all that happened then was the police shoved her in a van with a bunch of other kids, drove them around for a while and then let them go) and then returned to the chair she had been sitting in, where the female officer handcuffs her to an iron ring attached to the armrest. The officer tells her that once they determine what she is going to be charged with, she can make a phone call.

What she's going to be charged with? Maybe Carolee wants her to be charged with murder. Janet can imagine her coming up with some convoluted new-age explanation of why destroying some tapes containing a person's image is like murdering their soul. But that won't work if she's channeling Jorge Castelan, because Janet knows that he doesn't believe in the concept of a soul. The very idea is something he would scoff at as a religious misapprehension, a non-thing, weightless and invisible. And if a thing such as a soul did exist, it would be useless for a sorcerer: too weak, too pious. It would be quickly gobbled up by the spirit guides that Georgie has around him: the crows that appear in murderous flocks, the coyote that walks alone. Janet would enjoy having a conversation with Carolee about how she would put those particular companions of the last nagual on video, perhaps with flashes of blue lightning in the background.

Janet manages to distract herself with these thoughts while she waits for someone to come back and tell her what's going to happen next. She's actually feeling much calmer than she has since she woke up this morning. In fact, it's as if all the fire has temporarily gone out of her; she's feeling bored and even dozy. There is something both decidedly unreal and ridiculous about being handcuffed to a chair in the quiet, under-populated police station in Woodstock, New York, facing a poster advertising the importance of the neighborhood bear watch. It feels like something that would happen in a movie, or a dream. In fact, it's so hard for her to take the situation seriously that it lends itself to flights of fancy. If they keep her here much longer though, Janet thinks, she may just decide to turn herself into a big, black crow herself and fly away. Fly right through the walls.

Finally, the female police officer comes back and tells Janet that they haven't clarified, yet, what she's going to be charged with: it may be a misdemeanor or it may be grand theft, depending on the value of the tapes. There is some confusion about that because the actual value of the Beta tapes is one thing; the value they represent in terms of what their purpose was—masters meant to be reproduced as DVDs that will reap great profits according to a statement they apparently have from Carolee—is another. In the meantime, she is going to be able to bond out of custody for two hundred and fifty dollars and will be contacted later about making a court appearance at which the charge will be set. The officer tells Janet she can call someone to bring the money, which can be handed over in cash, or charged on Visa or MasterCard. This also seems ridiculous: along with her hardware store purchases and items from the lumberyard, she can imagine her next statement from the credit card company including a charge for "bail bond."

But then she realizes it's not necessarily going to be her credit card statement that records this adventure, because she doesn't have her wallet with her. So, asking if she can make her phone call and being told yes, Janet dials Renna's number at the gallery.

When Renna picks up and Janet tells her where she is, and why, Renna simply says, "Well, I was expecting you were going to do something, but I never pictured anything quite so creative."

"Will you just please come?" Janet says.

"Half an hour," Renna tells her.

And true to her word, she soon breezes in, wrapped in what Janet supposes is her bail-your-friend-out-of-the-police-station outfit—skinny jeans and a black poncho, her silvery blonde hair tied up with a piece of sober black lace. The money is paid and Janet is handed a sheaf of papers, which she folds up and puts in her back pocket; she'll read them later, when she's more interested in what they say.

Outside, Renna takes her arm and leads her down Tinker Street. She pushes open the door of the gallery and says, "Why don't you hang out here for a while? I'll close up in an hour or so and then you can come back to my house. I'll make something to eat, we can have a glass of wine…"

"No," Janet says, "but thanks." She leans over and gives Renna a kiss on her cheek. "You're a good friend, you know that? Not what I expected."

"Well Jesus," Renna says, "I don't know if I should be insulted or burst into tears."

"I just thought I'd tell you."

Renna gives her a strong look, eyebrow raised in the usual signal that she's not necessarily going to believe what she's been told. "You sound like you're taking off or something."

"Nope," Janet says. "I'm going home. No farther than that."

"I'll call you later," Renna says, as Janet turns and starts heading down the street. "I mean it," Renna calls after her. "I'm going to check on you."

Dusk, in this season, lasts until long after dinner time. Janet isn't very hungry, so she eats peanut butter out of the jar as she sits on the front steps of her house, watching the mountains turn the color of the sky as the sky changes into deepening shades of gray, building the night out of darkness and stars. Each star glitters like a rivet in the vast halls of the universe where, she imagines, doors are opening and closing. Messages are flying around like meteors, hers among them. She does not believe it is simply sitting at the bottom of a rocky void. She imagines it has already been received.

☽

Once, not long after he'd met Yamon, the old nagual walked his new pupil out into the desert. They trekked for a day and a night until they came to a bare plain with a flat horizon. A place of nowhere, of nothing: cold at night, hot and dry during the day. "Too hot, even, for scorpions," Yamon said, "too hot for snakes and lizards." He gave Jorge Castelan a drink of water from his canteen and then said, "I am going back now, to my house. You wait an hour, and then follow me."

"How can I follow you?" Jorge Castelan asked. "I don't know the way."

"Well," said Yamon, "you should have been watching. You should have made a map in your head."

"But you didn't tell me to do that!" Jorge Castelan protested.

"It is not my job," said Yamon, "to tell you everything. Some things you have to figure out for yourself."

Jorge Castelan got very angry at his teacher then. He was a city boy, a student of anthropology used to classrooms and the occasional field trip, complete with a tent and bottled water. Nothing had prepared him for such physical hardship or to be put to an extreme test of wit and endurance in an environment that was still alien to him. "Yamon," said Jorge Castelan, "you're being very cruel to me, even putting my life in danger."

Which made Yamon laugh. "If you think your life is worth so much," said the old nagual, then find your way back to my house and tell me about it. Tell me why I should care."

At that point, seeing that his teacher was serious about leaving him alone in the empty desert, Jorge Castelan was reduced to pleading not to be abandoned. "This isn't what you said would happen!" he cried out. "You said you would be my teacher. That I would learn the secrets of the universe."

Yamon shrugged. "Maybe there aren't any," he said.

"You are a liar," said Jorge Castelan.

"Of course," replied Yamon. And then he asked, "are you frightened?"

"Yes," Jorge Castelan admitted. "I'm very frightened."

"Good," said Yamon. "Secret number one: many things in life are frightening. In fact, just about everything is. Whatever frightens you, bare your teeth at it. Growl back."

"Growl at what?" asked the terrified anthropology student.

"At whatever comes," said his teacher, who waved at him and then walked away.

)

This story is not in any of Jorge Castelan's books. It's something he told Janet one day shortly after she moved into the apartment above his garage, in the house in Westwood. Now, Janet remembers how enthralled she was by the story—doubtful, too, but still intrigued. *So what happened?* she asked, and Georgie told her, *Nothing much. Not that time, anyway. I just practiced growling for a while and then did what Yamon said: I followed him.* When Janet asked how he managed that, he said that it was easier than he had expected: the old Indian had left a trail of energy behind him. *Once it got dark*, said Jorge Castelan, *it glowed like a string of lights, and I just strolled along until I got back to his hut. At first I thought that Yamon didn't know his own power: he didn't know that energy was literally leaking out of him. Later, I realized that of course he knew; he knew every detail of everything he was doing. He was just testing me. He wanted to see if I would even last the few hours until the sun went down.*

So Janet sits on her front steps, and considers the idea that she might practice growling. But then she remembers the poster in the police station that warned about how living in the country, with hungry bears waking up from their winter's hibernation, requires caution and sensible habits. Probably, thinks Janet, that does not include growling in the dark. So she refrains from making any noise at all as she waits—will wait through the night, if that's what it takes—for her own sorcerer to find his way to her.

X

If this was another one of his stories, probably a bus would appear out of the darkness, some old rattle-trap with worn tires, covered with dust from the desert roads. But instead, he shows up in a cab, one of the nondescript black and gray cars that belong to the taxi service that answers calls in Woodstock and the other small towns in the surrounding area. Janet, still sitting on the front steps, sees the car at the end of the driveway and watches Jorge Castelan climb out of the back seat. He pays his fare and then walks up the driveway.

Wordlessly, he sits down beside Janet and leans against her. She knows what he's doing: he's making sure that she knows he's there—really *there*. And she does.

Some time passes. Then, looking up at the sky he says, "No moon tonight."

"No. No moon."

He nods, as if they have established some important fact that they both agree on. Then he says, "There are other tapes, you know. Copies."

"If there weren't, I just figured you'd make new ones."

"Well, she's not going to press charges."

"She?"

"We."

Janet shrugs. "It doesn't really matter. I was going to plead civil disobedience."

Jorge Castelan likes her answer. It makes him chuckle. But, he says, "That doesn't apply."

"I would have tried it anyway. This is Woodstock. Civil disobedience is a justification for forgetting to return your library books."

"I know why you did it," Jorge Castelan tells her.

Janet turns to look straight at him. "No," she says, "you don't."

She gets up and walks into the house, which is dark. She lights one lamp in the living room and then continues on into the kitchen. Jorge Castelan follows her. If Janet just challenged him, he seems disinclined to acknowledge it. He seems serene, untroubled. As calm as still water.

"Are you hungry?" she asks him.

"Yes," he tells her.

She gestures for him to sit at the table and then begins looking through her cabinets, opens the refrigerator. "I have brown rice and beans," she says. "Hippie food. Which seems to be the theme lately." Janet realizes that Jorge Castelan probably has no idea what she means, but he doesn't ask. "And some kind of fancy cheese Renna gave me," she continues. "I never keep enough of anything here."

"Whatever you've got is fine," he tells her.

She heats up the rice and beans on the stove, puts the cheese on a plate with a small knife. The cheese is a hefty yellow wedge that, when unwrapped, releases the tangy sweet smell of cherries.

Georgie feeds himself slices of the cheese and accepts the bowl of rice and beans when it's ready. Janet gives him a spoon and seats herself across from him. She lets him eat some of his dinner before she says what she has to say. At least, the beginning of it.

"Zella's alive. Renna and I went to see her."

Georgie continues to eat. "I know," he says finally. "I found her. I've been talking to her."

"No you haven't," Janet says.

"Because you don't know it and even she won't acknowledge it means nothing. I have been talking to her. I speak to her…elsewhere."

"Stop it."

At last, Jorge Castelan sits back, pushes his food away. "Janet Planet," he says. "What's the matter with you?"

Exasperated, she replies, "I'm upset."

"Why?"

"Why? I keep trying to tell you why, but you don't listen."

"Of course I don't listen! You are full of complaints, which are a waste of time. Besides, everything you want to complain about has to do with my life, not yours."

Complaints? Could he think of a more dismissive way to describe how she feels or what she's done? But by trying to diminish her *intent*—if that's what he's doing, playing sorcerer's tricks—he gives her courage. And it occurs to her that this must be courage arising from the same source that he relied on when he was a young man, arguing with Yamon. A young man in the desert, following a string of leaking energy. *Just who do you think you are, to bully me?*

"Those tapes," she says. "Let's begin my *complaints* with those. Is that really how you want to end your life? As an infomercial? As a package that Carolee Carter Enterprises will market on…what? Cable TV? The Internet? Sorcery for beginners—just follow these few easy exercises."

"They aren't easy."

Janet takes a breath. Inside, she's shaking. "Georgie," she says, "We both know I'm not stupid so don't talk to me like I am, or I'm going to ask you to leave. Right now."

He seems unimpressed with her threat. "You left once," he says. "I could leave now. We would still come back together."

"That's right. As long as I live, one way or another, whether I like it or I don't like it, knowing you has defined me. It will go on defining me. But not the Jorge Castelan that's on those tapes."

"I don't see…"

"Yes, you do see. You're just pretending not to. Lily and Namuria are dead. Zella is…I don't know. Weaker. *Not* fearless. And I am still struggling to understand you—my life with you and without you because no matter what you say, everything about you affects me. And one thing I'm sure of is that all that time, all those stories, all those words and ideas have to mean something. Who you are, who you've been to me—and to the witches and Zella and to everybody else who has ever read your books—has to mean something more important than what's on those damn tapes. Or else…"

"Go ahead," Jorge Castelan says. "Or else what?"

"Or else it's all a lie. And I couldn't stand that. I don't want the best part of my life to have been just a part of some fantasy of yours. Something I'm going to end up being ashamed of."

Jorge Castelan closes his eyes. He is silent for what seems to Janet like a very long time. In her mind, she is replaying the last thing she said to him and almost can't believe the words that came out of her mouth. She is horrified at herself, but angry enough to know that what she said is true. It's how she feels. The years with him were the best part of her life—the time she felt most loved, most purposeful—but they were followed by decades of confusion and, sometimes, rage. These are memories she does not often visit, but also cannot deny.

None of this is what Jorge Castelan chooses to address when he finally speaks to Janet again. At least, it doesn't seem that way.

"I am not ill," he says. "Centered Movement is not the end of my life."

"Then why are you doing it?"

"Evolution," says Jorge Castelan. "Everything changes, evolves."

"That's what you're writing about in *Flying Through Walls*."

"Am I?" he says. "Is that how you read it?"

"Yes."

"Well, I haven't made much progress on that book. Maybe I can only write in California. Or in Mexico, in a hut." He barks out a laugh, signaling a change in mood. He's through being serious and he's heard enough from her for now. But he has heard her; Janet is sure of that. "You know what I think?" he says. "I think I'll stay here tonight, if you don't mind. I'm not in the mood for the princess."

"I'd like you to stay. Because I want to take you to see Zella tomorrow. She needs to see you, Georgie."

He stands up, stretches. "I am so tired of women," he says.

"You don't act like it," she says, still feeling combative.

But he, apparently, feels differently. He walks over to her, pats her on the head. "Not you," he says. "I am not tired of you, Janet Planet."

Is that a yes or a no? Will he go with her to see Zella—not *elsewhere*, but at Harmony Road? It may be that Janet will have to wait until morning to find out. She stands up and is about to say something about getting sheets and blankets to make up a bed for him, but before she does, he simply walks over to the couch, takes off his shoes and lies down. Almost immediately, it seems, the last nagual is asleep.

☾

In her dream, she is walking along the red fence again. She looks down at her hands to remind herself that she is dreaming, but that this is an active dream, a dream in which she is traveling from one point of awareness to another. She is still looking for the assemblage point, which remains unknown, but that is not a cause for concern; the assemblage point—the location of both exit and entry—can change depending on what is learned, what progress is made when one is awake. The coyote still watches from his hill above the dry fields and says nothing, but she expects that he will, someday. It does not have to be now.

Suddenly, unexpectedly, she wakes up with a feeling that something is wrong. In the dark, she walks through the small house on bare feet. Midnight is chilly; spring in the mountains is still a cold season on a moonless night. The floorboards creak as she makes her way from her bedroom in the back of the house to the living room, where Jorge Castelan is asleep in his clothes, under a blanket she tucked around him before she went to bed.

As she enters the living room, he sits up, waking as suddenly as she did—if he is awake. She isn't sure. But he speaks to her as if he is. He says, "Let's go somewhere. Let's leave here and go someplace else. Not back to California. Somewhere."

Should she even answer? Do you speak to a dreamer? Do you respond to the dream words of the last nagual?

"Janet?" he says, as if he's not sure she's in the room.

He's spoken her name. Awake or asleep, he must expect an answer. "I'm here," she says, which seems to be enough. He lies down again and pulls the blanket across his body. He goes back to his dreams.

)

"And so what happened when you got back to Yamon's hut?" Janet had asked Jorge Castelan when he told her the story of being left in the desert to find his own way home.

That's when he told her the part of the story that is in one of his books: when Yamon said, You are an idiot, but teachable, I hope. I was expecting someone different.

"There was a point when I could have walked away from him," Georgie told Janet, *"from what he was teaching me, and then there was a point when I could not. For a long time, it was as if he was trying to get me to give up. He gave me ridiculous tasks to perform, telling me it was a way to teach myself discipline, to be alone with my own thoughts. He made me drive around the towns just above Baja until I found a motel with a wall made out of glass bricks. 'Why,' I asked? 'Because I like glass bricks!' he told me. 'They are important to think about. They have an interesting dual nature: glass is eminently shatterable and yet it can be made into strong bricks. That's amazing.' Well, it took me days to find the motel he*

meant—someplace he had seen once, passing by on a bus and then I had to rent a room and stay there for a week. No TV, no walks, no reading, no distractions; I was just supposed to sit in my room and think about the contradiction inherent in glass bricks. But what I really was thinking was, what is the point of this? Only a fool would sit in a crummy motel room for a week and think about construction materials because some old Indian told him to. Maybe he was just having me on, seeing how much he could fuck with my mind. Let me tell you, I got very angry."

"But you did it," Janet guessed.

"Oh yes," Jorge Castelan said. "I did it. I wasn't going to let him think that I couldn't do anything—anything!—he told me to. Then he told me not to bathe for a month—except that every other day I could pick one part of my body and clean only that. Do you know what happens? You begin to feel like your arms, your legs, your toes, your rear end—every separate part of your body that you depend on to just do its job and not bother you begins to talk to you, to take on a separate life. Your thumb begins to vie for your attention, your left elbow moans and groans. They all want to be attended to! Then Yamon made me read the same book over and over again, a child's book of nonsense rhymes. I got so sick of that!

"After a while, though, I began to realize what he was doing; he was forcing me to see how easy it is to be stuck on the surface of life, to keep skimming information from just the top layer of what's right at hand, right in front of your eyes. I could spend my life trying to figure out everything about those bricks, reading that book, arguing with my nose about whether or not it's had its turn with the washcloth yet. Because Yamon kept me on the surface, I wanted to go deeper than that, beyond that—and then he had me. The more stupid tasks he gave me to send me away, the more I wanted to come back. I fought to become his pupil. I fought to learn everything he could teach me. And then, once I knew a little, I had to know everything. I couldn't stop. I still can't."

"But you also said he lied to you," Janet said.

"Only sometimes," Jorge Castelan told her. "But then, once I learned to adjust the attention of the universe, to have some control over my own experiences and to understand them not only in this world but on many other levels as well, then I lied, too. We were liars together. We were always trying to trick each other. Tricks make good lessons for sorcerers."

Suddenly, then, Jorge Castelan changed the subject. He said, "you've heard so many of my stories, but you never tell me any."

"I don't have any," Janet said. "None that are interesting."

"Of course you do," said Georgie. "Everybody does. For example, why did you leave home?"

"Because I was miserable there," Janet told him. "I didn't belong. And I wanted something else."

"Like what?" Georgie asked.

"I don't know," Janet stammered. "Something."

"And what if there's nothing?"

Janet was taken aback. How could Jorge Castelan possibly say something like that? "Then everything you've written about what happened to you isn't true. You would be lying. Are you?" Janet asked. "You just told me that you lied all the time."

"Of course not," Jorge Castelan said. "I only lied to Yamon, and that was for fun." And then he tapped her on the head, that familiar gesture that Janet had never seen him use with anyone else—not the witches, not the Fearless Guide, no one. "But think about it," he said. "All I can do is try to explain what Yamon taught me, what I learned. Maybe if it had been you in that bus stop, you would have learned different things. Or nothing."

"You keep saying nothing, as if that is a possibility."

"Nothing is always a possibility," said Jorge Castelan. "Nothing, anything, something, everything. It all depends on the bus stop, right?"

And then he tapped her on the head again and laughed. He laughed loud and long.

☾

In the morning, the gray dawn, Jorge Castelan coughs so much that the sound wakes Janet, but when she goes to him, he's still curled up on the couch, coughing in his sleep. It seems hard for him to wake up, and when he does, slowly opening his eyes, Janet thinks that he looks like he has collapsed overnight: grown thinner, smaller. She tells him that she will make tea, and when it's brewed, she puts lemon and honey in it, feeling like a girl in a folk song from some time very long ago. Tea and honey, lemons, oranges, Chelsea mornings. Silver ships on the water, Michael row your boat ashore. Very, very long ago.

When she goes back into the living room, Jorge Castelan is sitting up. He drinks his tea, then asks for a towel so he can take a shower. He takes a long time in the bathroom, but when he comes back he is dressed again and looks a little better.

"Alright" he says, "how long is this trip?"

"A couple of hours," Janet tells him.

"You're going to drive?"

"Yes," Janet says, though she realizes that this is part of her plan that she didn't think through. When she had considered asking him to go see Zella—which is what she had thought about, in fact, almost the whole way back from Harmony Road Farm—she never got past the point of imagining that she would have to somehow persuade him. But now that he has agreed with no argument at all, she is left with a whole blank set of space to fill up, an empty package of time that contains no words, no images except two people standing in a room, looking at each other.

It is Georgie who moves them into the next moment, the next experience of the morning. He says, "You never liked to drive. Can I trust that you won't kill us both?"

Janet hears this as a horrible reference to Lily and Namuria driving to their death in the desert, forgivable only if it is unconscious. But she cannot believe it is unconscious since Jorge Castelan would say that he does not have an "unconscious," having long since opened all the closed doors of his awareness. She chooses, therefore, to push back at him, to respond to him in what she thinks of as his own terms.

"I have evolved," she says, but it was a wrong choice. She succeeds only in making him irritable.

"Is this going to be a day where you repeat to me everything I've ever said?"

"No," Janet replies. "I'm sorry." And she decides actually, that she is. She feels depleted herself; the roiling emotions of last night have subsided and she doesn't really want to argue with him anymore. Besides, she doesn't think she's good at it; she never has been. The night, or perhaps simply his proximity through the hours of dreaming, seems to have marked a clean division between yesterday and today. All Janet wants is to get on the road.

Georgie, too, seems inclined to let that last skirmish be their final one, at least for now. He starts fussing over the kind of small things he would normally leave to the women in his life: do they have road maps, bottles of water, change for the toll roads? *Yes*, Janet says to all his questions. *Yes, yes, yes.* She thinks he is procrastinating, but finally, he simply stops picking things up and putting them down and says, "Let's go."

After they leave Woodstock, but before they get on the highway, Janet tells him that she wants to make one stop. In Saugerties, she finds a store that sells cell phones and buys one with prepaid hours, which she intends to give to Zella. Janet wants to be able to stay in touch with her and this will be the easiest way to do it. When she gets back into the car, Georgie has fallen asleep again. She doesn't mind; she feels quite content to be navigating the roads herself, taking him where he needs to go. She heads toward the highway that will take them west, and then north, and drives on.

He sleeps for hours, coughing and groaning in his sleep. Janet is concerned that he may really not be well, but she doesn't want to wake him. Finally, he opens his eyes as they are crossing the bridge to Canada. He stretches, looks out the windows.

"How are you?" Janet asks him. "You were coughing a lot. Is there anything you need?"

He hears her concern but does not acknowledge it. "So," he says, his gaze still on the passing scenery. "Another country. It doesn't feel like it."

Janet allows herself to laugh at his comments. "You want to see another country? Wait until we get to Harmony Road. It's 1969 all over again."

"That wouldn't be so bad," says the last nagual. "Except I'd miss cable."

Janet laughs again, remembering their old life, perhaps because now they are just an hour or so away from seeing Zella. She says, "I want my MTV?"

"Not any more" says Jorge Castelan. "But I still like movies. Movies all the time. Remember, in Westwood, every time they offered us a new channel, we subscribed to it?"

Janet does remember, and they spend the rest of the trip reminiscing about their favorite films. Jorge Castelan seems to have recovered his vitality—at least he seems stronger, and some color has come back into his face. His mood has also lightened—in fact, it seems to Janet that he is in relatively good spirits and not in the least bit concerned about seeing a woman—his wife—whom he hasn't seen in several years and who even he must guess is in a fragile state. Well, *lovey, dovey, wovey:* once again, Jorge Castelan seems not all that interested in the bothersome effects or even lingering echoes of mere human love.

When they reach the sun and moon sign, Janet turns onto the dirt road that leads to Harmony Road Farm and, as before, drives past the painted buildings, heading for the cottages by the creek. There seem to be more people out and about today, strolling between the residences or doing some lazy work in the various small garden plots around the smaller houses. There are even a brace of recreational vehicles parked at the edge of a field, apparently housing tourists.

Watching out the window, Jorge Castelan does not seem all that taken with the place. "Too many dogs," he comments to Janet.

"Most people like dogs," she reminds him, because that's something she remembers saying to him dozens of times before. Jorge Castelan is not a big fan of pets. She continues, "People like this, in particular."

"People like what?"

"You know. Like half the people you run into in Woodstock. Hippies. There are still a couple of us around."

"Don't think I haven't noticed," he says.

Janet is highly amused by his distaste for his current surroundings. The new-age guru does not, it seems, like new-age destinations.

When they reach the cottages by the creek, Janet points out to him which one is Zella's. "Why don't you go in alone?" she says. "I can just wander around for a while."

"Don't get lost," he tells her firmly.

"No sir," she says, with deadpan seriousness that makes him shake his head in mock exasperation.

She watches as he walks up to the cottage and knocks on the door. It opens, and he walks in. Janet has no concerns about whether or not Jorge Castelan and the Fearless Guide will achieve a reconciliation—of course they will. Janet cannot imagine Zella turning away her lifelong companion; there is no question that she will be anything but overjoyed to see the last nagual, and that whatever explanations he chooses to give her—if any—for his behavior, she will accept. The real question is how the princess is going to take the reappearance of the Fearless Guide, since she seems to have gone to great lengths to get Jorge Castelan's women out of his life, and had succeeded—up to now. In fact, as Janet gets out of her car and begins to stroll along the edge of the creek, enjoying the spring day, it occurs to her that if anyone is responsible for Lily and Namuria's death, maybe Carolee Carter deserves even more of the blame than Jorge Castelan. If she hadn't tried to get them out of the house in Westwood, the women probably would have just stayed there, waiting for the last nagual to come home. And maybe he would have, eventually. Janet's idea of going traveling is a week's vacation; perhaps in the sorcerer's world, an absence of two years—maybe five, a decade—is the same thing.

And that, Janet thinks, is very much a Jorge Castelan idea: that you have to consider the possibility of undescribing what has been described to you as normal. Years ago, that was the reason behind creating the place where she is now—Harmony Road Farm. It was itself conceived of as a kind of alternative reality, a way of stepping out of the everyday world to live by different principles. Who's to say how far those alternatives can go? For Georgie, Zella, Lily and Namuria, time, relationships, the natural and physical world had different parameters than for anyone else—most anyone else. Maybe the princess was willing to buy into that idea when all she had to deal with was the sorcerer: but what if, after today, she had to incorporate the Fearless Guide into some new description of reality? Well, Janet decided, that was Georgie's problem. He said he was tired of women? Too bad. She doesn't think that they are tired of him.

The creek is widening now and its banks are getting steeper, and slippery. This is an area of the property that Janet is not familiar with, so she decides to turn back. And then she does exactly what Georgie told her not to do, what she promised, jokingly, to avoid: she gets lost. Though she's sure she's just been following the creek as it meanders through thick stands of water oaks on either side, she's been so lost in thought that maybe it actually branched off at some point and she's now walking along the edge of a different stream than the one she had been hiking beside.

She keeps walking, and in a few minutes, through a break in the trees, she sees planted fields and a weathered-looking barn. She's not sure if she's still on the Harmony Road property or on land that belongs to a neighboring farmer, but hopes that if she heads toward the barn she'll find someone to tell her how to get back to Zella's cottage.

She walks through a yellow field of barley, under a sky of such deep blue, such stillness, that it is as if the air has been flattened, the afternoon cut away from the rest of the day and placed before her framed as a separate hour, a separate place. She continues on until she reaches the barn, but it's empty—a worn-out shell of a structure that looks like it hasn't been used in a long time. And there seem to be no other buildings around, no people. Janet really has no idea where she is.

There's a low hill about a hundred yards beyond the barn and Janet thinks she'll climb it to get a better view of where she is—maybe, from a better vantage point, she'll see some landmark that will guide her back, if not to Zella's cottage, at least to the main part of Harmony Road, where the pottery kilns are, and the eating hall.

She walks around the back of the barn, heading toward the hill, and as she rounds the corner, is astonished by what she sees. For the first time in her life, she has a visceral sense of what the phrase *struck dumb* means, because she feels like her heart, her breath, have become as still as the air around her.

In the middle of a bare, brown field bordering the planted rows of barley is a red fence, about five feet high. It seems to be constructed of simple wooden slats painted a vivid shade of red. The first picket-shaped fence board stands about a hundred feet from the barn and then the line of red slats marches on for perhaps a quarter of a mile, where the fence abruptly stops. Janet can see the horizon beyond—the neighboring fields slice across the bottom of the blue sky like a scissored line—so there seems no purpose to the fence, no reason for it to be here. Except, of course, that it's the red fence that she has been dreaming about for years. More than that: for decades.

She sits down on the ground, with her back against the wall of the barn. Instinctively, doing as she had been taught, she looks down at her hands. *Okay*, she thinks, *here am I, here is that. What is going on?*

Is it possible that when she was a teenager, during the winter she spent at Harmony Road, she saw this fence and for some reason, the image of it has stayed with her all that time? She can't imagine that to be true. To begin with, she still can't recall ever having been on this part of the land before. On top of that, the fence actually looks new; not just freshly painted but newly built. Especially compared to the broken-down barn; the wooden slats look as smooth as if they have just come out of someone's woodworking shop, carefully sanded and completely uniform in size. Neither the wood nor the paint seem to have endured the slightest bit of weathering, as if somehow the entire fence had just been put up this morning, erected in this bare field for no reason other than for Janet to see it standing here. But as in her dreams, it is neither a menacing nor a welcoming structure: it is just a fence, painted red, standing in the middle of a field.

After a while—five minutes? half an hour?—of simply sitting and looking at the scene before her, Janet brings herself back to the immediate problem at hand: she still has no idea of where she is or how to get back to Zella's cottage. She can keep wandering or she can do something more expedient, and ask for help. Glancing at her watch, she realizes that it's over an hour since she left Georgie at Zella's; she doesn't want to interrupt whatever conversation they're having, but she doesn't know what else to do.

She dials the number of Georgie's cell phone and he answers almost immediately. He says, "We were wondering where you were."

We. One word, and just by the way he says it, Janet can tell that, as she expected, the last nagual and the Fearless Guide have said whatever they needed to say to each other to reestablish their bond as sorcerer and apprentice, perhaps even husband and wife. Georgie sounds like he often sounded to Janet, when she was younger, when she would call the house in Westwood if she was late getting home for some reason: like an impatient father, annoyed but tolerant, used to being told to wait a little longer for his wandering daughter to find her way home.

"Well," Janet says, "I need directions."

"I don't believe it. You *did* get lost."

"Just a little. I can't be that far, though. Put Zella on the phone, will you?"

Zella, too, sounds perfectly fine. Her voice has strengthened; she sounds focused, even vibrant. When Janet asks how she is she tells her, *never better. I'm glad,* Janet tells her, and then explains as best she can where she is—she describes the creek, the barley fields and the barn—and Zella tells her that she is no more than ten or fifteen minutes away. She is still on Harmony Road property and if she just goes back to the creek, and follows it again, she'll be back at the cottage in no time.

After listening to Zella's instructions, Janet asks her to put Georgie back on the phone. "Listen," she says, "how are you feeling? Are you up to a walk?"

"I feel fine," he tells her, the tone of his voice warning her away from any further questions in that direction. "Why are you asking me that?"

"Because I was wondering if you could come here and get me. I want to show you something."

He agrees, and now sounds affable on the phone, joking with her about how many more times in her life she expects to wander away and make him come find her.

Soon, while Janet is still sitting on the ground with her back to the barn, she sees Jorge Castelan walking up through the grassy field that borders the creek. He smiles when she spots her, comes to sit beside her and leans against her shoulder, as he had done the night before, when they were sitting on the stairs in front of her house.

"So," he says, "what's so important that I had to come and rescue you?"

Janet points toward the field. "That fence," she says. "That red fence is in my dreams all the time. I just wanted you to see it."

"Why?"

"I'm not sure," she says, since she's been asking herself this question since she called him.

Georgie laughs. "Maybe you wanted to be sure it's really there? It is. But why are you so surprised? You lived here before. You've probably had this fence in your mind forever."

"No. I've never been to this area of the farm before. I know it. And that fence looks new."

Jorge Castelan laughs. "What are you asking me, Janet Planet? Did I put it there? Is this a dream? Are we traveling together?"

"I don't know what I'm asking you, Georgie. I guess I was just shocked to see it. It's exactly the way I dream about it. A red fence, a field, a hill…"

She's about to add the last element—the one thing that's missing—but before she can, he interrupts her. "You want help in figuring out what it means? I can't. You put the fence there—not me, not anybody else. A fence divides one place from another—perhaps one time from another, one world from another. The fence is a signifier. Perhaps it marks an assemblage point for you: a place of decision. But it is interesting that you have been able to transfer it from one reality to another—from your dreams into the reality that we move through in our bodies. That takes real power. As I told you before, Janet Planet, you are becoming a powerful witch."

"Georgie. I am not a witch."

"No? Alright then. What can that fence mean? Why is it here? Hmm?" He rocks back on his heels, looks up at sky. "Well, all I can do is go back to what I remember from my psychology courses in school. But that was a long time ago. Do you think that will help?"

What game is this? Janet wonders. What is Jorge Castelan doing now? Playing the part of the dumb boy, the sincere but not-so-bright student with nothing to offer but his earnest study habits, which he will gladly draw on for whatever information, however outdated, he has stored away? Or has he, for some reason, suddenly cast himself in the role of Yamon and assigned Janet the role of Jorge Castelan, full of stupid questions that have self-evident answers—if only you had the insight to think them through?

"If I remember correctly," he continues, "one idea is that when you dream about deep water, for example, you're probably making some kind of contact with your subconscious fears. Fences are easy: fences can symbolize barriers, stalemates, an impediment that you cannot find your way around, or perhaps knowledge that you are blocked from acquiring. Perhaps," he says, patting her on the head, "you just aren't tall enough to peek over the top."

"Barriers, stalemates, impediments. That sounds like a tarot card reading," Janet says. "Not psychology."

Jorge Castelan says, "I am just making suggestions. I remind you again, you have created that fence. You can leave it there if you want. It looks pretty sturdy to me; it will certainly keep you from going any further."

"Going where?"

"I don't know. Do you want to find out?"

Without waiting for an answer Jorge Castelan stands up and, taking Janet's hand, pulls her to her feet. Then he leads her directly into the brown field. They seem to be barely disturbing the still air as they walk along the stony ground under the empty blue sky. When they reach the fence, Janet touches it, gingerly, and is almost surprised that it doesn't turn to powder as her fingers brush its surface. As Jorge Castelan said, it seems solid enough and, seen close up, Janet can conceive of it as nothing more than what it must be:

just a series of painted wood planks set one against the other and hammered into the earth.

With Janet following behind him now, Jorge Castelan walks the length of one side of the fence—about a hundred feet. When he comes to the end, he simply walks back along the other side, so that he and Janet end up exactly where they started. Was there a point to this? Janet wonders, but the last nagual seems pleased that they have completed this activity.

"There," he says.

"There, what?" Janet asks. "What did we do?"

"We just made a magical pass around your fence. It will help you, I think."

"Let's hope so."

Jorge Castelan frowns at Janet Planet. "You think this is silly?"

"No."

"You do. I can tell. But do you think he does?"

Georgie raises his hand to point at something in the distance. Looking in the direction he's indicating—past the barn, toward the top of the hill beyond—Janet sees a shape both dark and silvery, a shadow made equally of daylight and nighttime; a spirit, a traveler, an animal, a figure in a dream. Standing motionless on the top of the hill, standing as still as the still afternoon, is an enormous coyote.

Janet has been half expecting this apparition—if that's what it is—but still, she feels surprised. She thinks of what Georgie had said before: *Is this a dream? Are we traveling together?* Her confusion shows on her face, prompting Jorge Castelan to say, "You've seen him before?"

"Yes," Janet replies, softly.

The last nagual gives her an appraising look, deep and clear-eyed. He says, "That is interesting. As is the fact that apparently, he has nothing to say to me anymore. It seems that it's you he's come to see. I think he has a question for you."

"Does he?" Janet murmurs.

The afternoon seems to grow even quieter. A scrap of cloud sailing in from the horizon skids to a halt. Birds hold their breath.

"Yes," says Jorge Castelan. "He wants to know what side of the fence you are on."

The last nagual has a good laugh at his own joke, which he repeats for Janet, because he finds it so funny. Then, still holding her hand, he begins to lead her back to Zella's, back the way they came. When Janet turns to take a last look at the coyote, he is gone.

☾

In the night, she thinks she hears Georgie coughing again, sounding like he is in great distress. She is halfway down the ladder of the loft bed she's sleeping in before she realizes that's impossible. They're spending the night at Harmony Road, but Jorge Castelan is sleeping in a guest house back near the main buildings. Earlier, Janet had seen how much the day had drained him and had insisted on staying the night (besides, she may be learning to enjoy driving but is not going to fool herself into thinking she is capable of Renna's ten-hour feat of endurance). He had agreed without a fuss, but did object when Janet started phoning around, looking for a hotel room for him. He had told her that he was perfectly capable of "camping out with the hippies," so Zella had suggested the guest house. Janet had been assigned the loft bed under the eaves of the cottage that Zella shared with three other women.

Wide awake now, in the middle of the night, Janet realizes that it is her imagination that has brought her the sound of the last nagual in distress, but she decides to check on him anyway. It's a long walk from the cottages to the main buildings, but probably no farther than from her house to Meggie's bakery on Tinker Street. Though she would be unlikely to be walking the road in Woodstock dressed as she is now—in nothing more than a long tee shirt borrowed from one of Zella's house mates (*Canada!* it says in red and blue letters, *How cool is that?*) with her jacket thrown over her shoulders—at Harmony Road Farm, even if she runs into anyone, they are unlikely to give her a second glance.

The guest house is probably the original two-story farm house that was built on the property, which has had extensions and a wide, wrap-around porch added onto it over the years. The front door is open: nothing much has changed here in that respect, as well—doors are rarely locked at Harmony Road. Janet walks in through the entrance hall and then down the quiet hallway, treading carefully on the old floorboards. Around her, she can hear the sound of sleepers deep into their journey through the night: someone snores gently, someone turns in a creaky bed. Janet continues down the hall, because she knows which room Georgie is in: they have given him a large bedroom at the back of the house, one that, unlike most of the others, has its own bathroom.

    The door to his room is ajar, and Janet peeks in. Jorge Castelan is in bed, seemingly fast asleep. He is folded on his side, facing away from the door, but Janet's view is partially blocked by the other person in the bed beside him. Janet hadn't even thought to look before she left the cottage, but if she had, apparently she would have found Zella's bed empty, because she is here, curled up against the last nagual. She must have come in after Georgie fell asleep, because she isn't under the covers with him but wrapped in a separate blanket. The dark blue quilt, one of the products made by the craftspeople on the farm, is probably from the stack of a dozen or so that are kept in the communal linen closet on the first floor. The nightlight in the hall provides just enough illumination for Janet to be able to see the decoration on the quilt, which is a variation of Harmony Road's signature design and perfect, Janet thinks, to protect the Fearless Guide in her dream travels: onto the dark blue fabric someone has sewn a round, cheery sun and a smiling moon accompanied by a seemingly infinite pattern of swirling stars.

XI

They leave early the next morning and head back to Woodstock. Zella and Georgie share what to Janet seems like a restrained good-bye on the porch of the guest house, but, as before, Janet is more effusive. She gives Zella the cell phone and again promises to keep in touch with her—and means it. She throws her arms around the Fearless Guide and holds her tight for a few moments before getting into the car.

Georgie goes back to sleep before they even get to the Peace Bridge, but wakes up about an hour later and wants to stop to get something to eat. Janet gets off the highway, finds a diner, and they spend some time dawdling over their breakfast. Georgie seems to be enjoying this sojourn—he's full of light-hearted stories and memories, mostly about life in Westwood. Perhaps, Janet thinks, it was being with Zella that has set him off on this train of thought and she just lets him talk. He reminds her of a time they all went to a favorite restaurant not far from their house that had suddenly become trendy and watched, with surprise, as the tables around them filled up with movie stars. He remembers a particular dress he gave her once, to celebrate her birthday. He does not talk about spirits or illness or the attention of the universe or Centered Movement or flying through walls. As he talks—but eats little—Janet butters her toast, eats scrambled eggs, asks for more coffee. They could be any two people on any road trip, stopping off along the way.

Back in the car, Jorge Castelan falls asleep again and doesn't wake up until hours later, just as they're about to turn off Route 212 and drive into Woodstock. He asks Janet to let him off on Tinker Street, and she tries to insist on driving him home, but he says no. He tells her that he has an errand, which she does not believe, but neither does she expect to suddenly be privy to all his intentions. So she stops the car near Meggie's bakery and lets him out.

He motions for her to roll down the window and taps her on the head. "You're a good girl," he says.

At first, Janet thinks he's teasing her, talking to her like he might have many years ago. But he sounds too serious for that, so she's not sure what to say in reply. Her hesitation prompts Jorge Castelan to answer for her.

"Just say, thank you," he tells Janet.

She smiles at him. "Okay. Thank you."

"You're welcome," he tells her. "For now."

What signal is he sending? Those last two words, small as they are, hardly seem to add up to a casual remark. "I don't understand," Janet says.

"For now," he repeats. "You know what now means."

Jorge Castelan is looking at Janet very intently—so much so that he completely captures her attention in a way that he might have done when she was much younger. And so was he. "I don't know," Janet says softly. "Do I?"

He smiles at her. "Nena," he says, "Do you have it in your mind that I'm trying to trick you? Well, sometimes I play games, I suppose. But there are times when I mean exactly what I say. *Now*," he continues, "is when we are here, on this street, in this town, having this conversation. But now comes and goes in a flash. See?" he says, tapping her on the head again. "It's already gone. But here comes another *now*, and in this one, I have things to do and so do you."

And then, still smiling, he simply turns and ambles away.

When the phone rings in the middle of the night, the sound drags Janet from what feels like a deep, almost drugged sleep, without dreams. After leaving Georgie, she had gone home and stayed in the studio late into the evening, trying to catch up on the work she'd been neglecting. After dinner, she had fallen asleep on the couch, in front of the TV, which is where she is when she wakes up. She has to walk into the kitchen to answer the phone, which gives her a minute to focus, and when she does, her first feeling is that she's been through this before because she knows—she just *knows*—who's on the phone.

"Where is he?" asks Carolee in a voice that sounds like it has been sharpened on the edge of a knife.

"Georgie?" Janet says. "I have no idea. I dropped him off on Tinker Street hours ago."

"What are you talking about?" Carolee says. "What do you mean, dropped him off? Where were you?"

It had crossed Janet's mind yesterday to wonder whether Georgie had told Carolee anything about Zella, or if he had phoned her at some point, when Janet wasn't around. But the answer, apparently, is that he told her nothing. In a smaller way, he's evidently done to her what he did to the witches and the Fearless Guide: he just left. But Janet sees no reason to keep any secrets; besides, he didn't suggest that she should.

"I found Zella," Janet says. "We went to see her."

"That's right, that's just what he needs," Carolee says. "To be back with the old ladies."

Old ladies. Women maybe ten or fifteen years older than Janet. "There is only one *old lady* left," Janet tells Carolee. "The other two are dead, remember?"

"So where is she? Where is *he*? Did he stay with her?"

"I told you. We came back to Woodstock—that was around one o'clock. I let him out of the car near the bakery. He said he had some errands to do."

"He doesn't do *errands*," Carolee says.

"Yes," Janet agrees. "I know that."

On opposite ends of the phone, at opposite ends of two different towns, they listen to each other breathe. What is left to say?

All Carolee can do is keep asking the same question of Janet. "So where is he?"

"I haven't a clue," Janet tells her. "I really don't."

"I don't believe you," Carolee insists.

"Then don't," Janet says. "But I'm going back to sleep."

She hangs up the phone, turns off the television and pads off to bed. She doesn't expect to be able to fall asleep again but she does, almost immediately. When she wakes up a few hours later, once again, she can't recall having a single dream.

She makes coffee for herself and then picks up the phone in the kitchen. It's eight a.m.—would Zella be awake yet? Probably, Janet thinks. She isn't particularly worried about Jorge Castelan and doesn't feel she owes Carolee anything in the way of a good deed, but just in case there's something she herself needs to know, Janet decides to find out if he's gotten back in touch with Zella. She dials the number of the cell phone she gave the Fearless Guide but listens to it ring and ring in the far north until it finally goes to voice mail.

Janet goes out to her studio, puts everything but work out of her mind for half an hour and then calls again. Still, there is no answer. She tries throughout the morning, and by early afternoon, she comes up with another idea.

She dials information and asks for the number of the police station in Downey. It turns out that there is none, so Janet goes to her computer, pulls up a map of the area, and calls information again, asking for the police station in the town that looks closest to Downey. There, the phone is answered promptly by someone who identifies himself as Officer Keller.

"Hi, there," Janet says, not really sure how to begin. "I'm wondering if you can help me. I'm calling from New York."

"Oh?" says Officer Keller. "Whereabouts?"

"Woodstock. Anyway, I was visiting someone the day before yesterday nearby where you are…do you happen to know Harmony Road Farm?" Janet asks.

"Sure."

"Well, I told my friend I'd keep in touch with her—and I know she wants me to—but she's not answering her phone, so I'm a little worried."

"What's your friend's name?"

"Zella," Janet tells the policeman and then, cautiously, amends what she just said. "Zella-Zed." Officer Keller has no reaction to this—maybe he's used to oddly named people living at Harmony Road—so Janet continues. "I've been phoning for hours, and I don't have anyone else's number there, so…"

"I can help you out with that," Officer Keller says. "I can make a few calls."

"Would you?" Janet says. "That would be really kind of you." But since she's dealing with the police—again; who'd have thought *that* would happen twice in the space of a few days?—she's also a little cautious. "I don't want to cause anyone any problems," she says.

Officer Keller seems to find that amusing. "Hey," he says, "what year do you think this is? I'm not going to race over there and bash in anybody's head or whatever you're thinking. I *like* those people."

Janet apologizes and thanks him profusely. After she hangs up, she thinks about going back to work, but instead, picks up the phone and dials Renna, at the gallery. When she answers, she sounds like she's in a cheerful mood.

"What's up, cookie?" she says.

Janet doesn't even try to match her ebullience. She barely even says hello. "Listen," she says, "I think Georgie is gone."

"What?"

"Gone. Vanished. *Traveling*, he'd probably say. And I think Zella might be with him."

"Honey," Renna says, "back up a few steps."

"I drove him to see Zella. We spent the night and came back yesterday. I left him on Tinker Street but Carolee says he never came home. And I gave Zella a cell phone, but she's not answering it."

"When you say they're traveling," Renna prods gently, "what do you mean? Traveling like normal people or traveling like, well..."

Janet spares her the attempt to find words to describe either the mystical or the tragic. She says, "I don't know."

"Well, how about this?" Renna says. "I'll come over and hang out with you for a while. Just in case."

"Okay," Janet says. Just in case of what doesn't matter. She'd like Renna's company right now and is glad of the offer.

Janet goes back to the house and sits in the kitchen, staring at the phone. Twenty minutes later, she hears Renna knocking at the front door.

She comes in carrying a bag of sandwiches from the grocery store next to her gallery. Then, she shows Janet something else that Janet hadn't even noticed her friend was holding.

"Don't you pick up your mail in the morning?" Renna says. In her outstretched hand she dangles the strap of a dark brown backpack, threadbare with use.

"Where was that?" Janet asks. She is aware of how quiet her voice has suddenly become.

"It was hanging over your mailbox." Renna takes a look at the look on Janet's face and says, "You recognize it."

"I've never seen it before," Janet tells her. "But I know who it belongs to."

Together, they go into the living room and Janet puts the backpack on her coffee table, where it sits like a talisman. "I'll bet he's had this for forty years. Maybe more," Janet says.

"Georgie?" Renna says, catching on.

Janet nods. "He always told the story about throwing some things in a backpack and getting on a bus from L.A. to Mexico, and then getting off at the station where he met Yamon."

"And you think it's *that* backpack?" Renna says, with wide-eyed incredulity. "Do you know what you could get for that on eBay?"

Janet does what Jorge Castelan would do: she laughs. This is an iconic object; the idea of auctioning it off with collectible lunchboxes and used baubles is so absurdly disrespectful that it's actually funny. Besides, in just the few minutes it's been in her house, the backpack has been giving her the feeling that it may have intentions all its own.

At that moment, the phone rings. Janet hurries into the kitchen to answer it and Renna follows, making no pretense about the fact that she wants to eavesdrop.

It's Officer Keller, who has news for Janet: her friend Zella-Zed, he says, left the commune yesterday evening, telling her housemates that she wouldn't be coming back. She had hitched a ride into Downey with a Harmony Road resident who was headed for one of the stores at the crossroads and said she was meeting someone. The commune member had left her standing outside the store and by the time he had completed the purchase of a sackful of groceries and gone back out to his truck, Zella had vanished.

"I knew it," Janet says to Renna after she thanks the policeman and hangs up the phone. "They're gone. After I left him, he probably just turned around and went back."

"How?" Renna asks. Janet just looks at her. "Okay," Renna says. "We'll leave that one for later."

Janet returns to the living room and seats herself on the couch, and Renna joins her, leaning against her arm, as was Georgie's habit. What Renna means as a gesture of comfort, to Janet seems like another message. A companion to the backpack, which is also a traveler, now come to rest.

"I think he's sick again," Janet says to Renna.

"Then maybe he went back to Ivinger."

Janet shakes her head. "I don't think so."

"Why? Did he say anything to you?"

"No, but I think he showed me something." She is remembering the fence, the hill and the silvery coyote. "I thought it was me, my dream. But maybe it was his, as well."

She tries to explain what she means to Renna, who sits back and says, "Wow."

Janet simply nods. She is trying to process the idea, which, apparently, she has been trying to avoid by working as thoughtlessly as possible through yesterday afternoon and this morning, that on the grounds of Harmony Road Farm, Georgie had created for her—or in collaboration *with* her—the kind of lesson that Yamon had created for him. Symbols, dreams, spirits and challenges, presented as opportunities, not commands. The teacher can only offer information and experience. The student must choose how, and if, to act on what has been revealed. To jump the chasm, cross the boundary—or not.

"Well," Janet says, "let's see what else he has to say."

She reaches into the backpack and pulls out what she has already guessed is inside: a manuscript of maybe a hundred or so pages, bound with a rubber band.

"What is it?" Renna asks.

"*Flying Through Walls.*" Janet shows Renna the title page on top of the manuscript. The print is smudgy and the paper feels much-handled, evidence that Jorge Castelan has had these pages with him for quite a while. "It's the book Georgie was working on. He said he was having trouble finishing it, and I guess, now, he isn't going to."

Janet removes the rubber band and begins to leaf through the manuscript. She hands Renna the chapter she has already read—*Infinity for Grownups*—and, after taking a sandwich from the bag her friend brought, settles back on the couch to read the next two chapters, which are entitled, *Growling Back* and *A Traveler's Guide*. She leafs through the pages, and reads:

☽

You may think that all these years I have been writing the volumes of some kind of tourists' guide to infinity. That is not so. These books are a traveler's guide. There is a difference: tourists wander. Travelers prepare. It is possible that I have been successful in preparing only myself—and even that remains to be seen! But a lesson I learned early in my training was the importance of growling back at what growls at you: I think, as Jorge

Castelan, I have not always done this. In fact, I know that I have not. But perhaps as a traveler, I will do better than I did here. I hope you will too.

How does one begin to prepare for travel to the infinite? To begin with, dispense with the notion that I am describing life after death: I have no idea what death is—other than the cessation of physical functions—so I cannot prepare for what comes after it. But I can prepare for an active journey, a wakeful state of transitioning from here to there. How does one begin? First, by reviewing one's memories, both real and imagined. The things that you imagine have happened to you, and that you wish had happened, may be as important in evaluating who you are as those things that "really" took place. And by the way, that is such a stupid word: "really." It suggests that there is one meaning to everything when, of course, there are multiple interpretations of all events. It is up to you to pick one, to choose what is "real" for you.

After you have reviewed all the events of your life, you will probably be overwhelmed. All the time that seems to have passed so quickly will seem, now, to have gone on much longer than you expected: how else to account for all the many, many things that have certainly happened to you? It will turn out that your life has been more eventful than you thought, more full of experiences. And though you have learned very little—trust me, I have spent my life trying to learn everything I can and even I remain much more ignorant than wise—you have learned enough to begin an assessment. What do you want to do next? It doesn't matter how old you are when you begin this process, or how strong or weak your body is; those are meaningless and irrelevant conditions. What have you learned so far, what have you accomplished, and what do you want to do next? These are the questions the active traveler must ask himself. And then you will be ready to begin.

Oh yes. And practice growling. Strange and dangerous things may happen along the way. That's all right. You will be surprised how well a loud growl works in frightening away anyone—or anything—that may be inclined to impede your progress.

☽

That's as far as Janet gets when she hears a car pull up outside and a door slam. Renna asks, "Who's coming to join the party?"

"I have an idea," Janet says. She makes a kind of grumbling noise in her throat and says to Renna, "How did that sound?"

"Like you need a bag of cough drops."

"So I need to work on it," Janet says, as she gets to her feet.

She walks to the door and opens it to watch Carolee Carter striding across her patchy front yard. The big Mercedes is parked off to the side, its nose in the weeds.

"Come in," Janet says, as Carolee stamps into the front hall. She stops short when she sees Renna sitting on the couch amid the papers, but quickly turns her attention back to Janet.

"I want to know where he is," Carolee says.

"I told you on the phone, I don't know," Janet repeats. "But you're welcome to look around. Search the house if you like. Every little nook and cranny. Maybe you think I've got him bottled up in a jar or something?"

"He's gone off with that old witch, hasn't he?"

"She's the Fearless Guide," Janet tells her. "If you're going to run the Jorge Castelan industry, you need to get your facts straight."

"Don't start with me," Carolee warns.

"This is my house," Janet reminds her. "You came to see me."

"Which was obviously a mistake."

"Calm down, dearie," Renna says from the living room. "I'm sure you'll be able to find another boyfriend. Maybe you can upgrade to a wizard this time." She puts her hand to her chin, strikes a thoughtful pose. "Am I right, though? Does a wizard outrank a sorcerer?"

Carolee, who has turned to look at Renna, swivels back to face Janet. "Do you think this is a joke, too?"

"No," says Janet, who suddenly feels like she's running out of steam. A few minutes ago, she thought she had an appetite for confronting Carolee, but the energy seems to be draining out of her *intent*. She's tired now. She wants to sit down.

She walks back to the couch and sinks into it, beside Renna. "Look," she says to Carolee, "I've told you everything. He came over here…what, three nights ago now? He slept on the couch and in the morning I drove him to see Zella. She was living at a commune in Ontario called Harmony Road Farm. We spent the night there and then I drove him back here…I mean, to town. I left him on Tinker Street. That's it. That's all there is."

"Bullshit," Carolee spits out.

In a different frame of mind, Janet might be willing to allow that she hasn't really been completely forthcoming. She has given

Carolee only the bare outline of a much more complicated series of events. In retrospect, it seems to Janet that even she may have been receiving only the surface signals of actions—including her own—and relationships so deeply intertwined that it's hard to tell where one ends and the next one begins. But she doesn't feel capable of digging down any further right now, and certainly isn't going to force herself to do so for Carolee Carter.

"Do me a favor, will you?" Janet says to Carolee. "Just go home. I feel like you and I keep having the same conversation and it's not getting either of us anywhere."

Suddenly, Carolee seems to spy the pages that are strewn across Janet's coffee table and part of the couch. She picks up some of the sheets of paper and asks, "What's this?"

Janet doesn't see any reason, at this point, to pretend that the manuscript is anything but what it is. "It's a draft of a new book that Georgie was working on. It isn't finished."

Carolee is leafing through the pages now, making a quick scan of what they contain. "Well," she says finally, "of course it's unfinished. It's missing the chapters about Centered Movement."

"Oh, I see," Janet says. "You know that's what he meant to include."

"Of course," Carolee tells Janet. "We had talked about that."

She begins gathering the sheets of paper together, picking them up and arranging them into a neat stack. Then she points at the pages that Janet is holding, though she didn't even realize that she still had them in her hand. "I'll take those," she says to Janet. "And what you've got, too," she tells Renna.

"What are you talking about?" Janet says to Carolee. "All of this is mine."

She stands up, feeling, suddenly, like her head has cleared. Like the fog of exhaustion that had descended on her is lifting. It's as if a river inside her has reversed direction; energy is flowing back into her instead of seeping out.

"Maybe Georgie never explained this to you," Carolee says, "but I have power of attorney over Jorge Castelan's estate. That means unpublished manuscripts, as well. Maybe he left them here but legally, you have to turn them over to me."

"His *estate*?" Janet says. "I saw him yesterday afternoon—don't tell me you've decided he's dead already. And by the way, in case

Georgie never explained *this* to you, sorcerers don't die. They burn up from within." She waves some of the pages at Carolee. "If you're nice to me, I might let you read some of this. He has a lot to say about transitioning from *here* to *there*."

And with that, Janet walks over to Carolee and snatches the manuscript back from her. "So, miss power-of-attorney," she says, "I think you're going to have to fight me for these." She makes a deep noise in her throat and then turns to Renna. "Was that better?" she asks.

"Much," Renna replies.

Carolee moves toward Janet, as if to grab the manuscript back, but Renna quickly springs up from the couch and positions herself between the two women. "Darling," she says, "just try it and I'll smack you so hard you'll end up on another level of reality. *That* I promise you. From here to there in a nanosecond." Then she nudges Janet with her elbow and in a stage whisper says, "See? I only read a couple of paragraphs and already I've picked up on the lingo."

Carolee won't even glance in Renna's direction; she keeps her eyes fixed on Janet. "You know," she says, "I let you off the hook once because Georgie wanted me to. But I won't do it a second time. Keeping that manuscript is theft."

"So have me arrested again," Janet says. "But for now, please: just go."

"You must be crazy," Carolee spits out as she turns to go.

"Not according to Jorge Castelan," Janet replies. "I'm actually just being witchy. But you wouldn't really know anything about what he believes, would you?"

After she's gone, gunning the big Mercedes so that it sounds like a tank ripping up the front yard, Renna dissolves into a fit of giggles.

"That was really fun," she says. "I do so enjoy seeing someone with that much straightening gel in their hair get mad enough to start sprouting curls."

"I'm glad you were entertained," Janet says, flopping back down on the couch. "But in the end, she's probably right. I'll probably have to give her the book. Zella pretty much said the same thing she did: she has power of attorney, so she's got control over everything."

"If Georgie doesn't come back."

"Renna. He's not. I know he's not."

"Then what difference does it make, really? What are you going to do with the book? You said it's not even finished."

"It's not," Janet says. And then, instinctively tapping herself on the head, she adds, "I don't know."

☾

And what is she going to do without him? Lost, found and then lost again: does she really believe what she told Renna? That Jorge Castelan is gone for good? Would he do that—just walk off in the direction of infinity and leave nothing behind? Well, why not: that is exactly what Janet Planet did to him. He has actually been more considerate: he did leave something behind. His backpack. The pages of his unfinished book.

In the evening, after Renna has gone, Janet goes back to the manuscript and reads it through. She reads late into the night, and finds much of it affecting. In fact, she feels that there are pages that he could have easily addressed directly to her. She understands that this is how many people have felt, over the years, when they read Jorge Castelan's books, but still, still. None of them were, are, Janet Planet. None of them, tonight, can possibly feel as restless as she does when she finally turns the last page.

Traveling, I must warn you—in the way that I have described it—is exhausting until you really settle into it. There may be times when you feel like it requires so much energy that all you feel capable of doing is crumbling into dust and letting the winds of the universe blow you away. That's because traveling is disturbing. The sorcerer's way is disturbing. In fact everything that has happened to me, for example, since I met Yamon in the bus station in Mexico is disturbing. That's because just opening your eyes in the morning can be disturbing—imagine if you have to have your eyes open all the time! Of course, you can open your eyes as wide as possible and stare and stare and stare, and still there's always the chance that there's nothing, really, to look for. That nothing will come. But what if there is something? What if something comes for you? Or if you happen upon what you never expected? What will you do? Such encounters may change you forever—or just for a minute.

But a minute might be enough. A minute, a glimpse, a shadow on a hill in the distance, might be enough to give you hope that you can progress. Or if not progress, at least stumble forward. Forward is good. Forward can lead to anything. Keep your eyes open. Growl as loud as you can when you feel stuck. And if you can't even stumble, then jump. What's the worst that can happen? And consider: what if it does? In that case, you can just start traveling again. Go in another direction. But certainly, go, go, go. Things always happen to a traveler, even up to the last day, the last moment—but only if you travel with a sorcerer's attention. What does that mean? That you must always hold in your mind the attentive idea that what you have been told is reality is only the current civilization's description of what is real. The description created by those who currently think they know everything but, of course, know very little. Consider: there have been other civilizations before this one that have approached reality in many different ways. Therefore, a sorcerer pays attention to the fact that the current description of reality is limited. And it is limiting. A sorcerer can revise that description at any time, and he can hold many versions of reality in his mind all at once.

Let me give you an example of what I mean. Once, Yamon saw me reading a magazine article about people who believed that they had been abducted by aliens. Why are you reading that? he asked me, and I answered that I was curious. I was willing to accept that the people who believed they had been abducted by aliens were experiencing some sort of delusion but I also felt perfectly capable of believing that what they thought had happened to them had, indeed, really happened. That these people had been transported from their beds, taken onto space ships, subjected to invasive physical examinations and then returned home. Now, though I was willing to believe that, I also could not imagine what the aliens' purpose was. Apparently, they did these things quite often. How many people did they have to abduct and examine in order to achieve their purposes?

Are you an alien? Yamon asked me after we discussed the article. Have you lived a life like theirs? Do you have their needs, follow their beliefs? When I replied of course not, he said, then why do you think you can understand their purposes? You are trying to figure out what they are doing, but you are imposing only your perspective on their actions, trying to fit their activities into your understanding of reality. Obviously, they originate not only from a different place but from a different system of reality; what is reasonable and purposeful to them is beyond your understanding in your current state. You, said Yamon, *have great distances to cross before you can begin to guess at what they are doing, or why. And of course, there is also the possibility that they are all insane.* (I assumed that he was joking about that last suggestion.)

It took me many years to realize that when Yamon spoke to me about distance, he did not mean to reference physical space or measurements of yards or miles or even light years. Nor did he mean distance to be a description of passing time. Distance, as I have come to understand it, is internal. How far have you traveled? How much have you learned? What else do you want to know? These are personal questions. No one but your teacher, if you have one—if you can even recognize who your teacher is—should ask these questions of you. And no one's answer matters but your own.

Hopefully, by the time you read this, you will have traveled enough distance to have at least achieved the ability to state, without hesitation, that you are probably not a complete idiot. At least not anymore. To attest that you are able to keep your eyes open some of the time. That you have developed a nice, healthy growl. And if these things are so, then I urge you to go, go, go—go as fast as a blue streak. Go where? Wherever you like. Wherever you have decided that it is time to set out for. And remember: you can follow these directions on a bus, in an office or in your own chair at home. But I give you one warning: you must begin immediately. A traveler never rests.

XII

A traveler never rests.

Says who? This is what Janet asks herself a hundred times—more—over the next few days, the next weeks, as she tries to let the sorcerer go. Maybe he thinks time and distance don't mean much, but to Janet, that is how life is measured, and the measuring goes on. With him and without him, she has traversed both landscapes and mindscapes that have required her to draw on every ounce of her strength, every corner of her spirit. She doesn't need to be reminded of how difficult this has been: who is he to leave her a message telling her that there is farther to go? She knows that. So she knows he means it not as a revelation, but as a dare.

A minute, a glimpse, a shadow on a hill in the distance.

There is that to consider, too. More messages to decipher about what happened at Harmony Road. But maybe nothing happened, Janet begins to tell herself. What a crazy thing, red fences popping up out of nowhere and seeing coyotes everywhere. Spirit guides, magical meanings. Walking through your own dreams, hand in hand with the last nagual. *Enough,* she decides. *I've had enough.* She tells Renna that she doesn't want to talk about Jorge Castelan. She works days, she works nights. She watches television. She drives to another town just to go to the movies, and drives back with one hand on the wheel. And she sits up at night, because she cannot sleep. When she does sleep, often nodding off on her couch in the living room, almost immediately, she is back at the red fence.

Barriers, stalemates, impediments.

That sounds like a tarot card reading. The tourist's guide for the traveling generation.

Things go on like this as spring officially turns into summer, and summer grows deeper. During the week, on the Village Green, locals play guitars and set up impromptu drum circles from morning until well into the night. On weekends, families come up from the city to go tubing on the nearby Esopus River. Janet often walks into town in the morning, to have coffee at Meggie's, but then she goes back home, to work. And just as often, she meets Renna for dinner or a drink in Woodstock or Bearsville (avoiding Phoenicia, because

Janet does not want to run into Carolee, who may or may not still be living in the house in the hills), but then goes home again to work some more. They know her by name at the lumberyard now. She has met a local craftsman and contracted with him to make intricately carved roses for the soundboards of some of the harpsichords in her shop, for which people, apparently, are willing to pay outrageous prices. At a yard sale, she buys a small air conditioner and installs it in the workshop so she can be comfortable all summer. So she can work without stopping. So she can do more than stumble forward. So she can progress.

Until an August morning when the postman brings her a registered letter. She can't remember ever even having seen such a thing before: it seems like a relic from some distant past, before the world was wired to run on bits and bytes. But she has to sign for it, and she does, and then sits in her kitchen reading what turns out to be some very harsh language from a law firm working—big surprise—for Carolee Carter enterprises. They reference the manuscript written by one Jorge Castelan and demand its return to Carolee Carter. Immediately. Posthaste. Not a second's delay.

"Or else what?" Janet says out loud. *Or else what?*

The letter disturbs her. It's intrusive, threatening. It unbalances the harmony she has established, or tells herself she has established, in the routine of her days and nights. Even sleeplessness, even the fence. They are part of a manageable whole, as long as they keep their place. But their place, along with everything else in her life, is spoken for. Her mind is full to the brim. There isn't room for one more thing, one more thought. Not even a crack in which to store away a nasty letter.

By the afternoon, the letter has taken over; she can think about nothing else. So when Renna calls, meaning just to say hello, Janet can't stop herself from immediately bringing it up.

On the other end of the phone there is a pause. "So let me ask," Renna finally says. "Am I allowed to talk about this now? Is *the name* once again to be mentioned in polite conversation?"

"Yes," Janet says, exasperated. "Georgie. Jorge Castelan. Talk about him all you like if you have any ideas for me because I don't know what to do.

"Give it to her," Renna says. "Give her the manuscript. I mean, we had our fun with Carolee, but what's the point of fighting her?

She's got the money, she's got the lawyers…" A sly note suddenly creeps into Renna's voice. "Unless you still want to take her on."

"It's not her so much anymore," Janet replies. "It's Georgie. I don't know what he expected me to do with the book."

"Maybe he didn't expect you to do anything."

"But maybe he did."

"And you resent it."

"You're right," Janet agrees. "Because it feels like I owe him something."

"All men think you owe them something."

"That doesn't help," Janet says.

"Well maybe this does," Renna tells her. "He isn't here, remember? You have free will—or maybe you don't in Jorge Castelan land, but we're in Woodstock, and I guarantee that you do. Have free will, I mean. So decide for yourself. He gave you the book but he didn't leave any instructions with it, so my guess is, you're on your own. Do what you want, Janet. Do what will make things easier for you."

Listening to the silence on the other end of the phone, Renna sighs. "I forgot," she says. "Nothing is easy for you."

"Not right now," Janet says. "No."

Later, after she's hung up with Renna, Janet reads the attorney's letter one more time. And again she asks herself, *or what?*

Then, suddenly, she has a thought about who else to talk to about all this. She goes into her closet, where the manuscript is still stashed inside Jorge Castelan's backpack, and takes it out to her car. Then she drives to the town of Saugerties, where there is a copy and print store, and pays to have every page of the manuscript scanned and turned into an electronic file, which is given to her on a CD. She then drives back home and marches into her workshop, where she sits down at the computer and opens her e-mail program. There are several new messages in her in-box but she ignores them because she wants to send a message of her own.

Dear Eli, she writes, *I don't know who you are, but I gather, from Zella's letter to you, that at least I now know your name. Since I assume it was you who sent me the first chapter of* Flying Through Walls, *I am now sending you the rest, which Jorge Castelan has left with me. He's gone; I'm sure for good. Apparently, you know him. Apparently, he must trust you, since I cannot imagine how else you would have gotten a copy of the first* chapter of this book. I gather, as well, that you must know Carolee Carter and what she seems to have done to the witches and the Fearless Guide. Well, now she has her lawyers demanding that I give the manuscript to her. Should I? Shouldn't I? There are intentions here; I know there are, but they aren't clear and I don't think that I can sort them out without some help. Can you *help me? Please let me know.*

One day goes by, and then another, and another. Janet checks her e-mail obsessively, but there is no answer to her message. What does arrive is another letter from Carolee's lawyer, containing more demands for the return of what they are now referring to as "the Castelan manuscript." Janet considers the possibility that Renna might be right: the easiest thing to do would be to hand over *Flying Through Walls* and be finished with it. But she can't make that decision yet. She's too stubborn. And too angry: at Carolee, at Georgie, and even at Zella, a little. And now, at Eli Bell as well, who may be her only remaining connection to the last nagual and to solving the problem he has left with her in the form of his last book. She is beginning to understand the impulse to crouch down on her haunches and growl as loud as she can.

Finally, about a week after sending the e-mail to Eli Bell, Janet is in her workshop when her cell phone rings. She doesn't recognize the number but she answers anyway, thinking she'll be speaking to a customer. But that's not who's on the line.

First, she hears the sound of throat clearing, like someone is hesitant about speaking. Then, at last, a man's voice addresses her with a simple, "Hello."

"Hello," Janet responds, and because the man says nothing else, she asks, "Who is this?"

"This is Eli Bell," the man says. "Are you Janet Harris?"

Janet sits down, leans back against a tall cardboard box holding the precut pieces of a harpsichord case. Her annoyance with the caller's delay in answering her message fades into the background as she searches her mind to see if the sound of this voice means anything to her—if she's heard it before. It's accentless, nonregional, nothing about it provides a clue.

"Yes," Janet says. "It's me. But do I know you? I mean, other than through the e-mails. Have we ever met?"

"I don't think so," the man says. "No." Again, he clears his throat, then seems to fumble with the phone, which clicks and gasps. Janet is sure they're going to be disconnected until he speaks again. "I didn't know if I should get in touch with you," Eli says.

"Why?" Janet asks. "Did you read what I sent you?"

"I did," Eli replies. He ventures no opinion about the manuscript except to say, "So I suppose this is the last we'll hear from Jorge Castelan?"

"Carolee Carter wants to turn it into some sort of self-help manual."

"Well, that's what those books are, in a way. Aren't they?"

"I don't think Georgie would ever describe his work like that."

"No," Eli Bell agrees. "He wouldn't."

"Let me ask you something," Janet says, feeling suddenly apprehensive. What if this man is another sort of trickster? A con man of some sort? "Do you actually *know* Georgie?"

If Eli Bell hears the note of suspicion in her voice, he does not seem to acknowledge it. Instead, he responds with a long sigh. "Well, sort of," Eli Bell says. "I don't mean to sound mysterious. Really. There's actually nothing about any of this that's mysterious. Just… odd, I guess."

Janet listens, hoping he will go on. He does, but not with information, just another protracted sigh. "Listen," he says, "I'm not all that far away from you, actually. I live in L.A. most of the time but I've been in New York for a while. I've been teaching at New York University for a couple of semesters."

"What do you teach?" Janet asks.

"Mathematics." He pauses and then says, "I know, you were expecting comparative religion or mythology or something like that. Anthropology, maybe. Wasn't that his field, originally?"

"Yes," Janet says. "Originally."

Again, Janet waits to hear where this conversation is going, but Eli soon clarifies that. "I was thinking, if you'd like to come to the city, we could get together for coffee or something. We could talk. Maybe that will help."

Janet gets the impression that what he means is, help both of them. Making a quick decision she says, "I can probably be there in a couple of hours." She glances up at a copy of the schedule for the bus that runs between Woodstock and New York that she keeps taped to the wall above her work table. She doesn't even consider driving herself because she isn't ready, yet, to brave the cutthroat New York traffic. "I can be at Port Authority at five o'clock. I'll take a taxi from there: where should I meet you?"

"Tonight?" he says, sounding startled that she means to come immediately.

"Yes," Janet tells him. "Tonight."

Recovering enough to think of a place to meet, Eli Bell gives her the name of a restaurant on MacDougal Street, near the university.

"I'll be there," Janet says, and hangs up the phone before he has a chance to say anything else.

She calls Renna to tell her where she's going—*just in case*, she has the feeling that someone should know where she is—but also says she doesn't have time to answer all the questions Renna starts asking her. The bus is due in town in less than half an hour.

"Call me when you get back," Renna says.

"It will be late," Janet warns.

"Call me anyway," Renna says. "I just want to know that you've made it back alive."

"Renna, for heaven's sake."

"It's just a manner of speaking, cookie. But check in anyway, okay?"

Janet agrees that she will, and then runs out to her car and drives into town, going much too fast. She parks in the back of Meggie's bakery and runs in for a minute to ask her if it's okay to leave the car there until she picks it up later tonight. Meggie says sure, and Janet practically sprints out the door and up the street to the bus stop. She can already see the bus making its way down Tinker Street, and when it stops, she climbs aboard with a sense of relief. A moment later, though, when she goes to reach into her bag for her wallet to pay the bus fare, she realizes that instead of taking her purse from the front seat of the car, she's grabbed Georgie's backpack instead.

Is this accident or intent? *Flying Through Walls* has been living in her car ever since she took it to the copy shop. With some idea about out of sight, out of mind, there had been a dozen times when it had occurred to her to put it away somewhere, but the pages—Georgie—have outwitted her. *A traveler never rests,* he wrote, and now, while she is on her way from *here* to *there*, his last manuscript is apparently coming with her. Unless, of course, she gets thrown off the bus because she doesn't have any cash with her to pay the fare.

"Just a minute," she says to the driver, and sits down on the seat right behind him, trying to figure out what she can do.

And then, without really thinking about it, she begins searching through the pockets of Georgie's backpack. It's had years of wear and decades more of sitting in a closet, probably—a silent, unseen resident of the house in Westwood—and the zippers of the many side compartments are stiff and rusty. Janet struggles with each one in turn, not even sure of what she's looking for—but what difference does it make? They all prove to be empty. Then, making one last hunt for any hidden compartments, she feels the edge of another zipper on the side of one of the backpack's thick straps. This one slides open easily, and as it does, a crumpled wad of Mexican money falls into Janet's lap. She picks up the lump of peach-and-blue hued notes and thinks, *Thanks, Georgie, but I don't think I can pay for this trip in pesos.* But as she pulls Jorge Castelan's small stash of traveling money apart, at the bottom of the wad, she finds three American twenty dollar bills. This is just about enough to cover a round-trip ticket.

Wordlessly, Janet hands the money to the driver at his next stop. Then she settles herself down again with Jorge Castelan's backpack beside her on an empty seat. It's a man's backpack; big and bulky in shape, with a hefty weight to it. As worn and well-used as it looks, it has a presence; to Janet, it seems to emanate a sense of anticipation, as if it is eager to be off on a journey once again. Though perhaps, Janet thinks, it is really the object within that is pulsing with a traveler's energy, because *Flying Through Walls*, with its few completed chapters—*Infinity for Grownups, Growling Back, A Traveler's Guide*—is beginning to feel almost like a living thing to her, an entity with a purpose and an intent. After all, it has gotten itself on this bus, it is coming with her to meet someone it may regard as an old friend, it seems to have even paid for its own passage. And in doing so, it also seems to have assigned her a task—or Georgie did, but isn't that the same thing? Her job is to discover what intent is really contained within the book's pages, and if they need to travel in order for that to be revealed, then she is supposed to make sure that they get wherever they're supposed to go. Or perhaps she is supposed to find the missing pieces of *Flying Through Walls*, the fragments of itself that it seems to be hungering for—is *that* what she's feeling? That it's breathing inside the backpack, gathering the strength it will need to be completed? As if the manuscript itself desires to be finished. It desires to know how its own story turns out.

When Janet finally arrives in New York, it's rush hour and the Port Authority Bus Terminal is crowded with commuters trying to get home. Janet finds a taxi outside and tells the driver to take her to the Village; many of the university buildings are set around Washington Square Park and the restaurant where Eli wants to meet is nearby.

It's a warm evening, slow to give up the heat of the day. Janet has asked to be let out of the taxi a few blocks from the restaurant, so she can walk a bit. She likes this old neighborhood, and though it has long since transitioned from the days of coffee shops and tenement apartments cheap enough to support a population of artists and musicians, there are still some remnants of the old days to be seen: Janet stops to look in the window of a favorite store she remembers that sells silver jewelry heavy on the dragon, skull and evil eye motif, and another stocked with handmade leather sandals and Tibetan incense. Finally, she moves on, and threads her way through the streets crowded with couples pushing baby strollers and with students who have stayed in the city for summer sessions.

The entrance to the restaurant where Eli wants to meet, an Italian place that has been a Village standby for countless years, is downstairs from the street. Inside, it's pleasantly dim; there are candles on the tables, but they haven't been lit yet. What light there is filters in from the back, where doors are open to a dining patio that was once somebody's back garden. It's only five-thirty; an off-hour for a restaurant even in a busy neighborhood, so most of the tables are empty—except for one, where a tall man with a narrow jaw, narrow cheeks and gray hair is seated. That must be Eli Bell. As Janet walks toward him, she thinks she can see the traces of a boy's expressive face caught somewhere behind that professorial visage. Not quite hidden, not quite contained.

She sits down opposite him, at the table in the middle of what is a purposefully plain room. Gray walls, white tablecloths, spindly legged chairs.

"Eli?" she says.

He nods. "And you're Janet?"

"Well," Janet responds. "Finally."

Eli Bell nods again, as if acknowledging either the inevitability of their meeting, or the surprise of it happening at all.

"Do you want something to eat?" he asks.

She tells him, "Not a lot. But I'll have a beer."

He calls over a waiter, orders appetizers and two bottles of draft. Then, when they're alone again in the dim room, in the empty hour of a city evening, he says, "I guess the only way to do this is to tell you the whole story."

"Okay," Janet says, trying to sound noncommittal. She can't begin to imagine what this man is going to say to her.

"He's really gone?" Eli asks

"That's what I think," Janet says.

"Burned up from within?" Eli says, but in a way that gives Janet the impression he's being sarcastic. Only very slightly, but nevertheless…sarcastic.

"I couldn't tell you."

"Right," says Eli, "but maybe I can." He smiles suddenly; suddenly he seems less distant, a little more friendly. "I think," he begins, "or maybe I should say, I've always thought, that all this is my fault."

"All what?"

"Old Indians in bus stations. Spirit guides. Visions of alternate realities. Sorcery, witches…all of it."

Janet stays silent now, waiting for him to go on. In the interim, the waiter brings their food, the bottles of beer. Eli touches none of it. Then, when the waiter is gone, he says, "In 1960 I was twenty years old. If you look back now, it was a kind of strange year, 1960. A halfway year. Halfway between the beats and the hippies. Halfway through college for me. UCLA, as it happens. I had a couple of friends, it was a restless summer—well, one of us had a van so we pooled our money, packed some stuff and drove down to Mexico. I think we got the idea from a line in *On the Road*." He pauses for a moment, takes his first sip of the Sam Adams and says to Janet, "You know who Jack Kerouac was?"

"Yes," she tells him.

"Well, in the book, somebody says to somebody else who's wearing jeans and a denim jacket, 'You look like a man on his way to Mexico,' or something like that. One day, one of my friends was dressed like that. It was enough of a reason, I guess, for us to decide to head south of the border. Maybe anything was enough in those days."

"It would have been enough later, too."

"I suppose," he agrees. "Anyway, I don't think we had much of a plan other than to have an adventure. And having an adventure meant getting high. So, we crossed over into Mexico—all you had to do, basically, was wave to border guards in those days—and drove around. We ended up in some town in Sonora, where we bought some food, and then we drove off into the desert to camp." He drinks a few more sips of his beer, picks at his food. Then he continues. "The second afternoon we were there, this guy came wandering out of nowhere. He was about our age, maybe a few years older, with a backpack slung over his shoulder. A kind of stocky guy with dark, curly hair. We invited him to sit down with us and have something to eat, and it turned out he was from UCLA, too—but in the graduate program. He had taken a bus to the town we had just come from and now he was looking for plants. Medicinal plants. He told us he was having trouble with his dissertation, so he'd left his wife at home and had come down to Sonora to do some more research. As it happened, we told him, we might be able to help him."

"Peyote," Janet says.

"Oh boy, yes. Peyote. We were able to buy more than food in that town. Peyote was like…I don't know. Like beer," he says, pinging his fingers against the brown bottle on the table in front of him. "Cheap. Easy to get. So we got a lot of it."

"He told you he was Jorge Castelan?"

"He told us his name was Georgie. I don't think he ever gave us a last name and why would we ask? Who cared? We were playing at being cool dudes. Stoner freaks, out there with the rocks and cactus and the red sun. Wowee, zowee," Eli says. "We stayed high for…I don't know. A couple of days. It could have been a couple of weeks, for all I know. I mean, if you've ever done peyote…"

"No," Janet says.

"Well, all I can tell you is you drift off into another place. Visions, hallucinations, you name it. Peyote is very powerful, and we had some primo buttons. You do enough of it and you start having some very spiritual experiences, let me tell you. God speaks from the rocks, you can walk through the clouds, things like that. It was happening to all of us. And Georgie stayed with us all the time we were getting high. Finally, one morning, he said he had to get going and he walked off in the direction of the main road. He said he was going to get a bus to the next town, and maybe we'd all see each other back at UCLA."

"Do you know what town that was?"

"No idea," says Eli. "But I gather that was where the…well, what should we call it? Where the fateful meeting took place."

He still sounds sour, which makes Janet feel resentful. And compelled to tell him that there was, in fact, a town, a destination, and it had a name. "It was Este Muralla. That was where he met Yamon."

"Really?" Eli says. "We drove all over Sonora. I don't remember anyplace with that name."

Right now, Janet isn't interested in Eli Bell's opinion about whether or not there really is a town called Este Muralla, so she nudges him in another direction. What she wants is to hear about what she doesn't know.

"Did you ever see Georgie, later, in California?"

"Not for a while—at least, not at school. I went back, settled down and got my degree. But a couple of years later, when that first book came out—*The Peyote Palace*—I put it all together. There were never any photos of Jorge Castelan on his books but it all sounded familiar to me. I wrote him a letter because I was curious to see if he remembered me—us—and eventually, he wrote back. He invited me to have lunch with him one day, and I did."

A few couples are beginning to wander into the restaurant and there's more activity now as plates are carried in and out of the kitchen. A string of colored lights are turned on out back, on the patio, but Janet pays no attention to any of this. She is completely focused on Eli Bell, on the story he's telling her.

"So," Eli goes on, "we had lunch. Jorge Castelan and me. There was this park, near an office he had when he was a grad student…"

"Yes," Janet says softly. "I think I know the place."

"It was a nice day and he wanted to eat outside. So we bought some sandwiches and sat on a bench and had what I guess you could call a pretty weird conversation. I mean, I didn't exactly say so, but I sort of was trying to ask him if maybe he'd dreamed up the whole Yamon thing while he was hallucinating in the back of our van and he kind of laughed me off. And then he told me the Yamon story. Pretty much word for word the way he'd written it."

"But you didn't believe him?"

"Not really. I remember being struck by the fact that, in *The Peyote Palace*, he said the first time he'd ever tried peyote was when Yamon gave it to him, and that certainly wasn't true, because I gave him plenty."

"So he fudged some facts," Janet said.

"There were other things," Eli Bell said. "I told you that before we did the peyote, Georgie was talking about how his dissertation had been rejected. Twice, I think he said. He made a couple of jokes about the fact that if he didn't find someone to show him something new about the medicinal or hallucinogenic use of desert plants—something that hadn't been written about yet by another Ph.D. candidate—he was just going to have to make something up."

"None of your other friends—the people who were with you in Mexico—ever made the connection? Between the man you met in the desert and Jorge Castelan? Just you?"

"Not as far as I know," Eli Bell tells her. "We all kind of drifted apart once we graduated, but they probably didn't even remember him. Like I said, we did a lot of peyote. A lot."

"So why didn't you tell anybody about this?" Janet asks.

"I don't know. I guess I kind of liked the guy. When I met him back in L.A., I thought he was a little strange, like I said, but also…I don't know. Funny. Likeable. A little bit of a bumbler, if you know what I mean."

"Yes," Janet agrees. "I think so."

"Besides, what was I supposed to say to who? That I thought he made everything up? Or dreamt it sitting in the back of my van? It did cross my mind once or twice, but I figured I'd be vilified. Who was that one academic who spent so much time trying to debunk Jorge Castelan's work…"

"Arthur Rivers."

"Right. I heard about the hate mail he got—even threats. I didn't need any of that. He had the anti-Jorge Castelan market cornered and I didn't need to get into that argument. And by then, anyway, we had developed this kind of odd relationship—me and Georgie. We kept in touch over the years—mostly by phone and then by e-mail. He used to send me parts of his books to read before they were published. And a couple of years ago, he asked me to put up that website for him…it's a kind of hobby of mine, web design."

Eli finishes his beer, calls the waiter over and asks for another. When the young man who's serving them has come and gone again, Eli says, "You know, it did occur to me, over the years, that I was being co-opted. Masterfully. I mean, I really appreciated the technique. By keeping in touch with me, keeping me involved with him—even peripherally—I guess he thought he was hedging his bets. Keeping me on his side so I wouldn't ever tell my story. And I didn't."

"Until now."

"He said I could tell you anything. Everything. In fact, I got the impression that he *wanted* me to tell you everything."

"Is that why you sent me the first chapter of *Flying Through Walls*?"

"He wanted me to do that. I think he wasn't sure, at that point, how you felt about him, or if you wanted to read anything else he wrote."

"Is there anything else I need to know?" Janet asks.

"Look," Eli says, "I'm just the messenger here. If there's something you need to know that you don't already—and I haven't told you—you're going to have to tell *me* what it is."

Janet considers this for a moment and then says, "Do you mind if I ask when's the last time you talked to him?"

"The last time I talked to him?" Eli looks thoughtful. "Well, that was kind of odd, too. We hadn't actually seen each other in years—I mean, face to face. He was always kind of reclusive, and as time went on, he just became more and more so. I didn't mind, you understand—I wasn't going out of my way to try to see him, either. But then, back in the winter—before all that terrible business about the suicides—he called me up out of the blue and said he wanted to get together. He was actually going to fly out to L.A.—I guess it was that important to him—but I told him I was already in New York, so we met here. I don't mean here, literally," Eli Bell adds hastily. "Not this restaurant. I don't have a thing about meeting members of the Castelan family in this restaurant."

The Castelan family. Janet can think of several different ways that Georgie might have explained their relationship that would lead Eli Bell to characterize it this way. But clarifying that point doesn't seem very important right now.

"What did he want?" Janet asks.

"Nothing specific, really. I just got the feeling he wanted to…oh, I don't know. Reestablish the connection? Maybe heal old wounds—or not so old—would be a better way to put it. When I was still in California, I'd gotten a letter from Carolee Carter's attorneys advising me that her corporation was managing Jorge Castelan's business enterprises, and I was to turn over any records of financial transactions relating to the website, things like that. It was pretty insulting. To begin with, that website obviously doesn't make any money, but they really hounded me about it for a while. Other than that, though, I don't think we talked about anything important, and believe me, we barely even talked about Carolee. He just said he'd been out of commission for a while and so he'd turned everything over to her to manage for him. The princess, he called her. I got the impression that he sort of found her amusing."

Janet thinks of a lot of observations she could make about how "amusing" Carolee Carter is, but she doesn't much care about any of that right now. There is something, however, that Eli just said that she zeroes in on. "Georgie actually said he was 'out of commission'?" Janet asks.

"No. He told me some nutty story about having left this world for a while but I told you, I take that stuff with a grain of salt. Many grains of salt. That was all the more reason why I was so shocked—I mean, really shocked—when I got the letter from Zella. I had only heard from her once before in my life: when she asked me to put that notice on the website that she and…uh…her friends were going traveling. To be honest with you, I never quite understood what was going on there. I mean, most men can barely handle one woman. Me included. I don't know how he dealt with three."

Janet gets the impression that Eli Bell is trying to be humorous but it's an off-kilter attempt and it makes Janet feel defensive again. Irritated.

"They weren't just *women*," she says. "They were witches and a Fearless Guide."

Across the table, Eli Bell regards Janet with a concerned look. She can't tell if he's feeling regretful or worried that she might… what? Bite him? What does a sorcerer's child do when she's pissed off? "I'm sorry," he says. "I didn't mean to say anything offensive."

"You didn't," Janet says, waving her hand to wave the moment away. And it works; anger passes from her like a cloud drifting away. "In fact, you're probably right. Not from Georgie's point of view, of course, but for Lily, Namuria and Zella...I guess they just had too much invested in him. Everything, really. When he left, I don't think they knew how to breathe." Surprised at herself, that she's saying these things, Janet still can't seem to stop. "It wasn't like that at first," she continues. "Not when I was there. Everything seemed to make sense, to be in balance. We were happy. We were a family."

"Maybe that's what he really wanted," Eli says. "And maybe he should have left it at that."

Janet finishes her last sip of beer, stirs herself to go, "Well," she says, "I need to thank you for helping me find Zella. And for everything you told me."

"Not exactly what you wanted to hear, I guess."

"You mean about how you helped him dream everything up? Do you ever think it's possible that it was the other way around?"

"Not really, no," Eli says. "Do you?"

Does he expect an answer? Janet isn't going to give him one. Instead, she gets up, scraping back her chair. Before she can say good-bye, Eli Bell stops her with another question—the one they started out discussing, hours ago, on the phone. "So what are you going to do with the manuscript?"

"I'm still thinking about that."

"You could always publish it on your website," Eli suggests.

"My website is about Guttenberg harpsichords," Janet reminds him.

"It doesn't matter what it's about. You've got Jorge Castelan's last book," Eli points out. "Well, let's assume that's what it is. His last work in progress—and you've got real provenance for it: after all, you're Janet Planet. Jorge Castelan's Janet Planet. That's a big deal. And if you publish it, you can outmaneuver Carolee—which is something I think I'd enjoy helping you with, now that I think of it. Put the manuscript on your site, and I'll put a link to it on Peyote Palace. She can't get me for that. On top of everything else, you'll probably get a ton of business before she puts you in jail."

"She already tried that," Janet tells Eli Bell. "It didn't work."

"So Janet Planet can fly through walls, too?" he says. And for the first time since they sat down together, he smiles.

I don't really use that name anymore, Janet is about to tell him, since he's now uttered it more than once. But something stops her. "I guess you could say that," Janet answers. "Yes."

☾

Half an hour later, Janet is back at the Port Authority terminal, climbing aboard a bus that makes its way through the Bronx, up to Westchester and beyond, where the roads have been cut through a spine of rock shelf and boulders that marks the beginning of the territory that belongs to the Catskills.

As night overspreads the sky, Janet watches out the window at the headlights of cars flashing by on the highway. Great clouds pile up on the horizon, or else they are the mountains looming into view; it's hard to tell because they are shadow-colored, shadow shaped. Stars arrange themselves into luminous paw prints, tracking the moon.

After ninety minutes or so, long past the boundaries that separate the city's northern suburbs from the upstate counties, the bus begins making local stops to let passengers off at a shopping mall and later, at the edge of a parking lot near a train station. Then it ventures through a few small towns where only a diner is still open, or a bar. Passengers disembark along the way until only Janet is left on the bus as it heads out of the last hamlet it will pass before it gets to Woodstock—still another half hour away.

Alone now in the back of the bus, Janet begins to drift into a kind of half-sleep. But suddenly, just as she's slipping deeper into her dreams, she is jolted into rigid wakefulness when the bus makes a sudden lurch, as if it has hit a bump in the road. Immediately afterwards, though the bus keeps on moving, all the interior lights go out.

"Are you okay back there?" the bus driver calls out to Janet.

"I'm fine," she tells him. "What happened?"

"Beats me," he says. And then he begins talking to his dispatcher on the radio, though Janet can hear nothing of the conversation but bursts of static.

They plunge on through the darkness, which quickly gobbles up the miles. Janet can see little outside her window except the silhouettes of a rural landscape as the bus travels along a country road that skirts the dense, wooded foothills pushing up against the night sky.

Finally, they come to a crossroads, where there are telephone poles planted on opposite sides of the road, each affixed with lights that combine to cast a sharp, radium-colored glow across the pavement. Just as the bus begins to pass through the crossroads, it shudders to a complete stop. The air brakes let out a deep sigh, as if they are expelling the last breath they will ever take.

"Goddamn it," the driver exclaims at last, jumping out of his seat. "Just stay put," he calls back to Janet. "I'm going to see if I can figure out what's going on."

The bus has stopped in the center of a wedge of light, as if it has been rolled onto a stage. Looking out the window, Janet can see only as far as the edge of the road; the shapes of the trees beyond blend into blackness. The beam of the driver's flashlight bobs briefly in her view and then disappears behind the hood of the bus. Soon, the ticking of the engine as it cools down begins to slow until it fades to nothing. Janet is now alone on the bus, in darkness and in silence.

Suddenly, there is a kind of shivering in the shadows beyond the trees. A twig snaps, a narrow wind fingers its way through the leafy branches overhanging the road. And then, slipping out of the darkness onto the platform of light surrounding the bus, comes a familiar figure—a coyote.

He is a huge animal, both frightening and familiar at the same time. Even in the strange light cast by the roadside lamps, she can see that he is silver colored; he has silver eyes. As Janet regards the coyote through the window of the bus, he sits down on his haunches, throws back his head, and lets out a howl.

The sound seems to echo back and forth between the mountains. When it finally recedes, the animal keeps his nose pointed toward the sky, opening and closing his mouth as if he is swallowing the night in gulps. Then, quieting himself, he turns at last and looks directly at Janet. When she meets his gaze, what she sees in his eyes is a challenge.

Her reaction is one that she would never have expected; not even in her dream encounters with this animal has she felt as she does now—excited; even exhilarated, and almost overcome with the impulse to howl back. Or better yet, to growl at the coyote—to show him that she's as strong as she needs to be, or maybe even stronger.

Or, it occurs to her, she could just get off the bus and follow him, see where he leads, because that's why he's here—she knows it. That's the challenge he's come to make. And there is no possibility that he is looking for anyone but Janet Planet. As Georgie said, *He has nothing to say to me anymore. It seems that it's you he's come to see.*

Well, who else? Janet finds herself thinking. Who else is left? Georgie is gone, the women are gone—whether they've crossed over landscapes or dreamscapes or both, they are out of reach. Perhaps, in some hidden part of herself—or not so hidden—in all the years she lived apart from Jorge Castelan, his witches and his Fearless Guide, she always kept open the possibility that she could go back to them, but not anymore. They have parted from her for good. Janet Planet is on her own.

As she keeps her eyes trained on the coyote, she hears the driver climb back on the bus. The intercom squawks again, he stomps down on the gas and suddenly, the bus shudders back to life. Even the interior lights turn themselves back on.

"Alright," the driver exclaims. "Let's see if we can get this old clunker moving on down the road again."

The bus, recovering from its torpor, begins to slowly roll forward, picking up speed as it goes. Keeping pace, the coyote rises to his feet and begins to run alongside the bus, loping beside it with seeming ease. He keeps up with the moving vehicle for about half a mile and then, letting out one more long howl, turns quickly toward the trees and disappears. For a while afterwards, Janet imagines him running through the woods toward the shadowy mountains that loom in the distance, nailed across the horizon like a gateway to the night.

The bus follows the last winding mile of country road that leads into Woodstock. On Tinker Street, it comes to a stop near the Village Green. With Jorge Castelan's backpack slung over her shoulder, Janet makes her way down the steps and watches as the vehicle lumbers away, seemingly none the worse for its unexpected sojourn at the crossroads.

It's late, but on a mild, summery night, there are still a few locals lingering around the green. Somebody is softly tapping on a set of bongos; a couple is lying side by side on the grass, watching the moon float by.

"Hey. Didn't you see me?"

Janet turns around and smiles. "Nope. But I didn't expect to. Have you been waiting for me?"

Renna is sitting on the bench near the bus stop. She's all in black—black jeans, a black blouse, even black sandals on her feet—an outfit she has accessorized with several long ropes of rhinestone necklaces and a collection of thin bangles on her wrist.

"I tried to call to see what bus you were on, but you seem to have had your phone turned off," Renna says as Janet sits down beside her.

"You look nice," Janet says to her. "Is that your Vampira outfit?"

"No, it's my waiting-to-hear-what-the-strange-man-in-the-city-had-to-say outfit."

"He wasn't so strange," Janet says. "And I guess I did have the phone turned off. I was thinking."

Renna sighs. "Oh, boy. I can tell this is going to be complicated."

Janet sits down beside her on the bench. As completely as she can, she relates the story Eli Bell told her about the young man who had been having problems with his dissertation and ended up sharing peyote buttons with Eli and his friends in the Mexican desert. Who had then said he was heading off to catch the bus to the next town down the line.

"So what does that all mean?" Renna asks. "That he made it all up? That the whole Yamon thing, alternate realities and sorcery lessons, started with some hallucinations in the back of some guy's VW van?"

"I guess that's always been one possibility," Janet replies. "On the other hand, maybe he continued on to a town called Esta Murella and, in the bus station, met an old Indian named Yamon. The real mystery, then, is what happened afterwards."

"And now you think you know?"

Janet shakes her head. "Because of what Eli Bell told me? Not really, no. But I can tell you my best guess. I think that Georgie started out looking for plants in the desert and ended up on a spiritual journey. Maybe that wasn't his intention, originally, but that's what happened. And I believe that he really did have some of the experiences he said he did. I think the problem was—is—that traveling along a spiritual path is something you do alone. Once you start trying to get all sorts of people to go along with you, the journey becomes something else. Something that doesn't ever seem to turn out well."

"Like Centered Movement," Renna offers.

"I suppose," Janet agrees. "Though that was really going to an extreme; even Georgie must have known that. But even years and years before that: once he settled down in California and began to involve other people—not just the women, not just me, but everyone who got caught up in his ideas and his stories—then what he created got out of hand. It got much bigger and more complicated than he ever expected, but he just went along with it until he couldn't think any other way or live any differently. I don't really believe that Georgie came back from Mexico convinced that Yamon had revealed that he was going to be the last nagual but by the time I met him, he was. And then the books were so successful that he had to keep on writing them. Still, there must have come a point where they weren't exactly what they started out to be. It's like he lost sight of his own goal—at least, what I think his goal was in the beginning—and maybe at the end. He was just writing travelers' guides. You don't have to try to do everything a guidebook says you should do or go everywhere it says to go, because it's just a *guide*. A bunch of suggestions about how to see things you've never seen before and how to have new experiences. Learn new things." Janet looks off toward the mountains and smiles. "The hard part is actually getting yourself to go."

She leans back against the bench and closes her eyes for a moment. Then she says to Renna, "You know, I really like it here. Woodstock. Sometimes it feels like a ridiculous place to live—I mean, tie-dyed tee shirts and peace signs everywhere? But I do like it; I have to admit that. And on top of that, I have a lot of work to do. It's not the best time in my life to go traveling. But I guess you don't always get to choose when to stay and when to go traveling."

"What are you talking about?" Renna says. "Go where?" Glancing over at the backpack that Janet has placed beside her on the bench, she suddenly knows the answer to her own question. "Oh no," she says. "What's the point? Even if you can find that town—what was it called? Esta Murella? You know he's not there. Georgie, I mean."

"Of course," Janet says. "I know he's not there."

"So you'll go on this big, long, uncomfortable trip on a rattley bus…"

"I was just on a big, rattley bus," Janet says. "I'm beginning to like them. Interesting things seem to happen on a long bus ride."

"Isn't that thrilling. Can I finish now?"

"Sure."

"So you'll go on this trip to find out—what?"

"How Georgie's last guidebook is going to turn out," Janet says. "Or maybe nothing. Maybe there is nothing to know. Or if there is something, it's too hard to understand. I mean, the way we're brought up, the way we live. Maybe we just can't understand anything else, and that's the way it's supposed to be. In that case, we can just buy some souvenirs and come home. It'll be like the old hippie days—we'll be on a road trip."

"We? Did you really say *we?* Why would I want to come with you?"

Janet smiles at her. "Everybody should go on some kind of spiritual quest once in their life, don't you think?"

"I don't know," Renna says dubiously. "I don't think I have the right clothes for anything like that. What *does* one wear to go searching for infinity?"

"Something comfortable, I would imagine," Janet tells her.

"Very funny." Renna looks down at her sandals—thin, shiny strips of black plastic—as if judging how far they might take her. "Didn't you just tell me that a spiritual journey is something you have to go on alone?"

Janet laughs. "Well, that's one useful thing I learned from Georgie—to lie once in a while. So there you go, I lied. I think it's actually okay for a traveler to take a friend."

She stands up, stretches, and then leans down again to give Renna a gentle but deliberate tap on the head. "I'll call you in the morning," she says. And then, with Jorge Castelan's backpack slung over her shoulder, Janet Planet ambles away.

☾

Other Recent Titles from Mayapple Press:

George Dila, *Nothing More to Tell*, 2011
    Paper, 100pp, $15.95 plus s&h
    ISBN 978-1-936419-05-0

Sophia Rivkin, *Naked Woman Listening at the Keyhole*, 2011
    Paper, 44pp, $13.95 plus s&h
    ISBN 978-1-936419-04-3

Stacie Leatherman, *Stranger Air*, 2011
    Paper, 80pp, $14.95 plus s&h
    ISBN 978-1-936419-03-6

Mary Winegarden, *The Translator's Sister*, 2011
    Paper, 86pp, $14.95 plus s&h
    ISBN 978-1-936419-02-9

Howard Schwartz, *Breathing in the Dark*, 2011
    Paper, 96pp, $15.95 (hardcover $24.95) plus s&h
    ISBN 978-1-936419-00-5 (hc 978-1-936419-01-2)

Paul Dickey, *They Say This Is How Death Came into the World*, 2011
    Paper, 78 pp, $14.95 plus s&h
    ISBN 978-0932412-997

Sally Rosen Kindred, *No Eden*, 2011
    Paper, 70 pp, $14.95 plus s&h
    ISBN 978-0932412-980

Jane O. Wayne, *The Other Place You Live*, 2010
    Paper, 80 pp, $14.95 plus s&h
    ISBN 978-0932412-973

Andrei Guruianu, *Metal and Plum: A Memoir*, 2010
    Paper, 124 pp, $16.95 plus s&h
    ISBN 978-0932412-966

Jeanne Larsen, *Why We Make Gardens (& Other Poems)*, 2010
    Paper, 74 pp, $14.95 plus s&h
    ISBN 978-0932412-959

Jayne Pupek, *The Livelihood of Crows*, 2010
    Paper, 86 pp, $15.95 plus s&h
    ISBN 978-0932412-942

Garnett Kilberg Cohen, *How We Move the Air*, 2010
    Paper, 110 pp, $16.95 plus s&h
    ISBN 978-0932412-935

For a complete catalog of Mayapple Press publications, please visit our website at *www.mayapplepress.com*. Books can be ordered direct from our website with secure on-line payment using PayPal, or by mail (check or money order). Or order through your local bookseller.

About the Author

Eleanor Lerman is a writer who lives in New York. Her first book of poetry, *Armed Love* (Wesleyan University Press, 1973), published when she was twenty-one, was nominated for a National Book Award. She has since published four other award-winning collections of poetry—*Come the Sweet By and By* (University of Massachusetts Press, 1975); *The Mystery of Meteors* (Sarabande Books, 2001); *Our Post-Soviet History Unfolds* (Sarabande Books, 2005); and *The Sensual World Re-Emerges* (Sarabande Books, 2010), along with *The Blonde on the Train* (Mayapple Press, 2009) a collection of short stories. She was awarded the 2006 Lenore Marshall Poetry Prize from the Academy of American Poets and *The Nation* magazine for the year's most outstanding book of poetry for *Our Post-Soviet History Unfolds* and received a 2007 Poetry Fellowship from the National Endowment for the Arts. In 2011 she received a Guggenheim Fellowship.